# New Beginnings at Lullbury Bay

## GEORGIA HILL

*For Jayne H.*

# Chapter One

May's bouquet
*Lilac – Syringa vulgaris*
*Love's first emotions, humility and purity.*

May the first. Spring had arrived! Daisy stood in the sunshine on the pavement of Lullbury Bay's steep high street and unlocked the door to *Va Va Bloom!* It gave with a slight wheeze. She sympathised; it was seven in the morning and she wasn't feeling all that awake either. Behind her, someone called out a cheery hello. Turning, she put up a hand in greeting, watching as he disappeared into the alley leading to the shoppers' car park. Tall and lean, he had luxuriant dark hair. A stranger in town. Suppressing the quick flicker of attraction, she reminded herself she'd sworn off men.

As she walked through the shop the air shifted and fragrance from her stock drifted up, zinging her senses awake. She had made the right decision to change career. Five years in, the shop was easing into profit. People always wanted flowers. No matter how broke folk were or how uncertain the economy, a small bunch of daffodils or a sweetly perfumed bouquet of freesias was a reasonably priced treat. And there were always special occasions to be marked: marriages, babies and, sadly, there were always funerals. The shop, on the main shopping street of the little seaside town in West Dorset, attracted more than enough tourists to keep the summer busy too.

Daisy loved living and working in Lullbury Bay. After the awfulness of the last few years, the town was shaking off the grey and depression and reviving. Not that you could ever be depressed for long when surrounded by salty sea breezes and stunning views across the bay. She'd definitely seen an increase in the sort of customer who bought flowers on a whim or as a regular weekly treat on their way to the bookshop-cum-coffee shop opposite. She was certain this year was going to see takings soar. At last.

It hadn't been straightforward. The pandemic, financial worries and the long days had all taken a toll. It was easier now she'd employed Marion, even if the woman was only in for a few hours a day. Now, on top of what had been a very steep learning curve, Daisy felt she was hitting her stride. She'd even grown to love this quiet time when most only had enough energy to glare sleepily at their alarm clocks. Flicking on the kettle to make a much-needed coffee, she leafed through the local paper which had been shoved through her flat's letter box. The headline shouted:

## NINJA KNITTERS STRIKE AGAIN!

Grinning, she scanned the top news story. The town had been hit by the renegade knitters again. For Valentine's Day, they had hung knitted pink hearts all around the cobbled square at the end of the promenade. Lullbury Bay was divided, with some thinking these knitting graffiti artists great fun, while others thought it a disgrace. This time they had covered three postboxes with knitted summer scenes. Daisy peered more closely at the photographs. They were like little hats stretched over the top of the postboxes; one a knitted image of a beach complete with chubby figures in old-fashioned costumes and a predatory herring gull, another had three knitted ice-cream cones and the third a fish-themed one in greens and blues complete with a dangling octopus. 'Sweet,' she said with a giggle, hoping she'd come across them in town. Putting the paper to one side she spotted the note left by Marion.

*This came with yesterday's post. I missed it – it was hidden underneath that ficus Mrs Catesby ordered. Sorry! Really got my imagination going, sweetie. Who do you think it's from?*

Intrigued, Daisy sat down with her coffee, took the letter out of the fat envelope and read. 'How bizarre! Oops,' she added, as she saw the time. 'If I don't get a move on and put some bouquets together, I'll miss the early morning trade.' As she opened the door to the cold store and the sweet overpowering scent of lilies hit her, her thoughts strayed. *Who could have sent such an odd request?* Then it was dismissed as she switched on the shop radio to hear it blast out the B-52s and 'Rock Lobster', and the familiar routines of the day took over.

'So, darling, did you read that letter?' Marion made a dramatic appearance at eleven. She was that sort of person; you always knew when Marion Crawford was around. She flung the door of the shop open, the rattling silver flower buckets and the chorus of seagull shrieks announcing her arrival.

It was the mid-morning lull. Time for a break. Daisy flicked on the kettle again. 'Yes, weird or what?'

'So I read it correctly. We've to follow the monthly orders all summer?'

Daisy came to the counter where Marion had made herself comfortable on the stool. 'Actually, it's different flowers every month until October. They're to be delivered to an address in Withycombe Lane. But the letter is headed with an office address in, hang on, where did I put it?' Daisy hunted under a pile of discarded leaves and found it. 'An office address in the Mailbox in Birmingham.' She frowned, puzzled.

'What, that chi-chi place?' Marion made a face.

'Isn't it a post office?'

'Not any longer, sweetie. They converted the building yonks ago. We had a look around while our Cassius had his interview at the university.' Marion examined her perfectly manicured nails, today painted in a rich burgundy. 'I didn't see anything worth buying but it's where they have all those swanky designer shops and offices.' She pulled a face at Daisy. 'Ooh,' she said, brightening considerably. 'This guy could be rich!'

Daisy laughed. 'Why does it have to be a man?'

Marion pointed a triumphant talon to the signature and printed name at the bottom of the letter. 'Mr W. Hamilton. W?' she said, thinking hard. 'William? Walter? Wesley? Warren?'

'Warren?' Now it was Daisy's turn to pull a face.

'You really must stop judging people by their name. It's an awfully bad habit, Daisy.'

'I'm not judging anyone,' she lied, knowing it was true, she *was* prone to prejudging people according to their name. Marion was right, it was a very bad habit. 'And whatever his name is, with this order all summer, he's going to bump up my profits nicely.'

'Daisy Wiscombe,' Marion said in despair. 'Get your head out of your profit and loss columns just for once. This is so romantic!'

Daisy looked at her employee with an exasperated fondness. She didn't have much time for romance. She, quite literally, didn't have *any* time for romance. Or any time for anything. Her business was all-consuming. 'How's that then?'

Marion rose to her feet and paced to and fro across the little shop, high heels tapping on the wooden floor. The newly arranged lilies quivered delicately as she swept past and her long, knitted coatigan threatened their petals. 'Oh, Daisy darling, come on. A man has paid upfront for a summer's worth of orders, the instructions in mysterious sealed envelopes. He could be a lonely widower, bereft at the loss of his wife, or a man trying to woo his long-lost love. Or,' at this she whirled round and pointed dramatically, 'he could have developed an infatuation for a lovely, lonely, raven-haired, blue-eyed flower seller and this is the only way he can get her attention!'

Daisy laughed, long and hard. 'Marion, you've got to stop reading those romance novels. Things like that never happen in real life.'

'Seriously though.' Marion sat back down and took Daisy's hand. 'Look at these. All chapped and work-roughened. About time you treated yourself to a day at the spa with me. All you do is work. Where's the fun, the romance?' She peered into Daisy's face. 'And you know, darling, you could be awfully pretty if you scrubbed up a fathom.'

'Rude!'

'You need to get yourself out there a tad more. Find yourself a man. Not necessarily *the* man but have a bit of fun while you're still young. Or youngish,' Marion added, with a twist of her lips.

'As I said. Rude!' Daisy snatched her hand away, uncomfortable with the turn in conversation. Marion was always trying to matchmake her with someone. Forty-something, smugly married Marion wanted the same for her friend. But Daisy had given up on romance. Her heart had been broken and she'd given up on men. In her experience all they did was lie and cheat. 'I had a holiday in January when things were quiet,' she said, defensively. 'Closed up the shop and everything.'

'And what did you do?'

Daisy had the grace to blush. 'Sleep mostly,' she admitted.

'Ha! You're never going to meet any men at this rate.' Marion pointed to Daisy's jeans and sober navy apron, emblazoned with *Va Va Bloom!* 'And look at the state of you! A haircut and a manicure wouldn't go amiss.'

'Marion, I've been at the wholesale flower market since five this morning, picking up a special order. They don't go a bundle on snazzy hairdos up there.'

'Hmmm.'

'Marion,' Daisy said, sighing. 'Look, you know I've been trying to get the business going.'

'There's more to life than money.'

For a second Daisy was speechless. Marion's entire lifestyle pivoted on being able to buy whatever she wanted, and whenever. 'Not when it pays your mortgage,' she retorted and then subsided. If she carried on she'd get really angry. Marion, for all her snobbishness, was a good friend and a surprisingly hard-working employee but she hadn't a clue. Her husband Barry earned enough to keep the whole family in the manner to which they had become accustomed. Marion only worked because she wanted to, as she was bored out of her skull in her luxury detached house in amongst the new builds on the edge of town. She had no idea how often Daisy had considered closing down, of the endless nights when she couldn't sleep for worry over the bills, the soaring cost of stock, the business rates and her fear of doing it all on her own. There was a frigid silence for a moment and then Daisy relented. How could Marion even begin to understand. 'How can I go out with anyone?' she asked, softening slightly. 'I get up at four most mornings and work all day Saturday. I'm so exhausted on Sunday all I can do is sleep.'

'I'm going to have to take you in hand. You're not getting any younger, you know.' Marion's head gave an indignant little wobble.

The anger burst through again. 'Do you mind? I'm thirty-three and very happy with my life. Can we end this conversation now?'

Marion took one look at Daisy's furious expression and finally took the hint. 'Ooh Saturdays! That reminds me. Brittany has a friend looking for a Saturday job. Are you interested?'

Daisy looked askance. Any friend of Marion's daughter would likely be loud-mouthed, lazy and spoiled.

As if reading her mind Marion chipped in with, 'Oh she's nothing like my Brit, don't you worry.' Marion was nothing if not realistic about her offspring. 'Apparently Mia is really hardworking.'

'Mia?' Daisy's lip curled at the name.

'Daisy, you're doing it again. Stop prejudging people. She's a perfectly nice girl from the Links Estate.'

'Oh, it just gets better!'

The Links Estate was a small enclave of social housing near the art school.

'Daisy Wiscombe, stop being such a snob! The poor girl can't help where she lives. Stop jumping to conclusions.'

Daisy thought it a bit rich Marion calling her a snob when the woman was the biggest one going. 'Remember before I gave up? I taught some of the kids from that estate. They made my life hell. It was one reason I wanted to get out of teaching.'

'Well, Mia's different. She's lovely, a bit eccentric maybe, a little too serious but she'll be an asset in the shop. I'm encouraging the friendship with Brit. Might do her good to discuss something other than shellac nails and fake tan. She's a nice kid,' Marion added as Daisy still looked dubious. 'And you know how busy Saturdays get.'

Daisy acknowledged the truth of this. With Marion refusing to work on Saturdays, Daisy struggled to do the flower deliveries and run the shop on her own. She even called in a favour every now and again from her mum now she'd taken early retirement, which was far from ideal. Still, she supposed the ex-office manager could deal with a stroppy Mia if she had to leave them together. Daisy's mum could deal with most things. Jan was an indomitable, no-nonsense character – and an even worse matchmaker than Marion – if that were possible.

'Go on then,' Daisy relented. 'Tell her to come in for a chat. If she's okay, I'll give her a trial run.' The shop door opened, letting in a 'shush' of briny sea air, and a customer entered. It was one of their regulars. 'Can you deal with Mrs Pearce? I'll make a start on the first of these mysterious orders.'

Daisy peered inside the large envelope which contained six sealed smaller envelopes, each marked with a month from May to October. She took out the first with a certain amount of excitement. Even if she couldn't buy into Marion's romanticism, it was intriguing and certainly something completely different from any order she'd ever received. She retreated to the little back room which doubled as office and kitchen – along with everything else. Looking around at the tiny table and rickety chairs, at the battered armchair, the shelves which held a haphazard collection of folders and the sink which was full of dirty mugs she hadn't yet had time to wash up, she had to admit the place was a mess. Jan would have a fit when she came in on Saturday. Daisy bit her lip and admitted defeat. Perhaps Marion was right, they did need an extra pair of hands. It was just that she wasn't sure they ought to belong to a twenty-two-year-old called Mia from the Links Estate.

# Chapter Two

June's bouquet
*Tulips – Liliaceae*
*Love's passion, perfect true love.*

**D**aisy was wrong. She couldn't have been more wrong. Mia turned out to be a treasure. She worked harder than any of them. True, her appearance was slightly unusual but, nose ring and blue hair aside, underneath she was as romantic as Marion.

'I'm saving up to get to uni,' she had explained on their first meeting the previous month. 'Mum can't afford to help and I really want to do English Lit at Exeter. I didn't bother much at school. Got in with the wrong crowd.' She screwed up her face. 'Learned my lesson though. So I'm taking my A-levels at evening classes. It's tough doing them this way but I'm determined to pass this time. I'll be older than most undergrads but, hey, I'm far more mature and ready for university now than I was at eighteen.'

Daisy had choked on her coffee and Marion had gloated – she'd popped in on her way to the spa for her weekly facial and, strangely enough, had arrived just in time for Mia's interview.

'Told you,' she'd mouthed.

Daisy had bobbed out her tongue at Marion and hired Mia on the spot. After a short trial period, it was agreed, they didn't know how they'd managed without her.

This Saturday, however, was unusually quiet. Jan had come in but wasn't really needed. She'd made herself useful by making endless, comforting mugs of tea, coffee and in Mia's case, Very Berry Crush fruit tea. After a hot May, June had blown in with unseasonable vigour and a sleety rain and it was affecting trade. The phone had been busy and Daisy had to go out later to deliver orders but shop trade had been non-existent. Tourists and locals alike were staying home. Bay Radio played in the background, but The Drifters were singing to an audience of only three.

'So, while it's quiet and we've got time, let's have a dekko at what this man Hamilton has ordered for this month then.' Jan pulled her cardigan firmly round her.

Mia, perched on the high stool, gripped her hands around her mug as if trying to extract its heat. 'I think it's so romantic.'

'Oh no, not you as well,' moaned Daisy.

'Come off it, Daisy, it is a bit unusual, you have to agree.' Jan took the letter with its bundle of sealed envelopes and examined it. 'You need to twang your romance muscle now and again.'

'Think it's withered away through lack of use,' Daisy muttered.

'What was the first order? For May?' Mia twisted a lock of blue hair around a finger. 'I'm assuming you've done that one already?'

'I was nearly late for May's order,' Daisy admitted. 'He wanted lilac.' She shrugged. 'It's not something I get many requests for, to be honest. I had to ring round like crazy to get it filled in time. Had to get in touch with a French supplier. That's the only place I could get it. The cold weather this spring affected the UK's stocks apparently.'

'Lilac?' Mia asked sharply.

'Yes, why?'

'You know what it means, don't you?'

'It has a meaning?' Daisy stared blankly. She hadn't a clue what Mia was on about.

'Love's first emotions,' Mia said dreamily. She sighed. 'That's so lush.'

Jan joined her daughter in staring at the girl.

Mia gazed back at them, misty-eyed. 'That's what it means,' she explained. 'Love's First Emotions.'

Daisy leaned against the shop counter. 'You're going to have to expand on that statement.'

'In the nineteenth century the Victorians believed every flower symbolised something. You know, the language of flowers. *Lingua Flora*. It's well cool. Lilac stood for first love. No Victorian lady would receive just a bunch of flowers, she'd read into the messages symbolised by the flowers. Just as no Victorian guy would give any old bouquet, it would be made up to reflect what he wanted to put over. It was a way of making his true feelings known if he couldn't get past the crusty old chaperone. It wasn't just for lovey-dovey romantic couples, either. A girl could reject some hopeless bloke, or someone could say how disappointed she was in a friend.' Mia warmed to her theme. 'It was literally a language. Even how the ribbon was tied was symbolic; to the left meant the message was about the sender, to the right it was about the person receiving it. An upside-down stem meant the opposite of the bouquet's message and if you left thorns on the roses it said there was everything to fear. It was all amazingly complicated and subtle. As I said, pretty cool, eh? And the Victorians would have known all the meanings, right down to the teeny, tiniest nuance.' There was a stunned silence. She gazed at the two bemused faces staring at her. 'What? Oh my eggs, Daisy, didn't you know flowers had meanings?'

Jan was first to recover and giggled. 'Yes, Daisy,' she said, enjoying her daughter's discomfort. 'Didn't you know about the language of flowers?'

Daisy gave her mother a dirty look. 'Don't forget I'm a scientist, Mum. My knowledge of flowers is restricted to their life cycle. And I reckon I probably knew as much about this as you did until ten minutes ago.' She shifted uncomfortably against the edge of the counter as Mia remained silent and slightly reproachful. 'Well, you know, been so busy setting up the business and everything. Besides,' she added defensively, feeling put on the spot, 'I don't think customers buy flowers on account of what they symbolise.'

'But you can't sell flowers without knowing what they mean!' Mia was horrified.

Jan hid her chuckles in her mug of tea.

'Done all right so far,' Daisy replied. 'Most of the businessmen who call in here on their way home just want a bunch of cheap, long-lasting carnations.'

Mia huffed. 'I hope they don't buy one of the mixed bunches then.' She wrinkled her nose, making her nose ring glint. 'Think I remember this right, yellow's contempt and the striped ones stand for a knockback! He'll go home with his hopes high and won't get lucky.' She sniggered.

Jan roared. 'Oh, Mia, you're a card.' She collected their empty cups and headed off to the kitchen, shaking her head as she went.

'Where do you get all this information?' Daisy asked, fascinated.

'Oh internet, books, the usual places,' Mia said airily. 'Could be great marketing, you know. I think you're missing a trick.' Plucking a bunch of pink roses from its silver bucket, she held them to her as water dripped down her leather miniskirt. She struck a pose. 'Take home some of these this summer. They represent perfect happiness.' She screwed up her face. 'Or the sun shines out of your behind or something.' Putting her head on one side, she added, 'Or was that daffodils? I'll have to buff my memory.'

Daisy slid away from the counter, ideas going around crazily in her head. It might just work. It might just be the unique selling point she could use to steal custom from the nearby supermarket. People were getting all too used to picking up a ready-made bouquet along with their carrots and she could never compete with the mass purchase power and therefore the lower prices of big supermarkets. Something like this would offer that distinctive personal touch little businesses like hers prided themselves on. 'You know you could be onto something.'

'Course I am. I'm not stupid, you know.'

'Believe me, I never *ever* thought you were stupid, Mia.'

'Yeah you did. Right after you clocked my nose ring.'

'I, well–' Daisy let the sentence hang. A wash of guilt flooded her. She *had* prejudged Mia and, worse, had made up her mind before even meeting her. It had been horrible of her and the girl hadn't deserved it. Mia could be far too perceptive sometimes. She wished she could let go of this fault but, no matter how hard she tried, it persisted. She wasn't proud of it. She really should take a chance on people but too often she remained cynical and expected the worst from them. 'Okay, I admit the blue hair and the black leather did throw me a bit. I have a horrible habit of being suspicious about people. I also prejudge them and don't give them a chance before getting to know them. It's my worst fault. I'm sorry. I did prejudge you but, now I know you, I'm extremely glad we're working together. And it's a fabulous idea to use the meanings of flowers to sell them.'

'What makes you so suspicious?' Mia asked curiously.

'I don't know.' Daisy shrugged but she knew exactly what lay at its source. A boyfriend who conveniently forgot to tell her he was married had something to do with it. She'd believed and trusted Neville implicitly and look where it had got her. A little prejudgment and cynicism would have come in handy with him. She changed the subject slightly. 'So, do you really think Mr Hamilton's orders all have hidden meanings?'

'Could have. What's he ordered this month?'

'Haven't opened it yet. The instructions said not to until the fifth, that's Monday, and then deliver the flowers on the tenth of each month. It's a bit annoying, to be honest. It doesn't give me much time to source something if he wants anything unusual. I mean, it's all so prescriptive but I can't figure out why. It's weird.'

Mia's eyes were as round as saucers. She wiggled her fingers in excitement. 'It's ever so thrilling. Is there a message to go with the orders usually?'

'There was last time. It was some poetry I think. The instructions are odd too. I had to drop off the flowers and the note at the house and put them on the back porch. It was creepy. Although there was a car in the driveway, it didn't look as if anyone lived there. Empty windows, you know? When a house isn't lived in.'

'It gets better and better.' Mia shivered delicately. 'So you didn't see Walter then?'

'Who?'

'Walter, you know, Mr Hamilton. I've decided the W stands for Walter.'

'Oh.' Daisy laughed. She supposed Walter was as good a name as any. 'No, there was no one at home.' A chill slid down Daisy's spine at the memory of the big old house at the end of Withycombe Lane. It had unnerved her and she'd driven away as soon as she could. 'Didn't look as if anyone lived there at all. But I'd hazard a guess at it belonging to someone older. No children's swings in the garden and there was a walking frame in the kitchen.'

'Open June's,' Mia said eagerly. 'Go on, no one will know you've opened it early. It might be something unusual again and you don't want to risk being late.'

Daisy leafed through the sealed envelopes until she came to the one marked June in the same spidery old person's handwriting. Ridiculously she found her hands were shaking. She wondered what to expect. Scanning the letter inside she said, 'Tulips,' with a disappointed sigh. After all the build-up the order seemed low-key and ordinary. 'They might be tricky this late in their season but Jakob, my supplier in the Netherlands, might be able to supply some. Shame. I was hoping for something more exotic.'

Mia was reacting rather differently. 'Forget all the practicalities.

It's *tulips*!' Her face glowed. 'Passion. Love. Passionate true love. Don't you see it's a story! It's a story of love. Lilac for when they first met, for the beginning of their romance. Tulips for their growing passion. Oh, Daisy, it is romantic. Here's Walter remembering his great love story. What colour though?'

'Why?'

Mia could hardly rein in her frustration. 'Different colour tulips have different meanings.'

'Really?' Daisy gave her a disbelieving glance and scanned the note again. 'Red, yellow and variegated.'

'Oh!' Mia exclaimed, giving a little scream. 'He *is* telling us the story of their romance. Yellow – there is sunshine in your smile. Variegated – you have beautiful eyes and red, well, red means passion and a declaration of true love.' She clapped her hands together in ecstasy. 'It's so totally emosh.'

'Hold on a minute. Aren't you getting a bit carried away? He could just like tulips and lilac.'

'Daisy Wiscombe, I'm ashamed to call you my daughter,' Jan called from the doorway. 'Have you no romance in your soul? Of course it's a story and this bright girl has solved the mystery. A Mrs Hamilton died at the beginning of March, aged seventy-five – it's here in the paper.' Jan held up a battered copy of *The Lullbury Bay Echo*. 'I thought the name rang a bell. It says she's survived by her husband and daughter.'

'Walter Hamilton must be her widower. I was right, he *is* reliving their romance. A flower through the months, each with a special meaning for them. Oh it's so lovely!' Mia's eyes sparkled with tears.

'Actually,' Daisy said suddenly, looking at the piece of paper which had fluttered out of June's order. 'Mia, look at this. This is what's going with the flowers this month.' She read the first few lines of the poem.

'It's Elizabeth Barrett Browning, *How do I Love thee?* I can't bear it, it's so poignant.' At this, Mia rushed out of the shop.

Jan and Daisy stared after her.

'She'll catch her death, it's pouring out there,' Jan said, practical as ever.

'Oh, Mum.' Daisy laughed.

'What?'

'Nothing.' Daisy went into the office to make the call to her contact in the Netherlands. Before doing so, she read the rest of the poem. 'Mia,' she said with a sigh, the romance of it all easing into even her hardened heart. 'You might just be right about all this.'

# Chapter Three

J an knocked on the front door of Daisy's flat, calling out, 'Only me.'

Daisy let her in. The flat over the shop was tiny but all her own and she prized the privacy and independence it gave her. Today though, she didn't mind her mum's invasion. 'Where did you park?'

'Behind the shop in the yard. I blocked in Primrose. Is that okay, lovie?'

Primrose was Daisy's ancient work van and her only means of transport. So-called because she was bright yellow. Daisy would love a van liveried in the shop's branded colours of silver and navy but wasn't sure she could afford it. 'Yeah, of course. I've closed up for today.'

'Not like you. Missing out on possible customers, but it's always nice to go along together.' Jan wrapped her scarf more securely around her neck. 'Wrap up, chickadee. Cold wind coming off the sea this morning. It'll be chilly down on the harbour.'

Daisy obeyed, lifting her best coat off the hooks behind the front door as a response to her mother's warning. It was true, she disliked having to close the shop on a working day, but the annual

Blessing of the Boats ceremony was something they'd always attended as a family when her father had been alive. Despite being a workaholic like her, he'd always insisted on taking the day off to go along. Then, they'd been a family of five. Now, with her older brothers working abroad, she'd kept up the tradition, even though it was just the two of them. A few hours' missed trade was trivial in comparison to how much it meant to her mum. 'Doubt if there'll be all that many customers around today. Too cold for tourists and most of the town will be at the ceremony.' She shrugged her coat on. 'And Mia's a bit too new to open the shop on her own just yet.' She peered at herself in the hall mirror. 'Do you think scarlet is the right colour? I haven't got anything else that's smart and warm.'

'You look a picture. And it's not as if it's a funeral. Mind you, they're naming the new boat and launching it today, don't forget. Going to be emotional for the Pengethleys.'

Avril Pengethley, her daughter Merryn and adult son Jago, had moved into Lullbury Bay the previous year. Avril's husband had died tragically whilst crewing for the RNLI and the new lifeboat was to be named after him.

Daisy glanced at her mum. It would be emotional for her too. The ceremony always made Jan teary as it stirred up memories of her own loss. 'It will.' She bit down on her own feelings and focused on the practical. Looking around, she found her cerise flowery-patterned gloves and tugged them on. 'Still, there's a wedding to look forward to later this year when Jago marries Honor, our esteemed and much-loved deputy head.'

'You still on to do the flowers?'

Daisy nodded, herding her mother out and locking the door. 'Going to be a huge wedding. Think most of the town's been invited, along with Honor's family, and there's quite a few of them too.' She patted her pockets checking for tissues and her phone.

'Come along, Daisy,' Jan said impatiently. 'I want to get a good spot.'

'It's not a spectator sport, Mum.'

'It's all right for you, you inherited your dad's height. If I get stuck at the back I won't see anything.'

Jan dashed a quick hand across her eyes and Daisy knew the brusqueness covered up sadness. She followed her mother down the outside steps at the rear of the shop and they turned left into an icy wind gusting up the high street.

'Told you there was a cold wind,' Jan said. 'Come on, let's walk quickly, it'll keep us warm. You'd never think it was summer, would you? They delayed the ceremony as the weather was so bad but I don't think it's much better today.'

At the cobbled square at the bottom of the high street, they turned right and marched along the promenade, heads down, following the crowds all heading in the same direction. The wind blew spray off the sea and sand kicked up in little whirls. Daisy felt she'd had an abrasive facial by the time they reached the harbour. Luckily, against the harbour wall and in amongst the crowd, it was slightly sheltered.

'Look, there's Jamie.' Jan waved.

Jamie had joined the Wiscombe family by marrying Daisy's cousin and was a stalwart of the volunteer RNLI crew.

'Oh and just look at Jago.' Her mother put a hand to her throat and gasped. 'It's not going to be easy for him, bless.'

Jago Pengethley stood, with the other RNLI crew. All were kitted out in uniform, as if about to go on a "shout" in a yellow which glowed blindingly bright in the sunshine against the contrast of their red life-saving vests. All stood to attention in a line in front of the new lifeboat. Jago, rigid in the face and staring into the distance, was obviously trying to keep his emotions in check. The boat, on its tractor launch, was poised high on the slipway behind them. Representatives from the Sea Scouts, marines smart in dress uniforms from the base in nearby Lympstone and town councillors stood in formation behind a table bearing three floral wreaths and draped with the Union flag.

'Lovely job on the flowers, Daisy,' her mother whispered as she took a programme of service off one of the young Sea Scouts who was handing them out.

'Thanks, Mum.' Daisy was proud of the three wreaths she'd made, all in crimson roses and sunshine-yellow lilies to reflect the RNLI working kit.

'Always find the Blessing of the Boats ceremony so moving.' Jan fished out a tissue and dabbed at her eyes.

'Me too, Mum, me too.' Daisy knew her mum was thinking of their own bereavement. She gave her a quick hug and then put an arm through her mother's.

The day was flawlessly blue. A hard light bounced off a sea frothing with waves. Gulls cackled and crooned above their heads, the wind lifting them off and over the churning water. Snow-white clouds scudded across the sky and the air was fresh with salty ozone and invigorating. A crystalline-clear day, the orange-ginger-biscuit cliffs at West Bay were clearly visible and the lighthouse at Portland could be seen on the distant eastern horizon. Daisy drank in a deep breath feeling the fresh air chill her insides. She loved her little town on days like this. A rough sea made her come alive; it blew the dust of the shop office out of her lungs. It also served as a reminder as to why they needed a lifeboat station in town; Lullbury Bay's waters were beautiful but deceptively treacherous. Although her dad had been a landlubber, he'd always been a staunch supporter of their RNLI and she was glad to be so too.

Verity, their vicar, hugged Avril and Merryn Pengethley and led them to the table where they sat as the guests of honour. Avril looked tense and pinched with cold but Merryn, her dark curls dancing, looked to be having the time of her life, completely unfazed by the solemnity of the occasion.

'Honor says Merryn's a real character,' Daisy bent and said against her mum's ear. 'She's in her class. Very clever and full of energy.'

'She's going to be a bridesmaid, isn't she? That's going to liven things up. But she's been through such a lot in her short life, I think we can forgive some high spirits. Ooh, here we go, it's all about to start.'

A brass band, sitting in the shelter of the lifeboat house, had been playing something soft. Now they struck up a rousing rendition of 'The Lord's My Shepherd'.

'Sing up, Daisy.' Jan prodded her with an elbow. 'This was your dad's favourite.'

'Think you're singing loud enough for the pair of us.' Daisy forced a grin as her mother sang loud and lustily, and very out of tune.

At the end of the hymn, Verity stood up. A tiny figure with dusty-brown hair, her clerical robes tugging and snatching in the stiff wind. Holding down her white surplice she began her address.

'Dear townspeople of Lullbury Bay. Dear visitors. Dear friends. May I welcome you to the Blessing of the Boats ceremony. This is an annual event where we give our thanks for the wonderful seaside place we live in, for the many opportunities it offers us: to fish, to work, for our leisure and enjoyment. It's also when we give thanks for our wonderful RNLI volunteers.' She paused. 'I'm going to keep this brief because it's very cold and I'm sure we want to retire to the warmth of the Old Harbour where Claude has prepared hot chocolate and bacon rolls. And they'll be much appreciated.' One or two people in the crowd cheered. Verity grinned and then sobered.

'As well as giving thanks, today we're also naming our new lifeboat.' She flicked a glance at Avril as if to see how she was holding up. 'The *Kenan Pengethley* is named after an incredibly brave man who gave his all. After a lifetime of service given over to the RNLI, Kenan went out on one last "shout" during which he tragically lost his life, not here in Lullbury but in the River Thames. He gave *his* life in order to save another's. In memory of his sacrifice, we are here to name our new lifeboat after him as requested by his family who are now firmly rooted in our little community. It is a fitting tribute to a man who was devoted to all that the RNLI stands for. Some here have probably needed our lifeboat's aid, most of you will have fundraised for our lifeboat, or been involved in some way with our lifeboat station. It is also rooted deeply in our seaside town. Kenan was a brave man. We have many more brave souls here who give up their time, who give up their precious family life and so much more, to volunteer to help keep our waters safe. We express our deepest gratitude to you all.' There was a ripple of applause and more cheers.

'I'm now going to hand over to Merryn Pengethley, Kenan's daughter, to lead us in our prayers.' She gestured to the little girl who stood, with Verity's arm supporting her. 'May we bow our heads and pray in remembrance of Kenan's sacrifice. After which, we will hold a two-minute silence to remember all those who have perished at sea.'

Daisy closed her eyes and listened to the young high-pitched voice recite a prayer and then lead them all in The Lord's Prayer. Afterwards the silence was punctuated only by the distant wail of a herring gull effortlessly gliding a thermal in the sapphire-blue sky. Her memories flashed back to her father's funeral when the same prayer had been said. A lump formed in her throat. It was unbearably moving.

'Thank you very much, Merryn,' Verity said. 'That was a very brave thing to do and you did it brilliantly.' Standing in front of the table, she made the sign of the cross. 'I bless all those who sail in our beautiful but sometimes dangerous waters. I bless the vessels they set sail in and I bless those who go to their aid. God be with you all.' Bowing her head in silent reflection for a moment she then turned and smiled broadly at the crowd. 'And now, we have the presentation of the floral wreaths,' Verity searched the crowd for Daisy and found her, 'which have been lovingly made and donated by our resident florist Daisy, from *Va Va Bloom!*' Applause rippled through the crowd and Daisy blushed. In unison and with military precision, the three wreaths were ceremoniously passed back from volunteer to volunteer until they reached Jamie on the boat. He laid them reverently on-board.

'Thank you,' Verity said. 'And now we're going to hear from Kenan's son. Jago is also a volunteer with our RNLI.'

Jago stepped forward. Daisy heard the crowd take in a collective and sympathetic breath. 'Thank you for coming today,' he began. 'My family has only been in Lullbury Bay a few months but we've been welcomed with open arms. I can safely say the decision to move here was the best we've ever taken. There is a very special community here and I'm incredibly proud to be part of it and to serve it. In some ways I wish my father was here to see this day. But, of course, if he was, this day would not be happening. The RNLI was his life, his work, his vocation. He gave his life to it, and his life was taken too soon. But now, in a way, he will still serve, still be at our sides when we need him.'

At her side Daisy heard her mother sniff hard. She searched for her mum's hand and gripped it hard.

Jago paused and thrust a hand across his eyes. Daisy could see his throat working. Eventually he took a deep breath and said, 'So I take enormous pride in naming this boat the *Kenan Pengethley*. May all who crew her serve her well and return home safe.' He pulled off the ceremonial cloth covering the boat's name. 'The *Kenan Pengethley*!'

'The *Kenan Pengethley*!' the crowd echoed.

The brass band struck up the Navy hymn, 'Eternal Father, Strong to Save'. This time Daisy didn't need her mother to nag to encourage her to sing out. She joined in with gusto. 'O hear us when we cry to thee. For those in peril on the sea.'

As they did so, a team of kitted-up crew members, Jago included, climbed aboard the newly named boat and the tractor rumbled down the slipway, releasing the navy-and-orange vessel into the water.

'Thank you all for coming,' Verity called out. 'That's all for this year. And now let's get ourselves warmed up and may God go with us!'

The crowd began to disperse, most heading to the pub on the harbour but Daisy and Jan stood watching the boat as it navigated the harbour entrance and sped out, bouncing hard on the choppy open water. They watched until it became a tiny speck far out to sea where it stopped to cast the wreaths.

Jan sucked in an enormous breath. 'Gets to me every time,' she said in a quavering voice.

Daisy hugged her. 'Me too, Mum. Me too.' She knew, for her mother, it brought back memories of a much more personal loss. Just as it had for her. 'Now, it's freezing out here,' she added briskly. 'What do you say to some of Claude's special bacon butties and hot chocolate?'

# Chapter Four

June's weather dramatically improved and with the sunshine came the tourists, the weekenders and the second homeowners. Trade picked up. Following Mia's suggestion, Daisy tried out a few carefully handwritten signs.

*Special Offer! Buy these alstroemeria to show her your devotion! Also symbolises wealth, prosperity and fortune.*

Daisy wasn't sure if she'd sold any more flowers but it was certainly a conversation starter and customers seemed to linger in the shop more. And if they lingered, the chance was they'd spend. A small bunch of carnations, the odd pot plant, some cactus feed, it all added up.

She had little time to ponder on the mystery that was Walter Hamilton and his long-lost love. If indeed Walter was his name. If indeed that was the story behind his order. She was busy and that's the way she liked it. If there was a gap in her life, she didn't leave herself enough time to think about it. She made sure she was so exhausted that she simply worked, ate to live and slept like the dead.

This summer would see the wedding of Jago Pengethley and Honor Martin. Jago, local artist and RNLI volunteer and Honor, deputy head at the primary school, were hugely popular figures in town. It was going to be a major event. Daisy was fond of the couple and wanted to get everything just right. She was only too aware it would also be a showcase for her business, an added pressure.

As the days grew warm and sunny and the happy couple popped in and out with their wedding plans, even she had to admit a longing for something undefined. For someone to love her enough to send her an Elizabeth Barrett Browning poem.

She delivered the bouquet of tulips, along with the poem, as instructed, on the tenth. This time she took in more details of the house. It was lovely, Victorian at a guess with small-paned leaded windows and an eccentric-looking turret on one side. Although it still gave her the creeps, she was beginning to appreciate what a beautiful house it was. The car, an old but immaculate dark-green Ford Focus, sat on a laurel-hedged drive and looked as if it hadn't moved since her last visit. Although there was room enough for several cars on the long drive, the Focus had been parked close to the house, giving the impression it wasn't used. She squeezed past it to the garden gate and walked around to the back porch. As before, it was unlocked so she propped the flowers against the kitchen door. It was a warm day and she worried they would droop so she looked around for something she could put water in. Spying a plastic bucket and an outside tap, she filled the bucket and then straightened and paused for a moment to appreciate the gardens; they took her breath away. A vast lawn stretched into the distance with a magnificent border of towering conifers. Birdsong filled the air and it all felt very peaceful, almost like something out of a fairy tale. All it needed was a scampering spaniel running around; a dog would love a space like this. But all was still, completely abandoned and slightly unnerving.

Daisy tried not to be nosy but couldn't help but glance through the patio doors and into a sitting room. One of those upright chairs designed for the elderly, with a footrest, a sagging sofa in an old-fashioned flower print, a few photographs on the mantelpiece over the gas fire. No stray cup on the coffee table, no discarded newspaper. It was tidy and completely devoid of human life. The house seemed to be holding its breath, even the dust motes were held in suspension. It was all very odd. She hoped whoever received the flowers would enjoy them and the poem. And she hoped they'd be back to rescue them soon.

She half-wished she could stay longer, partly to enjoy the tranquillity, partly to see if the mysterious W would turn up and she could meet him. Giving in to her pressing timetable, she sighed and went back to the porch. Putting the tulips into the bucket of water she hoped it might keep them going until they were collected. Tulips were prone to drooping. And just who was this W? She smiled. Mia was so insistent the W stood for Walter that they all called him that now.

As she got into her van and started the engine, she gave the house one last look. She didn't like the thought of it being left empty. It lay at the end of a private unadopted track and was isolated. An easy target. Weirdly, she was getting fond of Walter and his love for flowers and poetry; she didn't want anything to happen to his lovely old home.

After battling the tourist traffic to make the rest of her deliveries, Daisy arrived back at the shop in dire need of a cold drink and a shower. She vaguely heard Marion call out, 'Bye' on her way out, turned up the shop radio and sank a pint of water in the kitchen. Donna Summer's 'Hot Stuff' pulsed out sexily from Bay Radio replacing a Beach Boys classic. It was their local radio station and played nothing but golden oldies.

She tugged her apron over her head while stumbling through to the shop. Flicking back her hair from a hot face, she found herself face to face with a customer. He was dark-haired, tallish and lean; a stranger and the same man who had said hello that morning all those weeks ago. He wore chinos and a white shirt and looked as cucumber cool as she felt flustered.

'I'm so sorry, I had no idea you were waiting.'

'Not a problem. I've only this minute walked in.' He smiled, making some long unused muscle in Daisy's heart go twang. Crinkly dark eyes and the most sardonic pair of eyebrows she'd ever seen. The smile, creating a deep groove down one cheek, wasn't making her any less perturbed.

'What can I get you?'

'I'd like some flowers please.'

Daisy recovered herself and laughed. 'Well, you've come to the right place.'

He had the grace to look embarrassed. 'I suppose I have.'

'Have you any idea of type, or price?'

He shook his head, looking confused.

'What's the occasion? Birthday? Anniversary?'

'Apology.' He grimaced. 'Eating humble pie. My girlfriend and I had an argument and it's to say sorry.'

'Ah.' Of course a man as gorgeous as this would have a girl-friend. Daisy walked from behind the counter. 'We have some lovely globe chrysanthemums,' she said, pointing them out. 'The white ones mean truth and the red ones mean I love you, although I'm not fond of red and white flowers together.'

'Nor me.'

Daisy gave him a questioning look.

'I'm a Spurs fan. Tottenham Hotspur.'

She pulled a face. 'Now it's my turn to be bamboozled. What I know about football could be written on a pansy flower.'

'Our main rivals are Arsenal and they play in red and white.'

'Oh I see. I think. Sort of. Sorry. Football's not my thing.'

He laughed. 'Well, we're even then as I'm not a flower person. Why aren't you keen? On mixing red and white I mean?'

Daisy wrinkled her nose. 'I'm not sure. It's not a very subtle colour combination of course but I have some distant memory of it being unlucky. Something to do with World War One and blood on bandages.'

'Then I'll definitely avoid.'

'Oh dear. Was the argument that bad?'

'Oh yes.' He let out a low breath.

'Just how much grovelling do you have to do?'

'Let's just say price is immaterial.'

'Ouch! In that case, how about these beautiful gladioli? The pale pink and white look classy together and they make a very dramatic statement.' She reached down and plucked a couple of blooms from their bucket.

'They're great. Not sure they're quite Minty's thing though.'

'In that case, what about the classic combo of roses and lilies?' Daisy moved over to the lilies, and to the roses which had a touch of pink so subtle as to be almost not there. 'Lilies are always popular and these smell divine. The roses are in bud so will last.'

The man was obviously out of his depth. He shrugged. 'They look great. To me. There's one thing. I have an appointment before I can drive home. The flowers will be in my car for a couple of hours.'

'That's fine. I'll make them up into a hand-tied bouquet and put them into a gift box. It'll have a reservoir of water inside to keep the flowers fresh. Just keep them upright. Also, that way, your girlfriend won't even have to rearrange them if she doesn't want to. She can just pop them onto the table to admire.' She smiled. 'And forgive you.'

'Perfect.' He looked so relieved that Daisy's heart went out to him. He glanced at his watch. 'I'm half an hour early for my appointment. Do you want me to wait? Will it take long to put the bouquet together?'

'Not too long.' Daisy nodded to the bookshop and community café opposite. 'But instead of waiting, why don't you go over to Bee's Books? They do great coffee, the waffles are to die for and you can buy a book to read too. Give me thirty minutes or so and the flowers will be all yours.'

'That's brilliant.' He peered at her name badge. 'Thanks so

much, Daisy. Great name for a florist but I suppose that's been said many times?'

'Once or twice but you're right, it is.'

'Well thank you, Daisy the florist, you've saved my bacon.'

'They do a mean one of those too. Bacon butty that is.'

He laughed, looking relaxed for the first time since entering the shop. It was the most perfect sound. A deep rumbling which rose from somewhere around his knees.

Daisy felt her own wobble. He really was the nicest man. Whoever his girlfriend was, she was a lucky woman. Roses and lilies lucky. As he went to go, she called after him, 'I hope the flowers do the trick,' and watched as he put up a hand, and strode across the street to the café.

# Chapter Five

'Darling! Who was that gorgeous man I saw leaving here on Friday? He was positively swoony!' Marion perched on the stool, leaned her elbows on the counter and hissed, 'Spill!'

It was a glorious summer's day. Lullbury Bay's pavements thronged with sun-creamed tourists heading downhill to the beach. Happy chatter, the growl of traffic crawling along the main street and the cry of gulls filtered through the shop's open door. Walk-in trade was quiet, not many people wanted a bunch of flowers to take onto the beach. Daisy was content though. She had several standing orders from holiday-cottage owners who liked to welcome their clients with a small bunch of peonies or some fragrant freesias, and the second homeowners always picked up flowers for the weekends.

Daisy paused in her task of de-thorning some red roses. 'Morning, Marion. You keeping tabs on me?'

'Just happened to come out of Gladwin's as I saw him leave,' she said airily. 'Cass arrived home for the weekend and was craving a pasty so I had to come all the way back into town to buy a few. You know how much he likes them.'

Cassius, Marion's son, was a hulking rugby-playing student

with a legendary appetite. He often popped into the flower shop when at home and ate all the biscuits.

'I saw you,' Marion continued. 'You were all pally, doing that little wave you do when you like someone. And he was carrying the biggest hand-tied I've ever seen. Tell all!'

Daisy put the roses down. 'Well actually, I was quite proud of it. The Casablanca lilies with seven stems of the bud roses, a couple of green chrysanths and a stem or two of Irish Bells for luck. Plus some gyp of course. Some of that nice brown paper we've just had in and a raffia tie. Very classy, even if I say so myself.'

Marion rolled her eyes. 'Not the flowers you half-wit, tell me about the *man*. Six feet of edible manly goodness. Yum yum. Did you get his name? Is he local?' She slammed the countertop. 'Sweetie!' she exclaimed. 'I bet he's moved into the Coopers' old place. That's just been sold. Was having a chatteroony with Ellie at the estate agent's only the other day. It's the most marvellous house, sea views to die for. No parking though and in town that's an absolute must. Wedding ring?' she trilled in her nasal voice, returning to the matter in hand. At Daisy's blank look, she added hopefully, 'Mark where the ring was?'

'No idea. The only things I know about him is that he had an appointment in town, he's a Spurs fan, money didn't seem a problem and he'd had a row with his girlfriend. The flowers were to say sorry.'

Marion's face fell. 'Oh, a girlfriend.' Then she pounced, pointing a red talon. 'But, if they're having arguments, perhaps they'll split up and he'll come in search of a beautiful raven-haired florist?'

'Who would that be then?' Daisy put the roses in their silver bucket, trimmed a last few carnations and began gathering up the waste.

'Don't be a dunderhead. I meant you, of course!' Then Marion caught Daisy's look and sighed in exasperation. 'It's no good being all clever-clever. Men don't like that. You'll have to stop being so missy-ish if you're going to land the likes of Mr Spurs.'

'If not being myself is the way to get a man, I'd rather not bother.'

'No hope for you then,' Marion said gloomily and ducked as Daisy threw a carnation stalk at her. But she wasn't giving up so easily. 'You said he was a Spurs fan?'

'Think so.' Daisy began putting the carnations into bunches with some asparagus fern and gypsophila. They were always a popular impulse buy. Cheap and cheerful and lasted forever.

'Mmm. London team.' Marion narrowed her eyes.

'He said he had a couple of hours' drive ahead of him so he could be from London.'

'Not local then.' Marion's lip curled. 'Shame. We could do with some excitement around here in the shape of a hunky man. Not a weekender if he was going home on a Friday.'

'He didn't give the impression of being a tourist either.'

'Maybe he was scouting the place out for a business venture? Or he's moving out to the countryside and is looking to see what bargains West Dorset has to offer?'

Daisy laughed. 'He'll have to look hard then. Houses cost an arm and a leg around here.'

'You're so right there.' Marion subsided. She picked at a corner of the white wrapping paper stacked up in a wodge on the counter. 'Don't think we could get a new five-bed for the money they want nowadays. That's what I was chatting to Ellie about.'

'You're not thinking of moving away?' Marion could be irritating but Daisy was fond of her.

'Don't think so, darling. Will wait until the kiddiwinks are off our hands but it's always good to keep an eye on the market. You're so lucky you've got the flat upstairs, you know.' She pouted, returning to the subject close to her heart. 'If he lives in London, doubt we'll be seeing him again.'

'Oh, you never know,' Daisy said, wickedly. 'Maybe he liked

Lullbury Bay so much, he'll come back for a holiday. And bring his girlfriend!' As one of their regulars, pensioner Austin strolled in with his elderly German Shepherd at his side, she added wickedly, 'Look, here's one of Lullbury Bay's sexy hunks now.'

Marion's head jerked round in expectation. 'What did I say?' she muttered, as she saw who it was. 'Too sharp by half. You'll never get a man. Hello, Austin darling. Your Aggie out of hospital yet? Oh, that's such good news. What about a super bunch of flowers to help her feel better? We've some gorgeous roses that Daisy here has just prepared. I can put some scrummy lilies in with them to make it really special and some ferns too. I know Aggie will adore them.' She giggled. 'And you'll get lots of Brownie points.'

Daisy watched the exchange with amusement. She could forgive Marion a lot. The woman was a genius at upselling.

Over the next few days, however, Marion drove Daisy mad. With Brittany at a friend's villa in Corsica and Cassius now backpacking around Europe, she had time on her hands. She had decided to make 'Get Daisy a Man' her pet project. Not only did she force Daisy out to the pub on a work night, she tried to convince her to try out a club in Dorchester. The evening, sitting in the beer garden outside The Toad and Flamingo had actually been quite pleasant, although Daisy had fallen asleep over her third glass of wine. However, she firmly drew the line at the nightclub, even in the face of claims she was, 'So boring!'

Marion also insisted she kept spotting Mr Spurs. Once in the supermarket, once stuck in traffic lights at the top of the high street driving a sporty convertible, and once looking into the window of Berry-Francis the estate agents.

'I *told* you he's house-hunting,' she breathed excitedly to Mia, who had dropped into the shop on the way to her other job, a shift at the supermarket. 'Keep a look out for him, won't you, when you're at work.'

'It'll be a bit tricky seeing as I have no idea what he looks like, Marion.'

The older woman flapped her hands. 'Tall, dark, well-dressed.'

'Narrows it down.' Mia winked at Daisy.

'Tell you what, Mia, I'll get some cards printed with Single and Desperate and my phone number and you can hand them out to any eligible man who passes through your till.'

Marion tapped her handsomely capped teeth with a Biro. 'You know, darling, that's not such a bad idea.'

'Marion!' Daisy and Mia yelled in unison.

'What about speed dating then? Dating websites? Ooh yes,' Marion said, getting into her stride. 'Dating websites! Must be an absolute load of men looking on those. I'll sign you up for a few.'

'And all distinctly dodgy so don't you dare!' Daisy said. 'I'm not sure what I have to say to convince you but I am perfectly happy being On. My. Own.' She said it with emphasis but the image of Mr Spurs flitted into her mind, with those lovely sardonic eyebrows and the humorous gleam in his dark eyes and she wondered if she really felt that way anymore. The debacle that was Neville was five years ago now and she'd been on her own ever since. Maybe it was time to start dating again? But how? She hated the idea of nightclubs and always had, and didn't think the answer lay in dating sites. To change the subject, she addressed Mia. 'You're looking very different today.'

It was true. Gone was the blue hair rinse and nose ring. The only sign of the old Mia were the multiple silver rings on each finger and a subtle diamanté stud in her left nostril. She was also dressed differently. Much more soberly, in a nondescript denim skirt and blue vest top.

She smoothed down the skirt with distaste. 'These are the only clothes I've got which I thought suitable.'

'Has the supermarket introduced a dress code?' Daisy asked.

'Nah, as long as I'm doing the job okay, they're cool. I've just come from an interview at the school. The primary school that is. Don't think I'm ready to set foot in the grammar yet.'

'As someone who used to teach there, I know how you feel,' Daisy murmured sympathetically. 'And Mrs Arnold is a touch on the conservative side, isn't she?' she added, referring to the head-teacher at the primary school.

'Isn't old Hart still head of the primary?' Marion asked. 'He's been there years. I swear he was head when I was there.'

'Hardly likely, Marion, that was forty-odd years ago.'

'Well, thank you very much, Daisy, for reminding me of my age,' she answered, feathers ruffled. 'He was head when Brit was there, I'm sure.'

'And when I was there too,' Mia put in. She pulled a face. 'Mr Cold-Hart we used to call him. Mrs Arnold took over a few years ago. Bit of a stickler for looking the part I was told. Which is why I wanted to look as boring, I mean as normal, as possible. Wanted to make a good impression. I wasn't exactly a model pupil when I was there.'

'Ah, honeybun, you did okay at school,' Marion said. She put an arm around Mia's shoulders. 'Your dad leaving like that would mess up anyone.'

Daisy looked on. Marion could be the most awful snob some-times but underneath it all, she was wonderfully caring. Apart from her current obsession with matchmaking, of course.

'Thanks, Marion. And your Brit stuck by me, you know. All through primary school, even at the grammar when I really went off on one and didn't want to know her cos she didn't hang with the cool guys.'

'Well, you're back friends now, that's the main thing. And I, for one, am very glad of it. You bring her down to earth. Wish she had your work ethic, sweetie.'

'Speaking of work ethic,' Daisy said, 'have you got time to fit in another job? What about your A-levels?'

'Need the money, Daisy. The job at the school is only three afternoons a week. I'm going to support a little boy with behavioural difficulties. I can fit in my other stuff round it and, of course, it's term time only.'

'So, are you saying you got it then?' Marion hugged her again. 'Well done, you!'

'Brilliant news, Mia,' Daisy added.

'Yeah, I can start as soon as my DBS check comes through. They said it wouldn't take long. Don't worry, Daisy, I won't let it get in the way of working here.' Mia looked from one woman to the other. 'I love it here and I love you two. Besides, I want to find out the end of Walter's story.' She grinned at Daisy. 'And maybe meet Mr Spurs. Funny thing was, when Mrs Arnold found out I was an ex-pupil, it was that which swung it.'

'What do you mean?' Daisy asked, moving to the office to make a celebratory pot of tea for them all.

'She said, as I'd had a difficult time of it at school, it put me in a good position to see where this little boy was coming from. Oh, and the fact I was cheap!'

Daisy laughed. 'Always an upside.' She poked her head around the door. 'Got time for a cuppa? No? I'll just make one for me and Marion then. We'll have some of Bella's special cream cakes from On a Roll on Saturday to celebrate properly.'

'Thanks, Daisy.' Mia put up her hand. 'See you guys then. Oh hi, Mrs Pearce, you in for your usual? I'm just off but Marion will look after you.'

Marion shot her a look. Brenda Pearce was a very regular customer who, although perfectly charming, always took ages to choose and then usually haggled the price down. 'What can I get you today, Brenda?' she said, moving her to the back of the shop. 'We've got some lovely chrysanthemums in. I can probably get you a little off as some of them are in full bloom. Or should I say, darling, *Va Va Bloom!*'

From her spot in the back room making tea, Daisy could just

about hear Marion and Brenda have a muted conversation and then heard Marion call out, 'Customer, Daisy!' in an oddly strangled voice.

She came out to the counter to find herself face to face with Mr Spurs. As gorgeous as she remembered. Blushing slightly and very aware of Marion watching covertly, she stuttered out a greeting. 'Hello there. You're back again.' *Stating the obvious there, Daisy, good start.* This time he was in a navy shirt and it offset his tan beautifully, as did the designer stubble. Out of the corner of her eye, she saw Mia hovering by the shop's main door. She'd obviously passed him on his way in. Eyes huge, she was mouthing, 'Oh my God, is that him?' and pointing and giggling wildly. Daisy made shooing motions and then realised Mr Spurs was watching her, bemused.

'Wasp,' she explained. 'Such a nuisance at this time of year.'

'Absolutely.' He smiled, making his eyes crease up sexily. 'Minty's terrified of them.'

*Oh great, back to the girlfriend.* 'Is she?' Daisy said inanely. 'Well, they can give a nasty sting.'

*That's the way to wow him; with your sparkling wit. Go, Daisy. He'll shrug off his Minty, renounce his trendy London lifestyle and get down on one knee in an instant.*

'What can I get you today? Another apology bouquet?'

'Actually no.'

*Bugger. They'd obviously made up.*

'As you promised, the flowers did the trick. So much so, I'd like another bouquet of the same. Minty went into ecstasies over them.'

'Wonderful.' Daisy tried to concentrate on her profits and not on how her heart had plummeted into her Crocs. It was doing her no good, no good at all, to lust after a strange man who was obviously in a relationship. Perhaps she should get out more. Perhaps she should even try those dating sites Marion had suggested?

Pinning on a smile, she said, 'I haven't any of the lilies this week but I do have some beautiful gerbera in.'

'Gerbera?'

'In the bucket on the left-hand side of the door. They come in a range of colours as you can see. I could do you a stunning hand-tied in clashing pinks and oranges or you can go classy with the white and cream ones and I can add in some pale-pink roses.'

'I like the white ones with the pink middle bits.'

'So do I. Shall I add in some roses too?'

'Perfect. I'll come back in about half an hour?'

'That would be fine.' For some ridiculous reason she wanted him to linger. 'Are you heading over to Bee's Books again?'

He pulled a face. 'Regretfully no. I have some errands to run. But thank you for the recommendation, I'll definitely return. Despite all the teapots, I had an excellent coffee in there.'

Daisy giggled. 'The teapots are Bee's thing. She haunts every car boot within a fifty-mile radius to find new ones.'

'Will any more fit?' He raised a disbelieving eyebrow.

'Oh, she'd find a way. I'll put your flowers together for when you come back. By the way,' she added, as he turned to leave, 'if you want a specific type of arrangement, you can call ahead. Give me a couple of days' notice to get the stock in.' She plucked a business card from the little box on the counter. 'Here's the number. If your girlfriend likes roses and lilies, give me a ring and I can make sure I have some in for the next time you're in town.'

He scanned the card thoughtfully. 'Thanks. That's kind. *"Va Va Bloom! Flowers by Daisy",*' he read. 'Good name.' His face bore a slightly puzzled expression as if he was trying to recollect something.

'Well, I can't resist a pun. Mum suggested something simple and classy, so we compromised and chose both.'

'And it's a teensy bit more sophisticated than the shop's previous name which was *Chariots of Flower.*' Marion appeared at his side, a bunch of yellow and bronze chrysanthemums in her hands. She dropped them on the counter. 'Hi there.' Holding out a hand she said, 'I'm Marion, Daisy's assistant.'

'Rick,' he answered, taking it. 'Nice to meet you.'

'Rick!' she said on a long breath, turning to Daisy and making a wow face.

'Don't leave Brenda alone, Marion, please,' Daisy said through gritted teeth. 'I'm sure she'd like some greenery to go with those chrysanths.'

Rick smiled. 'I'd best go. I can see you're busy. Marion, Daisy,' he said, giving a little nod to each as he did so, 'I'll see you later.'

When he'd left and was safely out of earshot, Daisy hissed, 'Marion, how could you!'

'Well, darling, at least I found out his name! We'd have been here till Christmas before you did.'

'Marion, why would I need to know his name? He's a customer not a marriage prospect.'

'Shame,' said Brenda, coming up silently behind them. 'He's got a lovely bum!'

# Chapter Six

'So Mr Spurs is called Rick?' Mia asked on Saturday.

'Apparently.' Daisy wrapped the cactus in blue tissue paper, tied it with a white bow and handed it to the nine-year-old customer. 'There you go, Claudia. I'm sure your teacher will love it.'

'Thanks, Miss Wiscombe.' The child grinned. She turned to Mia. 'Bye, Miss Lodell. See you in school on Monday.'

'You seem to have settled into your new job quickly,' Daisy said as they waved Claudia off to where her mother was waiting on the pavement.

'I really love it. Mrs Arnold is being surprisingly okay, I love Honor, the deputy, and the rest of the staff are ace.' Mia blushed a little. 'I love it there. I'd like more hours.'

'Maybe, come September, they might be able to give you some.' Daisy watched Mia's face glow and wondered what she wasn't telling her. 'These affordable end-of-term teachers' presents are going down a storm. I'll have to order in some more thank-you cards. And some more Marguerites. They've gone well this week too.'

Mia wasn't to be deflected. 'So, Rick. Do you think it's short for Richard?'

'Could be.' Daisy ignored the way her heart skipped a beat when his name was mentioned. It was getting ridiculous, she really couldn't allow herself to be attracted to a man who had a girl-friend, especially after what had happened between her and Neville. Contrarily, she let her thoughts wander and focus on Rick. She hoped his name was short for Richard. She loved the name. Strong. Manly. Trustworthy. Unlike the name Neville which was none of those things. And the owner of that name had definitely lived down to it. She just wished she'd found out at the start of their relationship and not after two years. Two wasted years. How had he hidden his marriage for so long? Or perhaps he hadn't, and she'd been too infatuated to see the signs?

She'd begun seeing Neville at about the same time she'd become stressed at school. Her head had been full of a career crisis and it hadn't room for hunting down clues that her boyfriend was married. Especially when he told her he wasn't. Now, a Richard wouldn't do that. She wracked her brain trying to think of any Richards she knew. The only one she could think of was Dick who owned Gladwin's the butchers. And while he was certainly strong, manly, trustworthy and bought his wife a huge bunch of carna-tions on a regular basis, he couldn't be described as sexy. And Rick was definitely sexy, with those dark eyes and chino-skimming thighs, not to mention his behind which Brenda Pearce had quite rightly pointed out was lush. Oh God, she really needed to join a dating site. Blinking, she came to. Mia had asked her a question. 'What?'

'I said, do you know what his surname is?'

'No. He paid by cash.'

'Ooh that's unusual. No chance to take a sneaky at his credit card then.'

'No.'

'Shame.'

'Why?'

'We could have done a bit of cyberstalking. It's well cool what trails people leave. Could have found out more about him and this Minty girl.'

'That's a terrible thought,' Daisy protested, half appalled, half incredibly tempted. 'Not sure I want to find out about Minty. Ridiculous name anyway. Sounds like a toothpaste.'

Mia bit her lip, thinking. 'I'm assuming it's Araminta.'

'Araminta. She sounds posh.' Daisy curled her lip, aware she was, yet again, prejudging people purely on name alone. She scowled. 'Unlike me.'

'Oh my eggs, you've got it bad.' Mia waggled an accusatory finger.

'I know. I have. I've met the man twice. Twice!' She considered for a moment. 'Four times if you include when he comes back to collect his order. And the most riveting thing I've said to him is,' she put a hand to her hip and adopted an affected voice, 'did you know gerberas mean innocence and true love?' She sighed. 'I'm practically giving him the means to throw him into his girlfriend's arms.'

'Do you think he'll come in again?'

'Who knows? I don't know why he comes into Lullbury Bay in the first place.'

'Well, if he does, make him up a bunch of yellow carnations to give to her.'

'What do they mean?'

'Rejection! And if he's still buying her flowers in September, sell him a cyclamen. That means goodbye.'

'Oh, Mia, that's awful. For all we know she could be a lovely, generous woman who fully deserves Rick. Look, it's gone quiet. Let's shut the door for ten minutes, have a cuppa and indulge in what Bella calls a Belgian bun but which is really heaven on a plate. The gods blessed the day Bella moved into this town. She's a genius.'

'You're on!' Mia stuck her head out of the door to check the high street. It was deserted. The heat and sunshine had driven everyone down to the beach. She banged the door shut, content they weren't about to miss out on a customer, forgetting to flip over the Open sign. Going to the back room where Daisy had already filled the kettle, she sank onto the scruffy office armchair and opened *The Lullbury Bay Echo*.

'Ooh,' she said, to the background noise of Daisy clattering about finding mugs and plates. 'Have you seen the Ninjas are at it again?'

'What have they done this time?'

'Tied huge yellow knitted suns on the lamp-posts in the public gardens.'

Daisy perched on a rickety wooden chair. 'Love it! That'll certainly brighten the place up.'

'Not everyone agrees. There's a letter here complaining about them.'

'Oh, don't tell me Colonel Smythe is on the warpath again. He's such a grump. Do you know he moaned about the noise coming from The Toad and Flamingo when they had their live bands on?'

'He's not so bad. He's a governor at school. Bit crusty round the edges but decent enough underneath.'

'My goodness, Mia, did you swallow a sunshine pill? I've never known you to be so positive about everything and everyone. Working at that school is really suiting you.' Pushing a cake-laden plate over, she spotted a rosy colour rising in the girl's usually pale face. Something was definitely going on and it had started when Mia had begun to work at the primary school. 'So, tell me who works at the school nowadays.' She took a bite into the fresh-cream, pillowy-iced delight that was one of Bella's cakes and was distracted by Jan walking in.

'Slacking again I see, chickadees.'

Daisy cut her cake in half and slid the plate over. 'Hi, Mum.

You're in early, although I'm not sure you'll be needed. It's really quiet today. Have you seen what's in the paper? Knitted suns in the park this time.'

Jan peered at the double-page spread held out by Mia and chortled.

'Look good, don't they,' Daisy said. 'Huge yellow knitted suns can't fail to cheer you up. There's tea in the pot if you want one, Mum.' She heard a slight cough from the shop. 'Did you flip the sign back to Open?'

'No. Didn't touch it.'

'Oops. My bad,' Mia said, through a mouthful of cake. 'Soz. I forgot to change the sign when I shut the door. Maybe someone followed you in, Jan, thinking we're open.'

Daisy got up. 'I'll go.' She waggled her finger in warning. 'Don't either of you dare touch my half of that cake!' Going into the shop, she skidded to an abrupt halt. 'Rick!'

'Hi, Daisy. It's me. Back again.'

'It's you.' Daisy wiped a hand over her mouth hoping she didn't have any icing crusted around it. 'Back again. You can't need another bouquet already?' He was wearing jeans and a white T-shirt today and looked hot – in both senses of the word. Strands of hair were plastered onto his forehead with sweat.

'I might take a bunch of something with me but, actually, I'm in between appointments and could really do with a drink and something to eat. And I, well I know you're busy, but I wondered if you'd like to join me? Show me the best places to eat around here.'

Daisy didn't have time to answer.

'She'd love to,' called Jan from the door, looking Rick up and down with interest. 'Time you had a lunch-break, Daisy. We'll mind the shop. Take him up the Toad. Go on. Scoot!'

# Chapter Seven

Rick and Daisy took their drinks into the beer garden and found a spot in the shade. The umbrellas were up and fluttered in the sea breeze which whispered past. It was very hot for June and even the gulls overhead were wheeling slowly, too lazy to dip down for chips. The sky was the colour Daisy always thought of as Dorset blue. A vivid stretch of brilliant colour uninterrupted by any clouds, even the wispiest. She edged to the end of the bench and lifted her face to the sun; it was extremely good to get out of the shop and feel the sunshine on her face. As The Toad was a little way out of town, it escaped most tourists and its clientele were usually local. It was quiet today and they had the beer garden to themselves.

Rick collapsed onto the bench. He drank half his pint of shandy in one go. 'That feels better.'

'Busy morning?' Daisy sipped her spritzer, wishing it was a cold pint of cider but she had deliveries to do later. The sight of Rick's throat muscles working as he drank was doing something very alarming to her insides. Her heart was thudding so much she could feel its beat near the surface of her skin. She put a hand to her navy-blue *Va Va Bloom!* polo shirt and rubbed her sternum. *Get a grip, girl, all he's done is drink shandy!*

'Non-stop.' Rick noticed she was rubbing her chest. 'Are you okay?'

Daisy sucked in a deep breath. 'I'm absolutely fine. Just a bit peckish.' To distract him she asked, 'What do you do? For a job, I mean.'

'I run a company which caters to the restaurant trade.'

Daisy wrinkled her nose in confusion. 'What does that mean exactly? Are you like Speakes which does mass catering to some of the pubs around here?'

He gave a short laugh. 'Not exactly. I specialise in supplying pubs and restaurants with niche produce from unique producers. What that actually means is I'm permanently on the road checking up on my suppliers and finding new ones, sampling their stuff. I have a lot in the West Country. Cheters on the outskirts of Taunton for instance. They make a fantastic range of charcuterie. Then there's Tansy Gins and Vodkas in Tavistock. The restaurants I service can't get enough of West Country produce.'

'I thought it was all about cutting down on air miles, sourcing locally nowadays?'

'That's important too. I try to find really distinctive products that have a novelty value. The most successful I've placed recently is an English sparkling wine with lavender top notes.' He turned his pint pot around thoughtfully and ran a thumb through the condensation running down its outside. 'But you're right, people do want locally sourced food more and more these days. Lately, I've been uneasy with the air miles count of some of my stuff. I've been considering a change in career for some time. I'd always loved the being on the road aspect of my job. No confining office, no nine to five. Seeing different parts of the country. But lately I've got jaded. The driving takes it out of me, the roads seem more congested. All I seem to see nowadays is the back of the car in front in a motorway jam.' He rubbed the back of his neck in a tired gesture, his eyebrows rising in surprise. 'I can't believe all this is spilling out. You're very easy to talk to, Daisy.'

'Thank you.' She sipped her drink. It had been said before. It was part of her job, especially when dealing with the bereaved. Sometimes she'd listened for hours to a customer before arranging the flowers for the funeral of a loved one. She didn't mind. She found it the most rewarding aspect of her profession. They hadn't wanted to discuss the floral tributes so much as the person they'd just lost. And, even though her father had died years ago, she knew about grief. She understood. 'Are you thinking about a career change?' She knew about that too.

'Possibly. Maybe even settling down somewhere. Putting down some roots instead of living at Gloucester Services. It's a very nice service station, don't get me wrong, one of the best, but I find I'm longing to have a place in a community. Maybe one like Lullbury Bay.' He sighed heavily. 'That's one of the things Minty and I argue about. She wants me to go into the restaurant business. Open up somewhere in Birmingham or London, or maybe Manchester but I'm not sure I want that kind of city lifestyle anymore.'

'We haven't got a decent restaurant in Lullbury Bay, not anymore,' Daisy said. 'Cafés – there's Sea Spray down on the beach and Bee's Books but they only do snacks. Nice food, don't get me wrong,' she added hurriedly, 'but if you want to eat out anywhere interesting or unusual, you have to go into Bridport or even further. Of course, The Ship is famous for its pies and the pub grub is good here too but if you want a special sort of place for an occasion, you have to go out of town.'

Rick's lips twisted ruefully as he looked around the beer garden.

Daisy saw its scruffy benches and children's play area with its faded plastic cartoon characters forming the slide and see-saw through his eyes. It wasn't exactly the height of sophistication.

'I can't see Lullbury Bay being Minty's scene somehow,' he went on. 'She's very much an urban animal. Although, you know, I can really see the appeal of living somewhere like this. And, the more I come here, the more I think so.' He flicked a glance at her and Daisy felt heat rise in her cheeks. 'What sort of restaurant could you see being popular here?'

Daisy lifted her glass and sipped thoughtfully. 'Well, the locals like value for money and something not too pretentious and the tourists flock to the coast for seafood so fish is always popular. You wouldn't want to set up in competition with The Ship or The Toad–'

'How did it get its name?' he interrupted. 'It can't always have been called the Toad and Flamingo.'

Daisy grinned. 'It used to be The Green Man. Craig the landlord put names in two jars and got punters to pick a few out, then put the two least likely together.'

'Think I prefer the old name.'

'I'm with you but it's a talking point and people always remember it.'

'Point taken.' Rick nodded. 'What sort of food do they do here?' he asked, as Vicky, Craig's wife, came to take their order.

'Usual stuff but it's good. The burgers are legendary.'

'Shall I order two of those then?'

Daisy's tummy rumbled in response. She'd been up early as usual and hadn't eaten breakfast. Neither had she finished her cake. Maybe the lump lodged in her chest really was hunger and not lust? 'Yes, please. I'll have cheese on mine and a side of fries.'

'The same for me. And please could we have another round of drinks too?'

'No problem.' Vicky looked curiously from Daisy to Rick.

Daisy knew she'd be the topic of gossip for the next few hours.

When she'd gone, Rick reverted to their earlier conversation. 'So, in this imaginary restaurant of mine, nothing pretentious and nothing to compete with burgers and pies.'

'Or cakes and sandwiches. We've also got On a Roll.'

Rick laughed. 'Thought you said there was nowhere to eat around here?'

'I did, didn't I?' Daisy pulled a face. 'I meant the sort of place you go for a really special celebration. Birthdays, anniversaries, that sort of thing. Think there'd be a market for it too. We've got the new houses on Beaminster Road; they're all four- and five-bedders so we're looking at disposable income there and Uncle Dave's art school is gaining a reputation. After a dodgy patch, the town's having a bit of a revival. Have you been up to the castle ruins yet, just beyond the public gardens? There are plans to illuminate it and have an outdoor theatre there. It's all really exciting.'

'So all it needs is a destination restaurant.' His eyes glowed. 'It could be just the place, you know.'

'Less competition than in a city where there are lots of others.'

'You're right,' he said slowly. 'Maybe serving seasonal food, good quality local produce? Organic meat, cheese, local ciders and wines. Daisy,' he said, with mounting excitement, 'Lullbury Bay could be the place!' Going with what was obviously an impulse he grasped her hand, took it to his mouth and kissed it soundly.

Vicky chose that moment to return with their drinks. 'A pint of very weak shandy and a spritzer heavy on the soda,' she said, unable to take her eyes off them.

Daisy disentangled herself reluctantly. The kiss, ridiculous as it seemed, had sent her insides liquid with lust. She'd almost forgotten what it felt like to have the hots for someone. It was all spiralling crazily out of control, building from a simple physical attraction to a good-looking guy to something more. Something far more. Rick's enthusiasm for her hometown and his longing to create a perfect new business in it warmed her heart. She loved her little seaside town and was proud of it, and more than a little protective. She could see Rick was beginning to fall under Lullbury Bay's spell as well. If he was serious about opening a restaurant it could be just what the place needed. And, of course, there was the bonus he'd be around a whole lot more.

Remembering he had the fragrant Minty in tow, she blushed. 'Think you've just set the rumour mill running. It doesn't take much. That's the downside of living somewhere like this. Folk love a good gossip!'

# Chapter Eight

Over their burgers, Rick asked about the history of *Va Va Bloom!*

'I qualified as a teacher, scored a job teaching science at the grammar, thought my life was sorted.' That was the short version.

Rick looked surprised. 'Hadn't got you pegged as a scientist.'

'Not many do. Don't know why. Biology was my main subject.'

'And then?'

'I started hating it.' Another brief version of the truth.

'Okay. Why, if it's not a stupid question? Although forcing science into the heads of teenagers obsessed with acne and the latest TikTok phenomenon doesn't appeal in any way to me, I could see why it might be an attractive career to some.' He shuddered slightly. 'I couldn't wait to leave school. I went straight into work, had enough of studying by the time I was eighteen.'

Daisy chewed on a mouthful of burger before answering. 'The kids were mostly fine. There were always the ones who caused trouble and they could be difficult, really difficult at times,' she amended, 'and the paperwork was horrendous. The hours were long too but that was part of the job.'

'There was something else?'

Daisy puffed out a breath. 'I just wasn't very good at it.' She wrinkled her nose and laughed, embarrassed. 'It was weird. I was always very academic at school. Did well in exams, got my head down, didn't cause any ructions, got on with it. When careers suggested teacher training it seemed the obvious thing to do. I sailed through the degree, enjoyed the placements, got what I thought was my dream job back at the school I'd attended, in my hometown.' She paused, staring into the distance, remembering the exact moment it had hit her. 'There was another teacher in the science department. He wasn't head of department or anything, he'd been there since he joined as a twenty-one-year-old and was now fifty-three. Still teaching. Still in the same school. In fact, he'd taught me. He'd never done anything else in his entire life.' Picking out a stray piece of lettuce, she ate it absent-mindedly. 'Not that there's anything wrong with that if it's what you want from life.'

'It's just you didn't.'

'Yeah. Suppose.' She gave him a twisted grin. 'And then the more I thought about it, the less confidence I seemed to have in my teaching. And then I got a really difficult tutor group and they sensed the weakness, you know? They just knew my heart wasn't in the job. Caused me all sorts of problems which I couldn't handle.' *Plus the fact I'd just found out my boyfriend was cheating on me. With his wife.* Daisy didn't add that. It wasn't something she was particularly proud of.

'So, what happened?'

'I was put on a warning to improve. Had a bit of time off for stress and then my aunt died.'

'I'm sorry.' Rick's sympathy was heartfelt. It seemed he was okay in the listening stakes too.

'Thanks. Yeah, it was rough for Mum for a while, she was her only sister. She left me some money which was a huge surprise as I didn't know her very well; she moved to Scotland when I was a baby. So I made some decisions. The money meant I was *able* to make some decisions. Decided to leave teaching and open a business. So that's what I did.' She picked up her burger and resumed eating. The simple explanation didn't encompass the hard work and study, the expense in setting up a business, the sheer hard grind. Not to mention the loneliness. But she'd done it. She was proud of herself and deeply grateful to her Aunty Marie. Her inheritance had given her an opportunity she could only dream of.

'You make it sound simple, but it can't have been. It sounds incredibly brave.'

Daisy gave him a huge smile. He understood. He really understood! The thought was a thunderbolt: *I could fall in love with this man if I'm not careful.*

'What made you decide on a flower shop?' Rick picked up a couple of fries and ate them.

'Well, there was one for sale, for a start,' she said simply. 'It seemed the logical thing to do.' It wasn't entirely true but it was the flippant shortcut answer she gave out when asked.

'Are you always so logical?' He had a teasing look in his eyes.

'Maybe.'

'And you enjoy being a florist?'

'I love it.' No flippancy needed this time. It was the truth. 'I'm there at all the important times in people's lives. When they have a baby, when they're ill, birthdays, anniversaries, when they're getting married, when they die. I'm right at the heart of the community.' In her excitement she waved her burger around, threatening to spray tomato slices around the beer garden.

'When they need to say sorry.'

'That too. It's as if the whole town is my family and I can join in with all their key moments.'

'Some family.'

Daisy's eyes went huge. 'You can say that again. It gives extended a whole other meaning and, trust me, with the Wiscombe family being the size it is, I don't need any extra relatives. It's fun though. I know all my regulars, get to know the visitors and the second homeowners. I've quite a few businesses who have contracts with me. I wouldn't do anything else.'

'And, when I open my restaurant, you can supply the flowers. I like flowers on a dining table.'

'So do I. It's a deal!' She met his look and a beat of understanding passed between them. She put the rest of her burger down, no longer hungry. Her face felt suddenly very hot.

'I'm sorry, I didn't mean to make you the butt of gossip. Earlier on, I mean.'

'Trust me, if there was no gossip, this town would invent some. Don't worry about it.'

'I–' He paused. 'I like you, Daisy. A lot. I like talking to you like this. You make things make sense.'

Daisy blushed even harder.

'Minty isn't interested.'

Another thunderbolt but this one showered pure ice. It had the effect of bringing her right back down to earth with a resounding bump. Was he really offering 'the wife doesn't understand me' excuse? The disappointment lodged in her throat, solid and cold. After a frigid pause she asked, 'Are you serious about opening a restaurant here then?' Her voice fractured. Jigger, the pub's Labrador ambled over. She fed him fragments of burger which he ate greedily and then tickled his black ears, concentrating on his soft glossy coat. She didn't want to meet Rick's eyes. She didn't know what he was playing at. Neville's duplicity misted round her. She couldn't believe Rick might be the same.

'I could be.'

'You'd best get yourself to Berry-Francis then. They have commercial as well as residential property on sale.' Daisy kept her voice matter of fact. The hurt lodged in her gut.

'I will.'

It was no good, she couldn't stay and make small talk anymore. If he was trying to do the dirty on his girlfriend with her, he had another thing coming. Hot tears pricked. She had to get out of here before she embarrassed herself. Bloody men. They were all the same. 'Well, thanks for lunch but I really have to get back to work now.' Daisy stood up. 'Bye, Rick. See you around.'

It was only when she got back to the shop that she remembered she hadn't paid for her lunch and that Rick hadn't returned to collect his flowers.

'Well, tough titties, Minty,' she muttered. 'You'll just have to make do with a motorway service-station bouquet that your beloved can pick up on the way home, or go without for once.'

# Chapter Nine

The stranger beamed at her from across the restaurant table. He had spinach stuck between his front teeth.

Daisy was going to kill Marion, she really was. How had she ended up in this gastropub on the outskirts of Chard when she could be at home glugging down wine and Tom Ellis in *Lucifer*?

Marion had ignored her request to have nothing to do with dating sites and had enrolled her in a local-ish one based in Dorset and Somerset. She'd shown Daisy the profile she'd written on her behalf. Daisy had exclaimed in horror at the description of: 'Florist. Early thirties. Pretty. Looking for her evergreen romance' and had vowed never to go on any blind date. EVER.

Then she'd flipped through some of the responses on the evening after she'd met Rick for lunch and, still smarting from his 'my girlfriend doesn't understand me' comment, had found herself agreeing to meet Brett. Forty, in computer programming and divorced, he seemed fairly safe. Although, looking at him across the table now, as he waxed lyrical about the excellent pension plan he'd taken out, the profile picture he'd posted must be at least ten years old.

Daisy tried hard not to prejudge as instructed by Jan, Mia and

Marion who had ganged up on her and ordered her to meet him. She'd valiantly tried to forget Brett rhymed with wet and chastised herself for getting hung up on a name. And, I mean, comb-overs were okay, weren't they? Brett actually had attractive eyes. Admittedly they weren't dark and sexy like Rick's and were a watery pale blue, but he seemed nice. A bit desperate but nice. Besides, she reminded herself firmly, Rick was very much taken and in a relationship with the fragrantly minty Minty.

Their mains finished, Brett began to tell her about his children. Three. All girls. She began to warm to him slightly. He obviously loved them very much. As the wine flowed, mostly into his glass, he began getting more and more loquacious. Over her gooey cherry and dark-chocolate pudding, she heard all about how well they were doing at school, how brilliantly the eldest played the violin, how much fun the twins were. But by now Brett was getting very, very drunk. And morose. He slouched over his uneaten lemon tart, his voice getting louder and louder, declaring his undying love for his children and his hatred of the wife who had left him.

Daisy had had enough. Throwing down enough money to cover her half of the meal – she certainly wasn't going to pay for the expensive bottle of wine he'd ordered and drunk in its entirety – she had a quick word with the bar manager about arranging a taxi for her date and left.

As she drove home, she thought she might be able to fit in at least one episode of *Lucifer* and a couple of wines before hauling herself off to bed. From now on, her romantic life would purely be Netflix-sourced.

# Chapter Ten

July's bouquet
*Scarlet geraniums – Pelargonium spp.*
*I'm so sorry, stupidity, folly.*

'So, darling, what was your date like?' Marion asked, as she flounced into the shop the following morning and deposited her designer bag in the back room.

Daisy glared at her. 'Do not speak to me.'

'Oh, was it that bad,' she said, emerging from the office and deflating. 'I had high hopes for Brett. He came across as being lovely.'

'I'm sure he was before the wife he loved and who gave him three kids left him for a twenty-five-year-old graphic artist in Bournemouth. Still, I think he enjoyed the bottle of Rioja he sank.'

Marion perched on the edge of the stool by the counter and pulled a face. 'Oh lordy, he didn't get drunk, did he?'

'Oh yes. He got drunk. And oh lordy is right. He was as drunk as a lord.' Daisy thrust the arrangement of cerise-pink gladioli at her. 'He got drunk big time. And then he got morbid, a bit tearful and then his nose disappeared into his pudding as his neck was unable to bear the weight of his head any longer.'

'What did you do?'

'I came home, what did you think I was going to do?'

'I take it you're not going to see him again then?' The question was tentative.

Daisy's glare was answer enough.

'Oh well, just notch it up to experience, sweetie. Lots more lovely men out there.' Thick-skinned as she was, even Marion recognised the hand gesture.

Daisy stomped into the back room, flung herself down onto the comfy office chair and used a letter knife to open Walter's latest request. The sound of metal slicing through the paper was immensely satisfying but it did nothing to take the edge off her temper. 'Ruddy Marion,' she muttered. 'Ruddy matchmaking mother, ruddy Mia. Bugger them all.'

Opening the instructions, she scanned its contents. 'Scarlet geraniums,' she read, disappointed. 'That's not very exotic, Walter. Maybe I can jazz them up a bit?' Thinking through her stock, the image of a bouquet of geraniums, some soft asparagus fern and the firebox-red alstroemerias which had just come in began to form. 'I wish I knew where the flowers were ending up,' she murmured. 'If they're left at a graveside I could make it more robust and lasting but if they're given to an actual living person, I could concentrate on fragrance. Still, these are my orders and I am here to obey.' She heard Marion wittering on to someone and went back into the shop to find her head-to-head with Mia and in deep discussion.

'The date was a disaster and no, I do not intend on going on another!' she yelled.

The heads of her employees shot up guiltily.

'I'm sorry it didn't work out,' Mia said. 'Still, as my mum always says, plenty more fish in the sea.'

Marion's face glowed. 'Apps,' she cried, flapping her shellacs. 'Phone apps. Isn't there one called Plenty of Fish or something?'

She pursed her perfectly made-up crimson lips. 'Or is that the gay one?'

'Marion!' Daisy cried threateningly.

She put up her hands in surrender. 'Okay, okay, I get the message. I'm sorry. Look, darling, I'll pop over to On a Roll for some custard slices. On me. To hell with the diet.'

'Make mine extra custardy.' Daisy strode into the office, collected Marion's handbag and threw it over.

'Careful, darling, that's Prada,' she said as she caught it. 'Toodle-pip.' After she'd swept out, the shop immediately felt calmer. Marion was a human whirlwind and it wasn't always welcome.

Mia spotted the note in Daisy's hand. 'Is that this month's order?'

'Yup. Scarlet geraniums. Not very exciting.'

Mia gasped and flopped onto the stool. 'On the contrary. They mean sorry. Walt's done something stupid to apologise about.'

'Don't most men?' Daisy pointed out sourly, thinking of Neville, Rick and now Brett. It seemed even their lovely Walter wasn't immune.

'Oh my eggs, it's so frustrating not knowing the whole story,' Mia exclaimed. 'Wonder what he did?'

'Who knows? Lied? Cheated? Talked obsessively about himself, got drunk and fell comatose into his lemon tart? And did I tell you he had a comb-over?'

Mia winced. 'I'm so sorry, Daisy. But he was only one. There might be someone on there for you. Don't write all men off. They're not all dorks.'

Daisy slammed the note down and leaned against the counter. There was a box of snowy white chrysanthemums waiting to be collected and she nearly knocked it off. Rescuing it as it was about to tip over the edge, she said sullenly, 'Just the ones I meet then. Did I tell you Rick told me his Miss Toothpaste doesn't understand him?'

'No way!' Mia was aghast.

'Way. I couldn't believe it. He seemed so nice, so genuine.' Daisy growled in frustration. 'The one time, the one time,' she repeated, her voice rising to a crescendo, 'I didn't make any prejudicial assumptions about someone and he turns out to be a love rat.'

Mia giggled. 'He's so not a love rat.'

'No but he was heading that way.'

'Were you getting vibes?'

'Oh there were vibes all right. I'll tell you about the vibes. Along with a lot of hand holding and gazing soulfully into my eyes, he even kissed my hand at one point.'

'Ooh!' Mia's mouth fell open.

Daisy shifted irritably. 'It's not "ooh" at all. He's got a girlfriend, a longstanding one from the sounds of it and he was trying it on with me. I'm not going there again. I don't want a repeat of Neville.'

'Neville?'

'I forgot you don't know about Neville. He was the man who cheated on his wife with me. For two years, and lied to me, saying he was single.'

'Ouch.'

'Oh yes, ouch.'

Mia twisted her nose ring thoughtfully. 'I can't see Rick as another Neville somehow. He looks too trustworthy, too straight.'

'Mmm.'

'I think it's the chinos. You've gotta trust a man who wears chinos. And they look like expensive ones too.'

Daisy laughed for the first time since her disastrous date with Brett. I'll take your word for it, Mia, but I don't intend to find out. I don't intend on having anything more to do with Rick Whatever-His-Name-Is ever again!'

# Chapter Eleven

Saturday saw a whole van load of deliveries, including a wedding. Jan offered to man the shop and Mia rode shotgun with Daisy, hopping out and delivering when there was nowhere to park. Once they'd done the wedding order, they could afford to relax a little; being late with wedding flowers was not an option.

After two local deliveries right in town, their third drop-off was to a semi-detached house on the outskirts of Lullbury Bay. Compared to most weddings Daisy did, it was a small order and she'd been asked to deliver everything to the house. Along with trays of buttonholes and the bride's and bridesmaids' bouquets there were a couple of large arrangements which the happy couple were taking along to the room in the pub where the wedding breakfast was being held. Luckily, she was able to squeeze the van into a space on the street, so she helped Mia take the flowers in.

Daisy loved deliveries like this. A house on the morning of a wedding was usually happy chaos and this one was no exception. A slightly tipsy matron of honour greeted them and showed them where to stash the flowers in the garage to keep them cool, and then offered bubbly which they had to decline. This was all against a backdrop of hairdryers, the photographer trying to organise a clutch of giggly middle-aged bridesmaids and the babble of young children running off some steam in the back garden. The budget for this wedding had been tight but Daisy had been determined to do them proud and, with lots of white carnations clustered tightly together, some pale-green globe chrysanthemums, gypsophila, and feathery fern to bulk it all out, she was happy she'd done the best she could within their price range. She'd even been able to sneak a few ice-white roses into the bride's bouquet.

'Aw, that's going to be a sweet wedding,' Mia said, as she shoved the sheaf of delivery notes into the footwell and squeezed back into the van, clipping her seat belt on. 'Couple in their sixties. Were at school together, got married to other people, then got divorced, and found one another again on Facebook.'

Daisy thrust Primrose into gear. The van protested and she prayed she wouldn't need more expensive repairs.

'So you see,' Mia continued, 'romance isn't dead. You just have to keep looking.'

'Until I'm sixty apparently. What's next on the list?'

Mia fished out the notes from under her feet. 'Walter's geraniums, two birthday bouquets over Maiden Newton way and then we're finished.'

Daisy glanced in her rear-view mirror, turned Primrose round and headed to the western edge of town and the bypass. The traffic immediately slowed to a crawl and she reined in her impatience. A sunny Saturday had tourists flocking to the beach. 'I should have gone the other way.'

'Too late now. Besides, Lower Sea Lane is closed. It's why everyone's coming this way. Tourists and locals too. Roadworks, Mum said.'

Daisy pressed the window down and switched on the radio. As 'Walking on Sunshine' played, she tried to breathe in patience along with the salty sea breeze, and sang along. It couldn't be a better song to sing on a sunny day by the seaside, even if you were stuck in traffic.

'What *is* this?' Mia asked.

'Katrina and the Waves.'

'The who?'

'Definitely not The Who,' Daisy giggled, 'Katrina and the Waves. It's a band. They won Eurovision although not with this one.'

'Oh Eurovision.' Mia immediately lost interest.

'Do you mind? I love a bit of cheesy Europop. You might well hear 'Love Shine a Light' in a mo. Primrose's radio is stuck on Bay Radio and it only plays golden oldies. But seeing as Primrose is a bit of a golden oldie herself it's quite appropriate.' She ignored Mia's puzzled look; the girl was too young to appreciate good music when she heard it.

As the traffic ground to a halt Daisy stopped singing and groaned instead. She loved living by the sea but on days like this, you had to build in extra time to get anywhere, in any direction. She switched off the engine, staring vacantly at the car in front. Her mind drifted, inevitably, to the business and specifically to the shopfront. She was happy with the navy-blue-and-silver sign and the window frames hadn't long been repainted in the same dark hue, but she could never decide what to put out at the front. Lullbury Bay's high-street pavements were narrow; she wasn't allowed any A-boards but she wanted to create an attractive frontage to entice customers in.

A pair of manicured matching box trees in silver pots with white satin ribbons had done the job for a while but hadn't lasted a harsh seaside stormy winter. Maybe a marguerite shrub or two would do the job? Or perhaps she should put out some racks of flowers for people to help themselves. Or would that encourage people to *actually* help themselves? With Lullbury Bay's mini crime wave going on, she wasn't sure her profits could take the hit. As well as some of the yarn bombing being vandalised, there had been a more serious spate of thefts.

Katrina trilled off to be replaced by The Beach Boys and

'California Girls'. Daisy's thoughts were tugged back to Rick. The song had been playing on the shop radio when he'd first walked in. She remembered the immediate visceral effect he'd had on her and the gentle banter about football and team colours. Her bottom lip jutted out in what her mother would recognise as a sulk. It wasn't fair that the only man she'd met recently and who she actually fancied, had a girlfriend. A girlfriend who apparently 'didn't understand him'. She still couldn't believe Rick had come out with that old crap. She let the vision of him float up into her mind's eye. He'd looked less put together the last time she'd seen him but still edible. She loved how his dark wavy hair flopped over his forehead in a cowlick that he brushed back impatiently and that his cheek grooved deeply when he smiled, which was often.

Pushing out a frustrated sigh, she switched on the engine and let out the clutch; the traffic was beginning to finally move. The sunny vibe fostered by cheerful pop on the van radio, the hot weather and by having done a good job for the wedding couple disappeared. Behind her sunglasses a deep scowl developed, and her mood plummeted.

Eventually, she turned off Withycombe Lane and bumped them up the track leading to Walter's house.

Mia asked, 'What's the house like?'

It was the first time she'd spoken since they'd escaped the traffic jam. Perhaps she'd picked up on the tension. 'You'll see for yourself in a minute.' Daisy tried to shake herself out of her strop. It wasn't Mia's fault all men were cheating love rats. 'It's late Victorian I'd say,' she added, feeling guilty for her previous terse answer. 'All turretty bits and stained glass. It's impressive but there's something about it that gives me the creeps.'

'Probably just because there's never anyone around.'

'Yeah maybe. There's never been anyone in as far as I could see.'

'Maybe there's a first wife locked in the attic,' Mia suggested and made woowoo noises. 'You know, shades of Mr Rochester?'

Daisy gave her a sharp look. She'd had enough of mysterious wives – and girlfriends come to that – to last her a lifetime. She drew alongside the Focus which was still parked tight against the garden gate.

Mia hadn't moved. She was staring up at the house, wide-eyed. 'Oh my eggs, it's gorg! Daisy, you didn't tell me how gorgeous it is.'

They got out of the van and Daisy reappraised the building through the girl's eyes. Although it still gave off mad-woman-in-the-attic vibes, she had to admit, with its leaded windows and the fairy-tale turret which curled around the left-hand side, in the shimmering July heat it was spectacular. Leading Mia through the garden gate she noted someone had mown the grass and tidied the flowerbeds. The straggly verbena had been pruned and some of the cherries had been harvested off the trees. It was all looking far more cared for. 'I've always been in too much of a rush to notice before. And being on my own, it gave me goose bumps.'

'I can see why. It's quite isolated up here.'

'I'd kill for a garden like this.' Daisy lifted her face to the sun, enjoying having a moment out of the van.

Mia swept round. 'Lot of work. Mum always moans about ours and we've only got a little square patch of grass.' She shaded her eyes with her hand. 'Is that a summer house down there? Behind that purple tree?'

'The copper beech? Yes, think so. Lovely tree. Don't see many that colour, it's fabulous in full leaf.'

'Let's go and have a look. Have we got time?'

Daisy glanced at her watch. 'Can't be too long, not with the traffic being like it is.'

'Oh come on, Daisy. Everyone will be heading to the coast and we'll be driving inland and by the time we've done the drops, everyone will be on the beach soaking up the rays and blowing up their inflatables.' Mia was already strolling down the lawn.

With a slight pang of worry over the flowers stored in the back of Primrose who sadly lacked air conditioning, Daisy decided five minutes wouldn't hurt and followed her.

She was glad she had. The lower end of the garden was shaded by the border of conifers and the magnificent mature beech tree. She took off her Crocs and sank her toes into the cool velvety grass. It felt blissful to her hot feet. While Mia explored the summer house, she took time to appreciate the house from this angle. It really was beautiful. And odd. Its bricks glowed a deep rich red in the sunshine and its roof dipped and soared in a complicated manner. The hard, practical side of her worried about ancient guttering and leaks, but even though she was a self-confessed unromantic, she swooned a little.

She wondered if the turret had a staircase inside, as it had tiny windows randomly placed all the way up. She also wondered if the owner ever came back to fling open the French doors to the evening sunshine and the scent of a newly mown lawn. Despite all its eccentricities she could see it would be a wonderful house to live in. Was it Arts and Crafts? She didn't have much knowledge of architecture and vowed to google the style when she got home. Glancing at Mia who was staring intently through the summer-house windows, a hand shading her eyes to see better, she sighed a little. It was time to go. 'Come on then, better leave the flowers and get over to Maiden Newton before the birthdays are over.'

Mia peeled herself away reluctantly. 'Nothing in there except a few battered old deck chairs and a rusty table.'

'What were you expecting, treasure?'

The girl pulled a face. 'Thought there might be something to give us a clue who Walter is.'

'Or was.'

'Was?'

'I suppose he might be dead,' Daisy said, the idea only just forming. 'Perhaps this is a posthumous request. It would explain why the house is always empty.'

Mia's bottom lip quivered. 'Oh, that's so sad.'

Daisy shrugged. 'It happens.' They began to walk back to the house. 'People set up orders but die before they see them through.'

'Has it ever happened at *Va Va Bloom!*, to your shop?'

'No, but I remember my predecessor had a similar order. Told me a woman set up a standing order for flowers to be delivered to her aunt every month but her aunt sadly died after the first three bouquets were delivered.'

'What happened? Were the flowers cancelled?'

'No. Think the woman had them delivered to herself instead. There was no deep mystery about it all.'

'And *Chariots of Flower* knew who had ordered and who was getting them.'

'True. And Jean, that's the woman who owned *Chariots*, delivered them to a real-life person who received them with pleasure. Not like here.' Daisy retrieved the geraniums from the back of the van and led Mia to the porch where, as before, there was a bucket of fresh water. She put the bouquet in, tweaked it a little before being satisfied and stood back. 'That'll have to do. Wish I knew when they were being collected. I hate to think of them getting overheated and drooping, it's boiling in here with all those windows.' The perfectionist in her hated to think Walter would receive something substandard and think she wasn't doing a good job. 'Hang on a moment, Mia. I'll just take a pic.'

'Why?'

'To prove I've left them in good condition and fulfilled my end of the contract.' As she aimed her phone, sweat trickled down her back. It really was warm on the porch.

'Don't you lock it?' Mia asked, as they emerged into fresher air.

'No, it's always left open for me.'

Mia frowned. 'Let's hope they don't get nicked then. There was a warning online of a couple of dodgy blokes cruising houses and seeing what they can pinch. They've got a scruffy white transit. Load anything they can into it.'

'It's always worried me that the house appears empty.

69

Although, if your theory is correct about the wife in the attic, the dodgy blokes might be in for a shock.'

'Yeah!' Mia laughed and checked the garden gate was properly shut. 'Right, next stop Maiden Newton and then a cold drink please.'

'Sounds good to me.'

After the last two deliveries were done, one to a woman who had already started celebrating her fiftieth in style and tried to ply them with champagne, they headed back to the shop.

As Daisy stopped at the traffic lights just up from the church, she caught a flash of colour. It was a woman in red, her hair a swishy mane of white blonde. As she watched, Daisy saw her smile and turn to a man, put her arm through his and reach up to kiss him. The man wore a navy shirt and chinos. It was Rick. They got into a flashy sports car and drove off up the hill.

So that was Minty. The girlfriend who so misunderstood him. If so, they looked very cosy. It was a beautiful afternoon for a romantic drive in an open-top sports car. Her mood plummeted again. She thought back to when she and Rick had eaten lunch at The Toad. Had he actually used the misunderstood line or had he simply said Minty wasn't particularly interested in his restaurant plans? Perhaps she'd jumped on what he'd said, prejudged in her usual way and had misinterpreted it completely. Either way, Minty was stunning and she and Rick looked very happy. Why would he ever look at her? An overworked florist with dried leaves in her hair and fingers ravaged by rose thorns. A car horn hooted behind her.

'Daisy, wake up,' Mia protested from her left. 'The lights went green ages ago.'

# Chapter Twelve

'Ah, come on, Daisy. Come to the pub. Just a quick drink. It's the end of term plus I want to celebrate getting through the first year of my A-Levels.' Mia had popped into the shop late on Wednesday afternoon, just as Daisy was thinking of closing.

'I'm too tired, I've had a lot of work on,' Daisy complained. 'And it's Wednesday. All I want to do is go home, ping a microwave and open a beer. The last few days have been hectic with this funeral. People can't plan when they die, you know.'

She'd tried to shrug off her foul mood but it had persisted, hanging heavy and low over her ever since the weekend. And it was true, the funeral flowers had been a last-minute addition to everything else she had on. The mourners, let down by another florist, had panicked there wasn't enough time to create the floral tributes they most wanted. Daisy felt she couldn't let them down. For some reason, she'd soaked up their grief and flowing tears and had struggled to keep her usual professional detachment. The deceased had been a much-loved grandmother, the head of a large family, most of whom had, at one point, sat in the little back room sipping tea and sobbing. It had all been extremely emotional.

It had taken two very long days, working around her usual

hours, to get things done. She'd slaved over an enormous arrangement of white lilies and deep-pink roses to go on top of the coffin
and had constructed a display of white carnations to spell out the
word 'Granny'. By the time the flowers had been collected by the
undertakers, she'd been exhausted, physically and emotionally. The
last thing she wanted was to sit in the beer garden at The Toad and
Flamingo.

Mia was having none of it. 'And you need to come too, Maz.'

'Sweetie, kindly do not shorten my name to that revolting
nickname.'

Mia flung an arm around the older woman and kissed her on
the cheek with a resounding smack. 'You love it really.'

'Mmm.' Marion didn't look convinced but Daisy knew she
secretly adored being called Maz. It made her feel young. 'I suppose
I could do with getting out of the house with Brit and Cass still
away, even if it is just to The Toad,' she added. 'Which is hardly my
first watering hole of choice.'

'Ah come on, Maz. The Old Anchor will be heaving with
grockles and there's nowhere to sit outside at The Ship. The
Toad's far enough out of town for people not to find it unless they
know it's there.'

'And there's good reason for that. It's shockingly sticky-carpet-
ed.' Marion shuddered delicately. 'I can't ever be seen in there.
What would my tennis club say?'

'They'd say you know how to have a good time on a hot July
evening. And you, Daisy, it's time you stopped being a misery guts
and got yourself out and about.' Mia came to Daisy and wrapped a
thin arm around her, squeezing her closer. 'Please say you'll come?'
she wheedled.

Daisy gave an enormous sigh. 'Okay, just the one. Any more
and you'll have to provide matchsticks.'

'Why?'

'For the propping up of my eyelids.'

'Ace!'

Daisy saw Mia flick Marion a knowing glance and was suspicious. She soon found out why.

She and Marion found a table in the pub beer garden with difficulty. The weather hung hot and sultry; it was one of those rare evenings in England when it was possible to sit outside and not shiver.

Mia returned from the bar carrying three glasses of white. Putting them down on the table, she moaned, 'Busy in there. Good weather's brought everyone out. Must be rammed down on the beach. This place was the right choice.' Flipping a leg over the bench she sat down. 'Cheers!'

Marion brushed an imaginary speck off her immaculate white linen trousers and raised her glass. 'Congratulations on getting through your first year, Mia.' She sipped her wine and added in surprise, 'Oh, this is actually quite decent.'

'Yes, huge congrats,' Daisy added. 'The first step to your new life!'

They chinked glasses.

'Aw, thanks, guys,' Mia said, blushing. 'You and Marion mean the world. I love working at *Va Va Bloom!*' She waved at someone on the other side of the beer garden. 'Looks like there are a few teachers from school here. Oh look, they're coming over.'

Though they were in The Toad, Daisy was, by now, smelling a rat. A huge one.

'Hi,' Mia said. 'I didn't know you lot were going to be here.'

The girl may be clever but she couldn't act to save her life.

'I think we'll have to budge up, Daisy,' Marion said in a voice which brooked no opposition. 'Let them share our table. There's nowhere else to sit.'

Daisy glared but did as she was told.

Once everyone was settled Mia introduced everyone. 'This is

Lexi the music teacher,' she said as a petite redhead smiled and said hello. 'Sarika's sitting next to her. Sarika job shares with Honor. They're both going to be Honor's bridesmaids at the wedding.' Mia blushed furiously. 'This is Ben who teaches Year Five, and Pete.'

Everyone said hi. Ben squeezed in next to Mia, Sarika and Lexi struck up a conversation with Marion about the Greek islands and, as Daisy could have predicted, Pete sat next to her. As set-ups went, it was about as subtle as a flying brick.

'Hi,' he said. 'You're Mia's boss at the flower shop, aren't you?'

'Yes, I own it.'

'Fantastic! Owning your own business. Way to go!'

He was nothing if not enthusiastic. Daisy relented a little. He was quite nice in a beige sort of a way, with light-brown hair and brown eyes. 'And you teach at St Winifred's?'

'Year Six. I love it. Wouldn't do anything else.'

His nose was slightly sweaty and he pushed up his glasses in a nervous gesture. Daisy wondered if he was as much of a victim of the set-up as she. She could just imagine the conversation in the staff room:

*Oh, you're single? So is my boss. She's lovely. You'd really like her. We're going to The Toad on the last day of term, why don't some of you all come too and then you can meet her, Pete. Being in a group will take the pressure off. See how you get on.*

She tuned back in to listen to Pete talk enthusiastically about his current class. 'They're lucky to have such a devoted teacher,' she said, warming to him. She took a tiny sip of wine. She was so tired it was going straight to her head.

He blushed scarlet. 'I'm the lucky one. It's a fantastic little school. I was teaching in Yeovil straight after qualifying. They annihilated me.'

Daisy sympathised. 'I used to teach at the grammar. I know the feeling.'

Pete shuddered. 'Couldn't do secondary.' He gulped back

some beer and added, 'Is that why you went into the floristry business?'

'I suppose so. I needed to get out of teaching to save my sanity.'

'Now that I understand.' He nodded vigorously. 'Even though I absolutely love my job, by the time I get to this stage of the term, I'm poleaxed. Really looking forward to my six weeks off.'

Daisy laughed. 'I remember that feeling well.'

'So how did you get into the floristry business?'

'I dropped a couple of days at school and retrained at an evening class. Did my City and Guilds. Bought the premises in town and here I am.' It didn't quite encapsulate the sweat and hard work but she doubted he'd be interested in the unabridged version.

'Wow!' Pete said, impressed. 'That must have been hard. Teaching and training in something else at the same time.'

'It was,' Daisy admitted. 'But I was single-minded about it. Always am when I know what I want. It's deciding what I actually want that's the problem.' Sliding Pete a glance, she wished she could be as single-minded about romance. In so many ways she was happy with her life. Proud of her achievements with *Va Va Bloom!*, content with her friends and what little social life she had. Then Mr Spurs had rocked up and the eddies were still whirling, her mind and pulse racing and mixing her up as much as her metaphors.

Take Pete here. He seemed nice, far more stable than Brett, far less likely to cry into his beer, they had things in common, he was easy to talk to and not bad-looking. But he wasn't Rick. He didn't have sexy dark eyes that were permanently on the edge of humour. He didn't have that ability to make her knees wobble with lust. And he didn't have Minty the gorgeous blonde girlfriend, she reminded herself. Maybe Pete would be the perfect boyfriend but somehow she doubted it. She assumed he was single, hence the set-up. His next words confirmed it.

Swilling the remnants of his beer around his pint glass, he

cleared his throat nervously. 'I'm sure you're too busy but now term's finished, I'm keen to see the new Tom Cruise film in Bridport. I... um... I don't suppose you'd consider accompanying me? We could grab something to eat too, maybe?'

He was sweet. Old-fashioned. Safe. Daisy studied his open, honest face. He probably didn't have a wife or girlfriend secreted away somewhere but you never could tell. Ignoring the voice which was screaming in her head, *He's friend material, he's not Rick!* and telling herself Rick was most decidedly attached and, what's more, attached to the lissom blondness that was Minty, she made her decision. 'I owe you a chance,' she muttered. 'If only to prove to myself that I'm a terrible person who still hasn't lost the habit of prejudging people.'

'Sorry?'

Daisy sucked in a deep breath. What harm could it do? 'I'd love to, Pete.' She smiled. 'I'd love to see a film with you.'

# Chapter Thirteen

Despite seeming keen, Pete failed to ring Daisy. She put him to the back of her mind but cared more than she wanted to. The rejection stung. Luckily work was manic and she had two more weddings and another enormous funeral to organise. Plus, she'd applied for WebFlorist status and was panicking about the forthcoming inspection. If she passed, she'd be able to join a network where orders could come in via a website. She knew it would boost trade so there was a lot riding on it.

On the following Saturday morning Jan slid into *Va Va Bloom!* with a small brown-and-white spaniel on a lead.

'Hi, Mum, who have you got there?' Daisy looked up from checking the day's wedding order.

'This is Fleur.'

'Why?' Daisy glared as she squeezed another peach-coloured rose and fern buttonhole in the cardboard tray. She was relying on Jan to look after the shop while she delivered them.

'Why is she called Fleur?'

'No, Mum,' Daisy said impatiently. 'Why have you got her?'

Jan looked shifty. 'I'm just taking her for a walk as a favour for someone.'

'Who, Tom at the Animal Sanctuary?'

Tom Catesby ran a haphazard animal rescue centre at a farm on the outskirts of town.

'Sort of.' The answer was cagey.

Daisy cocked an eyebrow. 'Not surprised he'd want to keep her out of the way of Tiny. He'd eat a little thing like that whole.'

'Rubbish. Tom's Tiny is an Irish Wolfhound. Enormous but gentle as a lamb.'

'I'll take your word for it. Looks more donkey to me. He's huge.'

'Who, the dog or Tom?'

'Both! And since when have you been such an authority on dogs?'

'I read a lot. There's a thing called Google you know.'

Daisy came to stand in front of her mother. She bent down and tickled the dog under the chin. 'Have to admit she's pretty, with those huge eyes. What breed is she?'

'Cavalier King Charles Spaniel.'

'Hello, Fleur. You're very gorgeous.' The dog snickered a little, stuck out a dainty pink tongue and licked her finger. 'Cute.' Daisy straightened. 'When are you taking her back to her owner?'

'Oh I thought she could stay here for a bit.'

Daisy expelled a frustrated breath. 'How's that going to work, Mum? I've two weddings to get flowers to this morning. You'll have to man the shop while Mia and I do the deliveries.'

'She'll be no trouble.' Jan bent and picked Fleur up. 'You're as good as gold, aren't you?' She buried her nose in the dog's luxurious coat.

Daisy watched on indulgently. She'd never seen her mum so besotted, never thought of her as a dog person.

Mia came from the back room. 'Oh! Who's this?'

Jan repeated what she'd said to her daughter. To Daisy it rang even less true the second time but she was too busy to dwell on it.

'If you can stop fussing over a dog for a minute, we've all got work to do.'

'No need to be sharp, Daisy,' her mother reproved.

'Take no notice, Jan.' Mia tickled the dog's ears. 'She's been in a grump since opening up. Worried about getting the paperwork stuff done for the WebFlorist status.'

Daisy crammed one more buttonhole into the tray. Always paid to put in a few spares. 'Sometimes,' she said through gritted teeth, 'I wish the people around me and who profess to love me, wouldn't talk about me as if I wasn't here!'

'Oh, you loon, of course you'll be good enough to meet all the criteria for WebFlorist,' Jan said, in between crooning at Fleur. 'They'd be mad to say no. Although, if you want my advice, you're busy enough as it is, without all that bother.'

'It's just that people expect it nowadays, Mum. They expect to do stuff online. I know *Perfect Posies* in Dorchester do a lot of trade for over our way and pick it up having WebFlorist status. I need to update the website too,' she added gloomily. 'That's looking a bit dated.'

'Oh, lovie, didn't you do it just after you opened? That's been barely four years.'

'Five.'

'Has it? Time's flown.'

'And these things date so quickly, Mum.' Daisy ran a hand distractedly through her hair, leaving a rose leaf tangled in it. 'I need to present a good shopfront.' She chopped at the stems of some ginger-hued roses. Not her favourite colour, they'd been left over from a wedding order but would look okay bunched up with some dark-orange gerbera and maybe some yellow carnations. Bit autumnal for this time of year but she couldn't afford to waste stock.

'I thought *this* was your shopfront?' Jan gestured to the shop floor crammed with elegant silver containers of cut flowers, a cream-painted distressed dresser displaying scented candles and small gifts and the new acquisition, a greetings card rack.

'You don't understand.'

'I'm happy to have a look at the website for you,' Mia put in brightly.

'Thanks.' The reply was leaden.

'Are you all right, Daisy?' Jan handed Fleur to Mia. 'Find her some water, would you, my lovely? And then be an angel and pop to the post office. We need second-class stamps.' Mia looked from mother to daughter and took the hint. Jan came to her daughter and gently took the long-stemmed roses out of her hands. 'Let me do those, you're mashing the bottoms. They'll be good for nothing.'

Daisy flopped onto the stool. 'I'm fine.' She stared at her feet, hands dangling loosely between her knees.

'Yes I can see. Fine as mustard and twice as dandy.' Jan put the roses to one side and took her daughter's hands. 'There's more to life than work, Daisy. Look at what it did to your father. Worked himself to the bone and dead before fifty. Don't be like him, lovie.'

'I know.' Daisy shook her off and rubbed at her eyes. 'But I have a mortgage to pay, business rates, suppliers to keep happy whether or not I sell their stock.' She blew her fringe off her face. 'Sometimes it gets to me.' It wasn't the total truth but heartache over Rick and Pete's apparent lack of interest had compounded with her business worries and brought her low.

'If it's money you're worried about, I can chip in to help.'

'You've only got the cottage, I wouldn't dream of it.'

Jan shrugged. 'I could always remortgage it. I've often thought I would. You know, have some cash, go on a cruise. Invest in my daughter's business.'

'No,' Daisy said firmly. 'I am not taking your pension from you. You've got Drew and Luke to consider too,' she added, mentioning her twin brothers.

'If they ever come back from working abroad. It's about time they settled down and provided me with some grandchildren.'

Daisy mustered a smile. The grandchildren refrain was a regular one. She heaved a sigh. 'Things aren't that bad, Mum. I'm just having one of those days, you know. Just having one of those weeks, to be honest.'

'I know.' Jan gave her a hug. 'But the offer's still there. Don't be too proud to accept help. Don't be like your–'

'Father,' Daisy finished. 'Do you miss him, Mum?'

'Of course I do. I'll never stop missing him.'

'Did you ever think about remarrying? It's been a long time, nearly seventeen years. You know I wouldn't mind, not if he made you happy.' Daisy pulled a face. 'At least I don't *think* I'd mind, once I'd readjusted.'

'Me? Remarry?' Jan said, startled. Then gave a dry chuckle. 'Don't think anyone else would put up with me.' She leaned against the counter, burying her nose in a bunch of freesias, inhaling their heady scent. She was silent for a moment, her mouth twisting. 'Besides, I doubt I'll ever meet another man who will match up.'

Daisy saw the tears glistening. 'I'm sorry, Mum. I'm really okay, you know. The business is doing okay too. I'm just having a self-pity fest. I didn't mean to upset you by talking about Dad.'

'You can't upset me by talking about your father. He was the love of my life. I met him when I was sixteen and, from the minute I set eyes on him, there was never anyone else for me.'

Daisy gazed wistfully at the tray of buttonholes, all ready for a couple's big day. She wished she could kick herself out of this mood. It was unlike her but sometimes she felt her entire life was catering to other people's most romantic days. 'Do you think there's only one person for each of us?'

'I don't know, my lovely. I really don't know. Maybe. Maybe, if we're lucky we get to find love again. But don't take on so.' Jan straightened and became very busy. 'I'm absolutely all right. I enjoy

my life tremendously.' She gave Daisy another hug. 'I have the
most wonderfully clever, hardworking daughter, a nice place to live
and lots of friends. A lot of people can't say the same. I'm very
lucky.' She paused, seeming to be on the verge of saying something
important. 'Daisy, I've–'

'Yes, Mum?' Daisy looked at her. Her brisk and matter-of-fact
mother was unusually nervous. 'What is it?'

'Oh nothing. It'll wait. Cuppa?'

'Yes please. Can squeeze a quick one in before I get going.'

Jan went into the back room. 'Choccie digestives too, I think.
Weren't you going to go out with that chap you met in the pub?'
she called through. 'Might do you good to have something else
apart from work to concentrate on.'

Daisy could hear her rummaging about. 'He didn't ring me.
Mia says school had been manic though. End of term stuff, you
know, plays, concerts, sports days, parents' evenings. I expect he's
recuperating, and I don't blame him. It used to take me at least two
weeks to wind down and feel human again.'

Jan poked her head out. 'Who is this man who has stood up
my only-born daughter? Let me at him and I'll tear him off a strip.'
In the background Fleur yelped in agreement.

Daisy giggled, her mother's indignation finally cheering her up.
'He hasn't got as far as standing me up. He hasn't even asked me
out yet. Not properly.'

'What are you waiting for? Aren't we living through the great
age of equality? Ring him up yourself, you loon.'

'I'm not sure I want to.' Daisy sat on the stool again.

'You don't think he's The One?' Jan cocked a hopeful
eyebrow. 'Or even Mr Might-be-The-One? Or even a Mr Provide-
a-Poor-Old-Widow-with-Grandchildren One?'

'I don't think he's even Mr Potentially-a-Possible.' Daisy
pointed an accusing finger. 'And don't even get started on how
much you'd like grandchildren. I'm only thirty-three, I've plenty of
time.'

'Hate to worry you, lovie, but I had you when I was twenty-five. I thought there was plenty of time to have a whole football team but it never happened; your Dad and I wanted a big family. Don't take these things for granted.'

'I never knew you wanted more children. Weren't the three of us enough?'

'Yes, well,' her mother huffed. 'After the twins and then you, I wanted another girl but it didn't happen, so I made do with you.'

'Jeez, thanks.'

'You're welcome. So, if this teacher chappie isn't The One, who is? You've got to flex those romance muscles sometime or they'll wither and drop off.' Emerging from the office she stood implacable. Crossing her arms, she surveyed her daughter more closely. '*Have* you met someone, Daisy? Someone who might be special? Is that the real reason you've been so cranky this morning? Well, what's going on?' Jan paused then gasped. 'Oh no, it's not another married man, is it?'

'Get off my back, Mum,' Daisy answered, but softly. She was saved from further interrogation by Mia returning from the post office.

'Six booklets of stamps, all second class as instructed and I picked up some milk as we were running low.' Her nose twitched making the nose ring glint, obviously picking up on an atmosphere. 'Have I missed something?'

'No, nothing at all.' Daisy took the milk from her and nodded to the front of the shop. 'Customer, Mia. Could you deal? Mug of Very Berry?'

'Ace.' Mia gave the pair a troubled look and approached the customer. 'Can I help you? Yes, these lisianthus are pretty, aren't they? I like the deep-purple ones. They look really good with some cool green eucalyptus foliage and a spray of gypsophila.'

As Daisy followed her mother into the back room, they heard the girl continue.

'Did you know they mean charisma? Oh, didn't you know

flowers had meanings? Yes, lisianthus stands for charisma and congeniality. Nice, isn't it? Yes, of course I'll make you up a bouquet.'

Daisy took the chocolate digestive Jan offered and bit into it mournfully. At the beginning of the year she would have said she had no interest in romance whatsoever. And now, the unattainable Rick had turned that upside down. She couldn't even get a bloke she wasn't particularly bothered about to ring her for a date. Perhaps she should help herself to some lisianthus. If anyone was in need of charisma, it was her.

# Chapter Fourteen

To hammer home Daisy's resolutely single status, the happiest couple in Lullbury Bay came to their appointment to discuss wedding flowers. Honor was glowing with so much happiness Daisy didn't need to put on the shop's lights and Jago, who she could see was besotted by his fiancée, sat in the little back room sipping coffee. They should have been irritating but the love radiating off them was overflowing and genuine. Even the hardest-hearted, most jaded florist couldn't be cynical.

Wincing, Daisy glanced around the office with fresh eyes, thinking this was the next project; she could really do with a room where she could take clients to discuss flowers. She knew Honor and Jago pretty well so could get away with a meeting conducted over a ramshackle table with mismatched chairs, but it was hardly professional. She'd felt awful discussing flower arrangements for a funeral in here recently. Over the years the office had become more and more scruffy and cluttered, and it wasn't the image she wanted to portray going forward with her business. It would have to do for now, until she reassessed her profit margins, and at least Jan had worked her magic and it was clean.

A door led from the office to the walled garden beyond; her

workplace's best kept secret. If only she could afford a conservatory; it would be a suitably relaxing place to meet with clients. Her mind drifted as Honor and Jago looked through magazines for ideas. She could see it all now: tall ficus in enormous Greek pots, a leafy cheese plant or a delicate maidenhair fern. An antique rug on the floor and some good quality rattan furniture with lots of squashy cushions, doors open to the garden with the sound of trickling water from a water feature somewhere.

The image arose so clearly, she could smell the earth in the pots and feel the warmth of the sun beating down on the conservatory roof. She'd always considered expanding into selling more pot plants and it would be an ideal showcase. Sadly, the garden would have to stay as it was, underused and sadly neglected; she didn't have the time nor the money to invest at the moment. If only she had more confidence to spend more and take a chance on expansion. What was the phrase? Speculate to accumulate? Fear made her cautious and it was holding her back.

At least she'd finally decided on what to put either side of the front door of the shop. Two elegantly trimmed lavender bushes with fluttering silver and navy ribbons currently stood outside. They were in flower and the scent wafted in on the sea breeze. It was very calming. Her mind flickered to the dresser on which stood small gifts like teddies and scented candles. Some luxurious hand cream might go well, perhaps aimed at gardening hands, healing and maybe lavender scented. And she liked the idea of selling bunting too. Several customers had asked where they could get some, especially for big birthdays and baby showers which were becoming increasingly popular. She made a mental note to investigate some suppliers.

'I'm so sorry, what did you say, Jago? I drifted off there for a second. I do apologise.' She was surprised it was the groom-to-be and not the mother of the bride who'd attended but Jago was a renowned glass artist so perhaps he had an interest in how things would look.

'I said I don't think we really know where to begin.' He gestured to the magazines.

Daisy smiled at him, entranced by his grass-green eyes. He really was a handsome man. He sat, bunched up on the tiny chair, his knees up by his elbows. As well as being good-looking he was also tall and rangy. Far too tall for the chair she'd forced him to sit on. Biting her lip she said, 'I do apologise for the room, it's a little cramped.'

'It's cosy, Daisy,' Honor said. 'And the scent from your stock is wonderful.'

'Thanks, Honor. I would have come to you but it's easier this way. I can show you samples of some of the flowers and we can put a few colours and designs together.'

'I'd love that! It's all so exciting, I can't believe the wedding is only a few weeks away now.'

'I suppose you had to plan it for a school holiday?'

Honor nodded. 'Yes. The holidays are very welcome as a teacher but I don't have any flexibility when I take them.'

'It's late in August. Are you not having a honeymoon?'

Honor glanced lovingly at Jago. 'Oh yes but we're saving that for Christmas. We're going to Iceland.'

'Oh how fabulous. Now, flowers. Do you want small, large, traditional or a cottagey look, or something more sculptural.'

Honor blinked. 'I have absolutely no idea. Now it's my turn to apologise. My brain's still fried from the summer term. I don't think I've recovered yet. Another good reason to wait until the end of next month. At least then I'll be in a fit state to thoroughly enjoy the day!'

'I remember it well. I taught for a while too. Only began to feel human in mid-August.' Daisy laughed. 'Well, how about we start with favourite flowers. Is there anything special connected to when you first got together?'

Honor made a face. 'That was at Christmas too.' She giggled. 'I'm so sorry. We're hopeless, aren't we?'

'Not at all. I've closed the shop for an hour so we can take our time,' Daisy said. It meant she'd have to miss lunch but she didn't mind; she wanted to get it right for these two. She took in a breath. 'Let's start again. Colours?'

'The bridesmaids will be in a very pale pink.'

Daisy made a note. 'Have you a sample of the material?'

Honor scrabbled in her handbag. 'Yes. She handed over a scrap of oyster-pink satin. The grown-up bridesmaids and matron of honour will be in that colour and Merryn, that's Jago's little sister, will be in a slightly warmer shade.'

'That's pretty. We can put a whole range of colours against it. I can make the same bouquets for the bridesmaids and for you, or you can have something slightly different, or you can have a bigger version of the same.' Daisy saw the confusion and burgeoning panic on Honor's face. 'It's going to be in the church, isn't it?'

Honor nodded. 'Verity's marrying us.'

'She agreed even though I'm divorced,' Jago put in. He put an arm around Honor and hugged her to him. 'She knows I'm in it for life this time.' He kissed her cheek and she blushed.

Daisy watched them. They really were a gorgeous couple. Honor was a honey blonde with eyes so blue they were almost purple, the perfect foil to Jago's slightly piratical looks. There was something old-fashioned about her and she was going to make a stunning bride. 'Can I make a suggestion?'

'Please do!' The reply from Jago was heartfelt.

'With your colouring, Honor, and the bridesmaids' delicate pink dresses, I think you should go for something unstructured in pale shades. A simple bouquet of cream and very pale-pink roses, with maybe some peonies and some soft green foliage to set it off. Subtle and delicate. I can add lavender and freesias if you like to give it scent. Shall I put together a rough example?'

Honor clapped her hands together. 'Sounds perfect, Daisy.'

'Great. Once we've got the right colours and flowers, we can work from there for the church and reception. It's at Cheney House, isn't it? Over at Bereford?'

'Yes. In a marquee.'

Daisy pictured the lovely mellow stone walls of the Georgian house. Primarily a garden centre with a lake and beautiful grounds, they'd recently begun hosting weddings. It was the perfect romantic setting. 'If I'm right in remembering, there's a rambling rose, a Gertrude Jekyll that would be the perfect background for the photographs. Although it might have gone over by the end of August.' She tapped her chin, thinking. 'There's a superb Albertine too so we might be in luck. Janey, the head gardener, knows how to look after her plants so it'll be looking tip-top. Think the rose theme is the way to go. Have another coffee, help yourself to biscuits and I'll be just a minute.'

Going through to the shopfront, she put together a hastily arranged bouquet of delicate, shell-pink roses, some slightly deeper pink gerberas, three pure-white roses and added some silver-dollar eucalyptus. Wrapping some pale-pink satin ribbon in a broad band firmly around the stems, she returned to the happy couple.

She went unnoticed for a minute as Honor and Jago were chatting to one another. She couldn't help it. Loneliness pierced her. She'd spent the years since splitting up from Neville resolutely ignoring and dismissing anything romantic in any shape or form. She'd developed a hard shell, flippant on the outside but which hid the pain underneath. It was as if she didn't acknowledge her softer side, then it didn't exist. She saved her best cynical act for Valentine's Day, spouting her personal theory that it was a commercial nonsense and if you couldn't be romantic all year round, why save it up for one day.

She didn't miss the irony that it was one of the days, along with Mother's Day, when she made a good profit. The hard persona she'd built up since finding out about Neville's betrayal had become such a habit it could almost be her true self. But it wasn't. She spent her days making other people happy and romantic with the gift of flowers; she wanted just a little bit of that for herself. As she watched Jago hug Honor to him and kiss the top of her head in a gesture so tender it nearly made her weep, the emotions tumbling through her almost burst out. It was ridiculous, she'd done flowers for tens of weddings since she'd been in the business; what was so affecting about his one?

'Here you go,' she announced over-brightly. 'Not convinced the gerberas work but it gives you a general feel.' She plonked herself on the opposite side of the table and handed the bouquet to Honor. 'Some argue brighter colours work best for the photographs, but you can't beat a subtle colour palette and roses for a classy look. We can continue the theme for the buttonholes, the pew ends and the flowers for the wedding breakfast.'

Honor cradled the flowers to her, eyes sparkling with tears. She couldn't speak so Jago spoke on her behalf. 'You're a genius, Daisy. It's like painting with flowers.'

'From you, I'll take that as a deep compliment.'

'And it's meant as such.' He pushed over a flat tissue-wrapped parcel. 'This is a small token of our thanks.'

Daisy went very hot. 'Goodness.' With all this emotion flying around there wouldn't be a dry eye at the wedding. 'What is it?'

'Open it and you'll see. Only a very small gesture of our thanks for all you're doing.'

Daisy tore the white tissue and uncovered a heart made from blue glass. It was one of Jago's trademark light-catchers. He made small items in stained glass which were exquisite and in high demand. He also made large decorative glass panels for which people paid a fortune. She'd like one of those in the conservatory which, as yet, remained a distant hope. Holding the heart to the light, she twisted it this way and that. Made of shifting shades of blue, the glass was shot through with something magical and sparkly. It caught the light as she dangled it from her finger, sending reflections bursting around the dull little room. 'Oh my.' The tears she'd swallowed erupted. 'I'm a wreck.' Accepting a tissue from Honor, she scrubbed at her eyes. The glass heart could be her own; brittle to touch but fragile and easily destroyed. What was it about this particular wedding that made her so emotional? 'Bugger. What is it about weddings that turns on the waterworks?'

'I don't know.' Honor sniffed. 'I'm blaming it on end-of-academic-year exhaustion.' She blew her nose. 'Don't know what your excuse is.'

Daisy attempted a laugh and failed. The tears formed thickly and stuck in a hard lump in her throat. 'Thank you, Jago. I'll find somewhere in the shop window to display it and I'll treasure it. Actually, scrap that, I'll put it somewhere upstairs in the flat so it's safe and I can admire it.' Becoming brisk before she completely dissolved, she added, 'Now you have to go.'

'Why?' he asked, startled.

'Because Honor and I have to discuss her dress, her bouquet in detail and any possible headdress. So run along.'

'Yes, run along,' Honor repeated, merriment bubbling through the tears.

Jago put up his hands in defeat. 'I know when I'm not wanted. Come and find me in Bee's Books when you're done.' He stood and then bent to plant a kiss on Daisy's cheek. 'Thank you again.'

Daisy watched him go, clasping the glass heart to her own. At this rate a glass heart would be the only one she'd conquer. If only she could find a man half as nice, a fraction as loving as Jago, then she'd be all right. Aware she'd sighed, she turned to Honor. 'Now the man has gone we can get down to the really interesting stuff.' She leaned in, eyes gleaming. 'What's your dress like?'

# Chapter Fifteen

A s if to prove the job of florist was nothing if not varied and surprising, the following day saw Lullbury Bay's most feared pensioner come into the shop. Aggie Ruddick, doyenne of self-help manuals and an advice blog for the more mature, plonked herself down on the stool in front of the counter.

'How are you, Aggie? Hope you're feeling better now. What can I do for you?' Daisy shifted nervously. She was on her own having let Marion leave early. The woman had said something about needing to get home to FaceTime with Cassius. Daisy had no desire to get in between mother and son and, besides, she knew Marion had been anxious about Cassius deciding to leave Europe and travel to Thailand on a whim. She was right to be worried; Cass wasn't the sharpest tool in the box and easily led. The shop had been busy earlier on but had quietened and Daisy had planned to go over the paperwork for the WebFlorist inspection. She'd suppressed a groan when Aggie had marched in. About to ask her if she knew who lived in 'Walter's' Arts and Crafts house in Withycombe Lane, as what Aggie didn't know about Lullbury Bay wasn't worth knowing, she was taken aback when the woman began to speak without ceremony.

'I need some funeral flowers,' she demanded, flourishing her long purple cardigan and making her shoulder-length earrings rattle.

'I see.' Daisy reached for her order book. She flicked over to a clean page, Biro hovering. 'Are you happy to talk here, or would you like to go through to the office?'

'What? That poky room? No, I'm happy where I am, thank you very much.'

Although offended Daisy couldn't argue with the statement. 'Very well. May I ask who the deceased is?'

Most uncharacteristically, Aggie began to cry. She fished out a white cotton handkerchief from her enormous handbag, wiped her eyes, then blew her nose with a loud trumpet. 'It's Gretel.'

The name was vaguely familiar. 'And what relation is she to you?' Daisy asked gently. It was very unlike Aggie to show her vulnerable side. The woman was usually as hard as nails and twice as brusque. And that's if you were being charitable. Downright rude was another description.

'She's Austin's.'

'She's Austin's what?'

'She's Austin's dog, you stupid woman!'

A dog. Understanding dawned. Of course. For as long as she'd known Austin, Aggie's patient and long-suffering husband, he'd been accompanied by his German Shepherd. Man and dog were a familiar sight in town, owner plodding along with his equally aged pet faithfully at his side.

'Oh, Aggie, I'm so sorry. Austin must be devastated. He doted on Gretel.' She put a hand on the older woman's arm.

Aggie sniffed and batted it away. 'We're both devastated. Austin's had her since she was a puppy. No more loyal a dog.'

Daisy got up and switched off the shop radio. Alice Cooper yelling 'School's Out' didn't seem appropriate somehow. 'Can I make you a cup of tea?'

Aggie nodded curtly.

Daisy made them both tea and brought out a plate of chocolate digestives for good measure, then sat back at the counter. Pushing over a mug to Aggie, she said, 'I'm so very sorry to hear about Gretel.' Aggie nodded again and swallowed a great mouthful of tea. 'But what can I do for you?'

Aggie raised her eyes and blinked. Staring Daisy down, she said, 'I am obviously dealing with the hard of understanding here. How you ever run a business, I'll never know. And here's me listening to Brenda Pearce when she recommended you.'

Daisy quailed against the barrage of derision. 'I'm sorry, I still don't follow.'

'Are you stupid, girl? Do I have to spell it out?'

Daisy nodded. 'Yes,' she squeaked.

'I want you to do the flowers for Gretel's funeral!'

'You're having a funeral? For Gretel?'

Aggie slammed down her fist, making the mugs jump. She rose to her magnificent height of five feet ten and turned to go. 'I see I have come to completely the wrong place. I shall have words with Brenda. She said you'd understand, be sympathetic. But I can see we were both labouring under a misapprehension.'

'Aggie, please. Don't go. Come and sit back down. Finish your tea. I understand completely now. You took me by surprise, that's all. I've never been asked to do flowers for a pet's funeral before.'

Aggie stalled. She took in an almighty breath of indignation. 'This is no pet,' she thundered. 'This is Gretel. She was a member of the family.' Then she subsided, her shoulders began to shake and tears dripped.

'Of course. Of course she was. I'm so terribly sorry for your loss. Please sit down, have a biscuit and more tea and we can discuss the arrangements.' To Daisy's relief, Aggie sat down. Once the storm of weeping had finished, tea drunk and half a packet of chocolate digestives devoured, she was calmer.

Daisy picked up her pen once more. 'Now, tell me the details.' She didn't know whether to laugh, or cry along with Aggie.

'Well,' Aggie sniffed, 'her favourite colours were blue and purple.'

'Blue and purple.' Daisy bit the inside of her cheek to stop a laugh escaping and made a note. This was possibly the most bizarre funeral order she'd ever taken.

'And she liked hydrangeas. She was fond of a white rose too but only to nibble. Drove Austin mad, she did. He spent hours in the garden and she'd come along and destroy all his hard work.' Aggie's bottom lip quivered.

Daisy's heart melted. Aggie's grief was palpable. To many, dogs were more important than people and this was obviously the case with Gretel. 'You're going to miss her so much. We need to make her funeral the best it can possibly be. So,' she added, decisively, 'tell me more.'

Somehow Daisy scrabbled together flowers for Gretel's funeral. It had been very short notice. She'd had to work late into the night and beg a favour from Jakob, her favourite Dutch supplier, but she'd done it. Luckily, he was passing near Lullbury Bay on his way north so he'd popped by and dropped off her special order request.

The following morning Daisy slipped into the church early and placed two elaborate arrangements on either side of the ornamental casket containing Gretel's ashes. A large picture of the German Shepherd stood proudly on top and a lump lodged unexpectedly in her throat. The emotion caught her unawares. Jan was minding the shop and promised to meet her at Aggie and Austin's house later, where there was to be a wake. A dog's funeral wake was something not to be missed, Daisy thought as she tweaked a rose back into position and went to find a place to sit.

Mia slid along the pew at the back of the rapidly filling church to join her. 'Going to be quite a turnout,' she whispered, against the background of the organist playing 'Pachelbel's Canon'. 'I see Verity has agreed to lead the memorial service.'

'Don't think she had any choice. I've never known anyone say no to Aggie and live,' Daisy hissed back under her breath.

'True.'

'But Verity's wonderful and an animal lover. She would have agreed to do it anyway.'

'I approve of the flowers.'

'Gretel's favourite colours apparently.'

Mia gave her boss an incredulous look.

'It's true. Gretel loved blue and purple.'

'Okay,' Mia replied, on a long, disbelieving breath. 'Still,' she shrugged, 'heliotrope means devotion, the white roses are eternal love and the white poppies stand for consolation.'

'Glad you approve. I had to add some hydrangeas to bulk it all out. Aggie insisted the arrangements be large and dramatic.'

'Bit like her then.' Mia began to giggle.

'Hush. You can't laugh at a funeral.'

'Not even at a dog's funeral?'

'Especially not at a dog's, although I can't decide if the whole thing is incredibly touching, an insult to *people* who have died, or downright peculiar.'

Mia turned to Daisy horrified as a thought occurred. 'They're not going to bury the ashes in the graveyard, are they?'

Daisy wrinkled her nose. 'Not too sure it's allowed. But anyway, Gretel's remains are to be interred in the garden at Aggie and Austin's house. You coming?'

'Oh my eggs, you bet I am. Wouldn't miss it for the world.'

'I've had to do more flowers for the house too. It was a bit hairy, we'd got low on stock and it was all so last-minute. I had to call in a favour from Jakob.'

Mia nudged her hard in the side. 'Jakob, eh? Six feet three of blond manliness from the Netherlands.'

'He *is* gorgeous.'

'He's lush! Think he might like you too.'

'And he lives in Europe. Don't get any ideas.'

'*We're* in Europe.'

'Mmm,' Daisy said. 'That might be a moot point these days.'

'Moot?' Mia's top lip curled in confusion. 'Don't get you. I love his accent, all those soft "s" sounds.'

'Then you go for him. He's all yours. But you've got your cap set at someone else, haven't you?' Daisy watched with amusement as Mia's face crimsoned.

'Wish you'd talk English sometimes. You sound more and more like my gran every day.'

'After four hours' sleep, trust me, I feel like your gran.'

Mia poked her in the ribs again. 'Did the handsome Jakob keep you up all night?'

'I was working, Mia!' The girl didn't answer. Daisy could see she was distracted as Ben and Honor led in a group of staff from the primary school. 'Speaking of good-looking men, there's one now,' she teased. Mia's face turned even redder. 'Have to say Ben Townham is extremely gorgeous. Reminds me of that actor from *Fifty Shades*. Jamie Dornan, is it?'

Mia ducked her head and scuffed her feet on the wooden floor.

Daisy grinned, considered teasing her some more, then left her in peace and watched as more people streamed into the church. Jago walked in with Tom Catesby from the animal sanctuary. They were followed by Tom's sister, Ellie, and their mother. Ellie looked pin sharp as usual in a tight-fitting navy suit. Daisy's Wiscombe relatives shambled past, making a racket and she wiggled her fingers in greeting to her aunt and uncle. When everyone was seated, a sombre Austin led in Aggie dressed in top-to-toe black.

'Think the veil is a bit over the top,' Mia whispered.

'Ssh, the service is about to start.'

'Good, it's freezing in here.' Mia snuggled closer. 'How can it be so cold when it's boiling outside?'

~

Austin and Aggie's house was situated in the perfect spot. Set above and slightly back from the harbour, it commanded enviable and uninterrupted sea views. Today, the weather was glorious; a breeze softened the hot sunshine and fluffy white clouds danced in a sky so deeply blue it was indistinguishable from where it met the sea.

Daisy collected a glass of champagne and went to lean against the ornamental wall at the southernmost edge of the garden. There was a yacht race on and triangular specks of white sails bobbed and swerved as they raced out to the marker buoys before turning for the home run back to the harbour. The lifeboat, a bright-orange blob, hovered on duty and she wondered who was crewing today. All crew were local and most well-known and appreciated in the town. If you lived by or with the sea, the RNLI was part of the scenery.

Sounds of laughter and music drifted up from the beach. Lullbury Bay was in high tourist season and the town was crammed with holidaymakers. Daisy loved the bustle it brought. She watched as a family played a game of shuttlecock and the father face-planted in the sand, to shrieks of laughter from his children. School was out and the British holiday season was in full swing. Lifting her face to the sun, she closed her eyes and took in a great gulp of ozone, heavy with salt and seaweed, suntan lotion and vinegary chips. There was nowhere else like it in the summer.

Another scent, more subtle, drifted into her nostrils, lemony with notes of sandalwood. She became aware of someone standing next to her. Opening her eyes, to her surprise she saw who it was.

'Rick!'

'Hi, Daisy.'

He smiled and her heart flipped. He was wearing tortoiseshell-framed sunglasses so she couldn't see the expression in his eyes. Scrabbling about in her handbag, she put her own on, needing some protection – and not only from the sun. Suntanned and in a crisp navy linen shirt, he was irresistible. But resist him she must. 'What are you doing here? I didn't know you knew Aggie.'

'I don't. I've bumped into Austin and Gretel a few times when out walking in the early mornings and he invited me along.'

'I didn't see you at church.'

'No, sadly I had to be elsewhere but thought I'd try to come to the,' he paused, 'is it actually going to be a wake?'

'Part wake, part interment, I think. You saw the carefully dug hole just under Princess Anne?'

'Excuse me?'

'The massive pink rose bush.'

'Ah. For a minute I thought you meant Princess Anne was actually here.'

'With Aggie, anything's possible.'

He laughed. 'Remember I know nothing about flowers.'

'I remember. And I know nothing about football. How's your team doing?'

'It's not the football season yet.'

'Well, there you go then.'

Alice, Austin's granddaughter, came up with a tray of flutes. 'More champagne?'

Daisy took a fresh glass. 'I shouldn't, I have to get back to work this afternoon.' There was an uneasy silence and she wondered if she should offer her condolences. It was usual at funerals, wasn't it? Taking a breath, she launched in, 'I'm sorry about Gretel.'

Alice's eyes misted over. 'It's all terribly sad. Most of all for granddad. He loved that dog so much and with Aggie away working so often she was his constant companion.'

Daisy nodded, not sure how to answer. This sort of conversation was awkward at the best of times, but someone had forgotten to write the etiquette book for a dog's funeral. 'He'll miss her.'

Alice nodded vigorously. 'And if he doesn't get a chance to say it, can I thank you on his behalf for doing such gorgeous flowers. I know from what Aggie said it was all very last minute so it's even more appreciated. She came back from your shop and said how sensitively you handled it all. It can't have been the most usual of requests.'

Daisy was taken aback. She was pretty sure Aggie had said no such thing. Either Alice was the mistress of small talk, or she should be in training for the diplomatic core. 'You're very welcome. I'm glad they were suitable. And you're right, this is my first dog's funeral, but I was very pleased I could be of service.' Daisy meant it. At first she couldn't decide if this whole thing was over the top, farcical or in sheer bad taste but hearing the things Austin and Aggie had said about Gretel in the church, singing 'All Things Bright and Beautiful' and listening to the prayers, she'd changed her mind.

Alice smiled and glided on.

'What a lovely girl.'

Daisy started. She'd forgotten Rick was still there. 'She is. Very. And wise beyond her years.' She felt him staring at her hard.

'And this is a very lovely town. Daisy, I have—'

But his sentence was cut off. Aggie clinked a spoon to her glass. The next part of the service was about to begin.

# Chapter Sixteen

August's bouquet
*Sunflowers – Helianthus annuus*
*Pride and loyalty, wise thoughts.*

'So, what happened next?' Marion pouted. 'I'm fuming I missed it.'

'You're cross you missed a dog's funeral? Since when have you been a dog lover?' Daisy tried to keep her irritation under control; she could really have done without seeing her today. Especially after what she'd done. It was Saturday, a few days after Gretel's funeral. Marion was on her way to hot yoga, but Daisy strongly suspected it was to catch up with all the gossip. And not just from Gretel's funeral.

Marion shuddered. 'Oh, I'm not, sweetie but Aggie always throws a wonderful party and the champers is always top-notch so I wouldn't want to miss that.' She pulled delicately at her snugly fitting workout top. 'So, come on, what was it like?'

'The church service was surprisingly moving.'

'Totes emosh,' Mia put in. 'Amazing how many people turned

up. Lots of dog owners there of course. I mean, I don't go to church but Verity's actually all right, as far as vicars go.'

'I agree,' Daisy said. 'I wasn't sure how I'd feel but it was actually really lovely. Then we had a weird kind of wake at the house. Canapés and champagne catered by Tracy at the Sea Spray Café.'

Marion did a repeat shudder. 'Not that awful fat woman with the frizzy pink hair?'

Daisy pointed an accusing finger. 'Tracy's salt of the earth. She's done wonders for that café since she took over.'

'Suppose.' Marion huffed. 'Still, champers and bits on sticks is an ask above bacon butties and a mug of builder's.'

'The salmon tartlets and those Greek mini skewers with the goat's cheese and black olives were lush. I had three glasses of champagne too. Got a bit giggly on the till in the supermarket afterwards.' Mia began straightening the greetings cards on the rack.

'Hmm.' Marion gave her a very old-fashioned look, obviously miffed at missing out on champagne on tap and stylish party food. 'But what actually happened at this wake thing?'

'I found it very touching. Hi, Marion.' Jan came out of the back room carrying three mugs. 'Very Berry for you, Mia.' She handed round the mugs and gave Marion a baleful glare. 'As a dog lover, I can honestly say it brought me to tears.'

'Because?' Marion couldn't hide her impatience.

'Aggie and Austin read out memories,' Daisy intervened quickly, Marion and her mother didn't always get on. 'Some funny, some sad.'

'I loved the one about Gretel stealing Austin's slippers,' Jan said, blowing on her tea.

'And he bought nine pairs before she outgrew the habit!' Mia laughed. 'And her running off with his walking pole and chewing it.'

Marion looked at them as if they'd gone mad. 'Hysterically funny. Not.'

'You had to be there, Marion,' Daisy snapped out, losing patience. 'There was a book where people could write in their own memories about Gretel too.'

'Oh no! Really?'

'Well, she was a real character about town. Everyone local knew her and lots of tourists used to make a huge fuss over her whenever Austin walked her along the prom on busy days.' Daisy sipped her tea. 'And then her ashes were buried. There was quite a crowd. Lots of people there with their dogs. Jago with lovely Ivy, Tom Catesby with Tiny. Even Sid took time off from the farm shop and brought his Great Dane along.'

'I'm welling up now just thinking about it.' Jan fished out a tissue from the sleeve of her jumper. 'That lovely poem which was read out.'

'More Elizabeth Barrett Browning,' Mia added. 'She had a little spaniel named Flush. "Blessings on thee, dog of mine".'

'Oh that really did get me going.' Jan dabbed her eyes.

'It would get me going too. Right out of there.'

'Marion, don't scoff. They'd prepared a spot just under her favourite rose bush, with a view of the sea. They said she'd always be with them and they'd never leave her.' Daisy heard her mother blow her nose and Mia sank into silence. 'As I said, I really wasn't sure how I felt about the whole thing but I decided in the end it was the right thing to do.'

'Well, I think it's an insult to people dying. You know, actual humans.' Marion hitched up her sports bag.

'But it didn't take anything away from any person who's died,' Daisy replied. 'I reckon the more love there is in this world, no matter what form it takes, the better place it is for all of us. What?' she said, looking at the other women who were all staring at her open-mouthed. 'I can't have a soft side?'

'You can, my lovely.' Jan rubbed her daughter's arm. 'It's just we never get to see it.'

'Oh, hang on.' Mia's eyes, with their expertly applied flicky black liner, went huge. 'Didn't I see you talking to Mr Spurs at the wake? You know, the mysterious love-hunk who took you to lunch? You two looked very cosy.' She slurped Very Berry. 'Maybe that's why our boss has gone all slushy.'

'You mean the one who told me his girlfriend didn't understand him. That one? Yes, we had a weirdly stilted conversation about football and how nice the town is.'

'Oh,' Marion groaned. 'You will never get a man that way.'

'I don't need one,' Daisy said tersely. 'I wish you'd get that into your thick, interfering head.'

Marion gasped. She put a hand to her throat in an affected way. 'Well, really. I can see when I'm not wanted.' Striding to the door, she flung it open and strutted out, leaving it ajar and swinging.

'That wasn't very nice, Daisy,' Jan said. 'I mean, Marion's not my favourite person but whatever has she done for you to treat her like that?'

'Where would you like me to begin?' Daisy glared at her mother and concentrated her anger on drinking her tea. Slamming the mug down, she said, 'Now, can we actually start some work today?'

She marched into the office, missing Mia and Jan pulling faces at one another. Returning, brandishing the by now slightly battered Manila envelope, she read out, 'Sunflowers. That's Walter's order for this month. Along with Honor and Jago's wedding, I've two other weddings, plus the WebFlorist inspection to prepare for. Even without Gretel's funeral it was going to be full-on, so I cheated and opened up Walter's envelope early.'

'I love sunflowers,' Jan said. 'Love the way their heads turn to face the sun when they're growing in the field. Birds love the seeds too,' she added, nodding. 'Always striking. And pretty easy to get hold of in August, I would imagine. I approve of this month's choice, Walter. So, come on, Mia, tell us what the message is.'

'Pride. That's what they stand for. And they look like proud flowers, don't they? They can also stand for loyalty and the

Victorians would know they meant, "You are splendid". Wonder if it means he hasn't made it up to her?' Mia added thoughtfully.

'Made what up?' Daisy asked, already picturing what she could do with the sunflowers. They were one of her favourite flowers. She wondered if she could get some stalks of straw from somewhere or run some tall stems of solidago through. Tapping her Biro against her teeth she remembered she had some gold-sprayed twirly sticks left over from Christmas but then dismissed the idea. Keep it simple and natural, with some dark-green butcher's-broom and raffia. It would look gorgeous. She just wished she had a person to actually hand it over to. That was always the fun part. The bit that made the job worth doing; seeing the pleasure on customers' faces.

'Earth to Daisy. Remember last month he was saying sorry for something. An argument maybe?' Mia stamped her foot, making her purple hair fly. Now term was over, she'd returned to the dye. 'Ooh I wish we knew the whole story!'

'He probably just likes sunflowers. Lots do. I do. I think there's nothing nicer than a bunch of them. It's like giving sunshine.'

'And that,' Jan stated, 'is as romantic as my daughter is willing to get. Miss Romance crept from her cave, sniffed the air momentarily and retreated post-haste.'

Daisy gave her mother a filthy look. If only she guessed!

'Oh.' Mia clapped a hand to her mouth. 'I meant to say and I completely forgot! Pete says sorry but he got bogged down with end of term school stuff and he'll ring you as soon as he's back from Crete. Soz.' She giggled nervously.

'Just your luck, Daisy.' Jan laughed. 'What a shame.'

Daisy wrenched her thoughts from sunflowers and glared at them both. She'd had enough. 'I'm so glad you find the topic of my love life so amusing.'

'To be technically correct, it's your lack of love life we find so amusing,' Jan added unhelpfully.

Daisy pointed her pen at her mother. 'And your love life is all silver foxes and Viagra?' Jan gasped. 'No, didn't think so.' She knew she was being cruel but, now she'd started, she couldn't stop lashing out. She was fed up with being the butt of jokes. She turned to Mia. 'And you, not yet twenty-three and should have men falling at your feet.' She made a point of looking down dramatically at Mia's high-top Converses. 'No, don't see any. Not one.' Mia's mouth dropped open and then she closed it again, her bottom lip quivering.

'Daisy,' Jan said sharply. 'That's enough. Don't be so spiteful. What's got into you today?'

'Me? *I'm* the one being spiteful? What about you two? Not happy unless you think I'm pining over some unfortunate hunk of testosterone. Has it occurred to either of you I might be perfectly content on my own and that women have been known to actually exist and even flourish quite happily without a man hanging off their arm? And you asked what Marion had done? You do know she set me up with another online date last night?'

Pete's lack of interest and seeing Rick again at the funeral had decided her. She'd forced herself out there. After all, she wouldn't find love if she didn't make some attempt to look for it, so she'd agreed and had gone out the evening before. Taking in her mother's disapproving face and Mia's shocked one, she drew in a breath and then let it all out. It felt good to rant.

'Let me tell you about the delightful men out there who are just gagging to date me. His profile said he was a successful barrister, had a house on Sandbanks and was six foot three. Turned out he was an unemployed law clerk, lived with his mother in Weymouth and when he stood up, came to my armpit. But none of that would have mattered. I would have overlooked the fact he'd been economical with the truth. That wasn't the worst thing about him, you see. Oh no. I can top that. When it came to paying the bill, he went to the loo and disappeared. Permanently!'

'Oh, Daisy!' Jan looked aghast.

'Sorry, Daisy,' Mia muttered, scuffing her feet.

'Yes, sorry, Daisy,' her mother added.

Daisy felt better for having got it all off her chest, if guilty at upsetting her mother and Mia. 'Yes well,' she huffed. 'The best thing you can do today is keep an eye on the shop and I'll be out back making up Walter's sunflower bouquet. And don't, either of you, come near me unless you are bringing tea!'

Later, as she drove to deliver Walter's flowers, reproach overcame her. No matter how badly the date had gone, and it had been truly awful; as well as lying on his profile he'd been an utter bore. She now knew all she needed to about the Atco Commodore B14 grass mower. And who knew there was a grass mower museum in Southport? She hadn't and had survived so far without that scintillating little tidbit. Even so, she shouldn't have spoken to her mother and Mia that way. She'd pick up some cakes from On a Roll on the way back as a sort of apology. Glancing at the dashboard clock she could see it wasn't yet eleven. They'd have plenty left.

The date had been another disaster. She couldn't believe she'd let Marion talk her into it. With a heartfelt sigh she knew another apology was owed there. After the conversation about babies with her mother, witnessing Honor and Jago's loved-up state, all on top of the poignancy of Gretel's funeral and the weird encounter with Rick, a whole range of conflicted emotions had ambushed her. She felt thoroughly unsettled, itchy under the skin and raw.

Swinging Primrose onto the main road, she asked herself if she really wanted children. She thought she did. At some point. At some time in the future. But, as her mother had pointed out, time had a habit of running out. Daisy knew you didn't necessarily need a man around to have babies, but it would be difficult enough to run the business and raise children with a partner; it might be nigh on impossible to cope on her own. She had her mother, of course and her mother would jump at the chance to babysit but she couldn't see how fair that would be. Her mum wasn't yet sixty and had taken early retirement to enjoy life a little. Jan would love the chance to be a granny though and, with Drew and Luke working abroad and enjoying a fancy-free expat life, it looked as if it might be up to her to provide them.

She thumped the steering wheel as the traffic slowed to an inevitable crawl. So, if she wanted babies as an option, she needed to get proactive with finding the man to have them with. But did that really mean yet more drunken, lying idiots met online? Why couldn't she just bump into someone and have sparks flying? Honor had met someone. And someone gorgeous. Her cousin Lucie was happy with husband Jamie, although they bickered for England. Even Marion seemed vaguely content with her Barry, even if she did moan about the hours he spent away at work. Daisy let a sigh escape. Her mum had always made it clear she'd known right away when she'd met Rod. Why couldn't that happen to her? Where were all the good men? The men like her lovely dad.

Glancing down at the bunch of jewel-coloured peonies on the passenger seat, she made a snap decision. Turning left to head out of town, she deliberately stopped thinking about men and concentrated on the traffic.

# Chapter Seventeen

Daisy squinted into the sunshine as it beat onto the windscreen. The steering wheel was almost too hot to hold so, in an effort to cool down, she buzzed the window down. She turned up the volume on the radio and an old track from the eighties blared out.

'Nice try, Madonna. If only I had time for a holiday.' Daisy sucked in a sharp breath. 'Oh get a grip, woman,' she berated herself. 'When did you become such a misery guts? I'm even annoying myself! Come on, it's a beautiful day, I've got groovy tunes on the radio and it must be at least thirty Celsius out there. Life's good. I'll drop off the sunflowers first, deliver the bouquet to Crewkerne and do the peonies last before I go back to the shop.' Madonna slid into 'Girls Just Want to Have Fun' causing Daisy to growl out between gritted teeth, 'I'm trying, Cyndi my lovely, I'm really trying. It's just that I can't seem to stop being angry at everyone and everything.'

She'd driven to Walter's house so often now that she knew the route off by heart. Once she'd parked up on the drive, she punched in Bella's number to ask her to keep back a box of fresh cream cakes. Hopefully, that should go part-way to mollify her mother and Mia. She'd think of a way of making it up to Marion later, half resenting the impulse. After what the woman had done, it should be the other way round. It was the last blind date Marion arranged that she'd agree to go on. Ever.

The house was still sleeping and still unoccupied. The only change was the bucket which had been filled with fresh water and put by the kitchen door in readiness. It was a thoughtful gesture. Wedging the bouquet so it wouldn't topple over, she stood back to admire it. The sunflower faces tilted up at her, hopeful and cheery, their golden petals glowing against the backdrop of dark-green foliage. She'd been right to keep it simple. Flowers that dramatic deserved to let their beauty breathe. Any fussy adornment would be too much. The matte brown paper and thick raffia tie was perfect. Deciding to sit on the metal bench on the patio in the sun, she lingered a little, in the forlorn hope someone might be around and she could hand over the flowers in person. But, after five minutes or so, she became self-conscious. She couldn't just sit in someone else's garden; it seemed rude. Besides, she needed to go.

As she drove away, she glanced in her rear-view mirror, really hoping someone was popping in regularly and keeping an eye on the place. Being so remote, it would be an easy target for a burglary. Lullbury Bay was a quiet sort of place, but recent events proved it wasn't immune to crime.

The woman in Crewkerne was ecstatic to receive the bunch of deep-pink stargazer lilies. It was obviously unexpected; Daisy's favourite kind of delivery. She loved the joy a simple bunch of flowers could give, especially when coming out of the blue. Remembering the message the customer had dictated over the phone, he was in for some serious Brownie points. Grinning, her mood lifting, she got in the van and headed back to Lullbury Bay. Buoyed by the delivery, it reminded her why she was in the profession, she didn't even curse at the tourist traffic which made her journey twice as long. The good mood didn't last very long, however. Humming along to the Bee Gees' 'How Deep Is Your Love' on the radio, she remembered it was her father's favourite.

Daisy didn't visit the town cemetery very often, but when she needed it her father's grave gave her solace. She should visit more but she never seemed to have enough time. However, it was always somewhere she was drawn to when things were tough. And the last few months had been difficult. Work had been crazy busy and her moods and emotions all over the place. She needed its solace right now and always found the place peaceful, even at the height of tourist season when the grockles invaded every other space.

She parked Primrose in an empty car park and walked along the gravel path leading to her father's grave. The gardens were kept beautifully and despite the current hot, dry weather the grass was a smooth velvety green. The planting was a touch 'corporate' and unimaginative to Daisy's eye but she could see the geraniums and shockingly bright tangerine marigolds had been tended and looked after. Two avenues of purple sycamore trees gave shade and the gardener had dotted trays of water around for the birds. It was a truly tranquil spot. If given a choice, she'd rather have her father alive and with them but, if you had to lie somewhere, this was about as perfect as it got.

The grave was at the newer end of the cemetery where the headstones stuck up in regimented fashion, like a regular set of teeth, glowing a pearly white in the hot sun.

'Roderick James Wiscombe, devoted husband and father. Born 1960, died 2006,' she read. It didn't seem much to sum up a man's life. It should read that he was fun, was generous with his hugs and kisses, tickled her until she begged for mercy and did a spot-on Eric Morecombe impression.

'Miss you, Dad.' She knelt next to the headstone and poked the stems of the peonies through the holes in the flower container. Filling it with water, she knelt back and realised, with a sickening jolt, that her father had been forty-six when he died, not much more than ten years older than she was now. From her perspective of someone in her mid-thirties it suddenly felt very young. Much too young to die. If she wanted to find the love of her life and make babies, her mother was right, she might not have much time. For the first time it occurred to her that she'd deliberately sought out a career change to escape the future rut of being in teaching all her working life, only to dive into what might possibly be a new one. If all she had time for was work, was she really living?

Her father had certainly been robbed of his threescore years and ten. And she was sure he had much more to give the world than just working all the hours given. Was she like him? Yes, far too like him. She worked to the exclusion of everything else. But what else could she do?

Grief overcame her, suddenly and unexpectedly. The watering can rolled to one side, bleeding water onto the grass. She gave in to great gulping, hiccoughing sobs, covering her face with her hands. It all seemed so unfair. Her father had missed out on so much. She'd missed out on sharing so much with him. He'd never seen her qualify with her teaching degree. Would never see her business flourish. Would never hold his grandchildren. If she ever had time to make any. The tears fell uninhibitedly. He'd never been able to enjoy a retirement, or had enough years married to her mother. There was so much he would have gone on to do had he had the chance.

Great wrenching sobs bubbled up from inside and now she'd begun crying, it seemed she couldn't stop. She hadn't wept like this over her father for years. All her business worries, her feelings about Rick, the frustration over her unsuccessful dates, her loneliness – yes, she admitted, she was lonely – collided. Seeing Honor and Jago ecstatically planning their wedding had hammered that home. She was so lonely she could scream at the universe. Long repressed emotions hurled themselves out of her along with her shuddering sobbing. She clutched her sides and gave in to the pain.

Part of her was distantly aware of someone walking along the footpath behind her, their footsteps crunching on the gravel, but she was left undisturbed. Eventually, she fished out a tissue, scrubbed her face and blew her nose. Sucking in some deep breaths she tried to calm herself. Her father had been dead a long time; she'd thought the grieving was over but perhaps it never was, it just eased into a different gear. She sat there a while, staring into space and letting a peace descend.

Embarrassed, she collected the watering can and replaced it underneath the tap and then went to sit on a bench. A sycamore shifted overhead, its leaves giving off pattering sighs and a gentle shade. Daisy felt a tranquillity wash over her. Perhaps it was the after-effects of a good cry, or perhaps it was the surroundings. It really was a good place to end up in. A smooth open space on the western fringes of town, serene and immaculately kept. She promised herself she'd come more often. Closing her eyes, she let her mind drift, listening to the soothing sounds of gulls wheeling high above. Time passed and a sort of ragged hush descended over her.

'Hi, Daisy,' a quiet voice said.

Opening her eyes, she saw who it was. 'Rick!'

'Do you mind if I sit with you?'

Daisy shifted slightly away from him, not wanting to expose her tear-ravaged face. She stopped herself from pointing out it was a free country and he could sit anywhere, and simply nodded.

They sat in silence for a while. Daisy wished she could say it was companionable, but it was far from that. She wondered if his were the feet she'd heard when giving in to her crying jag. A blackbird dropped down and hopped about, head on one side looking for insects. It flew off disappointed, to be replaced by a fat pigeon who waddled about and then drank from one of the water trays. It was quiet, with no other mourners, only the distant rumble of traffic from the road and the odd keening gull to be heard.

He was first to break the frigidity. 'I think I may have upset you in some way when we had lunch at The Toad. I'm so very sorry if I did. Please accept my apology. I tried to say something at Gretel's funeral but it wasn't the right moment.'

It was a pretty speech and at least he didn't mention his uninterested girlfriend.

Daisy relented and eased herself round to face him. 'You didn't upset me,' she lied. 'I just remembered there was somewhere I needed to be.'

'That's good,' he grinned, obviously relieved, 'I hope you got there.'

'Where?' she asked, mystified.

'Where you had to be.'

'Oh. Yes.' Daisy winced. She never could lie convincingly.

'I've made some progress with the restaurant idea. I think I've found some premises that might suit.'

Despite herself, Daisy was interested. At least it took her out of her introspection. 'Where?'

'The place on the high street. It's all boarded up at the moment but looks as if it shares a courtyard with a chapel at the back?'

'Oh yes! Actually, it used to be a restaurant, but it closed down a couple of years ago now. Before that it was a school,' Daisy said with enthusiasm. 'But you'd have to ask Mum about that as it's before my time. Victorian, I think. School, that is, not my mum,' she added hastily. *Stop gabbling, Daisy, and concentrate.* 'That would work really well. It's been lots of things, even a carpet showroom for a while but somehow nothing stuck there or was successful. I hope it hasn't got too knocked about?'

'From the online details it doesn't look as if it has but obviously there would still be some work to do. The original features seem mostly intact. It makes sense you saying it was a Victorian school. The main hall is double height and I think the fireplace might still be there. There's a chimney but it's covered up. There are some rudimentary loos which will have to be spruced up but at least the plumbing's there. Most exciting of all is the kitchen.'

'The kitchen?'

'Must have been put in for when it was a restaurant. It's dated but the basics for a commercial kitchen are all there. It's very exciting. That's a major expense taken care of.'

'I went once, ages ago.' Daisy frowned as she thought back. 'It had tried to be a nouveau cuisine sort of place. Tiny portions and enormous prices. Priced itself out of the market as the locals refused to spend money there and for some reason it didn't appeal to the tourists. Seem to remember there being lots of offal and game on the menu.' She shuddered. 'Not my sort of thing. It had a beautiful parquet floor in the main room. Is that still there?'

'Hope so. Underneath all the carpet. Sanded and polished, it'll look fantastic.'

Daisy nodded. 'It's a pretty building. Victorian Gothic I think they call it. Bit odd for Lullbury Bay as most of it's medieval with a dollop of Regency on top. The mullioned windows are beautiful.'

'And it has that gorgeous front door with the hugest knocker and lock I've ever seen.' Rick paused. 'There's only one drawback.'

'What's that?'

'Parking.'

'Oh, I wouldn't worry too much. The main shoppers' car park is just round the corner. There's an alleyway that connects it with the main street and it's free after six.'

'Of course! I remember now. I used it myself on one of my first visits to Lullbury. Thank you. Local knowledge is always a godsend.'

'Happy to oblige. I suppose, with it being an old school, you'll have the name sorted.'

'School Dinners?' His eyes creased in humour. 'Doesn't quite work, does it? I'm hoping to offer something a little more sophisticated.'

'No,' she answered on a laugh. 'I was thinking more along the lines of The Old School Kitchen.'

'Daisy, you're a genius! I can have specials written up on a vintage chalkboard.'

'And waitresses in sexy school uniforms?'

'Well, maybe I won't go that far.' He grinned wickedly. 'Although it might get the punters in. There was a franchise in London that had that theme. Waitresses in St Trinian's uniforms and shepherd's pie and apple pie and custard on the menu.'

'That would *definitely* get the punters in round here but I'm not sure they'd be the ones you want to serve.' Daisy giggled. Her mood had dramatically improved. Maybe it had been the cathartic tears. Or perhaps some of Rick's enthusiasm was rubbing off on her. His energy was certainly contagious.

'And I wouldn't want to run anything so exploitative.' He shook his head. 'Not the vibe I want to go for at all.'

'Do you think you'll go ahead with it?'

'There's a distinct chance.' Rick rubbed his hands together. 'I'm seriously considering it, although I have one or two people to speak to first.' He pressed his lips together, almost talking to himself. 'I've got all my West Country contacts for suppliers. My diners would have the absolute best in local produce. It's all so exciting!' Turning to her, he gave her a mile-wide smile. 'Of course, once I'm up and running, you'll do the flowers? On a regular contract?'

'I'd love to. Seasonal ones in giant jam jars, on solid sanded-down pine tables. Informal with local herbs as greenery and with raffia bows to match the napkins. Lots of earth colours, cream, green and taupe with seaside blue shot through. Understated and subtle but warm and welcoming.'

'You really *are* a genius. I could hug you! In fact I will!' Rick pulled her to him and hugged the breath out of her. 'I think I'll ask you to be my style consultant.'

For a delicious second, she allowed herself to be held. It was so good to be embraced by a man and feel his hard muscles, smell the heat through his shirt: warm skin and laundry powder. She could stay like this forever.

Rick released her. He gave her a penetrating look. 'You were crying earlier,' he said, in a dramatic change of tone. 'I'm sorry, I don't mean to pry but I walked past you. I don't mean to intrude but are you all right? Visiting a grave?'

So it had been him earlier. Daisy screwed up her face. 'My dad's.'

He frowned. 'Oh I'm so sorry. I had no idea.'

'It's okay. He died a long time ago. I was only sixteen. Just about to begin at sixth-form college.' She sniffed. 'It just got to me today for some reason. It's coming up to the anniversary of his death. I suppose that's what did it.'

Rick nodded. 'It happens,' he said simply. 'It's hard to lose a parent, especially when they die young.' Slipping an arm back around her, he pulled her to him again.

She rested her head on his shoulder, feeling the steady thump of his heartbeat. It felt right. Utterly right. As if she were made to fit into him. There was comfort there and friendship but underneath, still, the insistent pulse of desire. The cotton of his shirt felt smooth against her cheek and a button gaped. She could glimpse tanned skin and a dark matte of chest hair. An image of Rick naked rose unwillingly – all right – very willingly into her imagination. She felt his head come to rest on top of hers and felt a whisper of breath as he gave the tiniest of sighs. This time the silence was companionable. And oh-so frustrating.

They sat together for some time. Eventually, he shifted. 'I'm so sorry, Daisy.' He gave another, deeper sigh. 'I have to go. I really don't want to but I have a meeting.' He kissed the top of her head and hugged her tightly for a second and then was gone.

Daisy sat, eyes closed, waiting until she felt able to move. Grief for her father mixed with the tumultuous emotions she felt over Rick was a heady combination. It was only as she heard the click of the gate to the cemetery shutting and, a moment later, a car fire up that she realised she hadn't asked why Rick was in the cemetery. Had he lost someone too?

# Chapter Eighteen

L ate on Monday afternoon Marion swept into the shop. 'Put
me together a bunch of those white lilies,' she barked, 'taller
the better and I'll have some palm leaves as greenery.'

Daisy bit her lip. Better get it over and done with. 'Hi, Marion.
I owe you an apology.'

'Yes you do.' Marion sniffed and looked away to the ceiling.

'I'm really sorry about the other day. You caught me at a very
bad time. I was,' she paused, not wanting to share the details, 'tired
and, well just a bit overwhelmed by everything.'

'Hmm.'

'I had no right to talk to you like that and I'm sorry.'

'Date didn't go well I take it?'

Daisy's lips twisted. 'I'll fill you in with all the deets another
time. But it was a disaster.'

Marion tottered to the counter, she sometimes wore the most
ridiculous heels. Her eyes moistened. 'Then it's my turn to be
sorry, darling.' She made a little moue with her mouth. 'I'm only
trying to help. Only have your best interests at heart.'

'I know. Thanks for the effort. And it's a lot of effort. Maybe
I've just been unfortunate?'

'Third time lucky then, sweetie?' Marion asked hopefully.

Daisy shook her head vehemently. 'Not for a while. But can I ask you something?'

'Fire away, honeybun.'

'No more matchmaking, online or otherwise.'

'Done.'

Daisy wasn't convinced Marion would keep her word, but it would have to do. And for all her – many – faults, the woman didn't hold a grudge. She curtsied. 'Now what can I get you, madam? Lilies, did you say?' She grabbed the bucket and began to lay some on the counter. 'Special occasion?'

'Barry is actually at home for three whole days and nights in a row so I thought I'd hold a little dinner party-ette. Want to impress a few of his clients. I've no idea why I do it to myself. So much work!'

Daisy smiled to herself. Probably the last thing Barry wanted was a load of people coming round to dinner and his wife in ultra-Stepford-wife mode. 'What does Barry actually do? You know, I don't think you've ever told me.'

'I have absolutely no idea, darling. As long as the bills get paid, I don't care.' She flapped her hands. 'Something to do with investments or finance or something.'

Daisy giggled. 'Anyone coming that I know?'

'Don't think so. We hardly mix in the same social circles, do we?'

'Ouch.'

'Well it's true. Actually, darling, you don't mix in *any* social circles. Maybe another date?'

'We've had that conversation and I made my feelings abundantly clear.' The reply was repressive.

'Not even with that nice teacher?'

'Marion!'

'Okay, sweetie. Point taken.' She pursed her lips as she surveyed Daisy putting the bouquet together. 'Actually, scrap the palm leaves. They don't look right, do they?'

Daisy patiently removed the palm leaf foliage she'd just added. 'Some gyp?'

Marion shuddered. 'God, no gypsophila. What about that round green stuff?'

'The penny cress?'

'I'll have some of that instead.'

'I can add some birch twigs too, that can look classy.'

'Yes, why not.' Despite her protestations of being uber-busy, Marion subsided onto the stool with a sigh. 'I've run myself ragged today. The caterers have been impossible.'

Daisy bit back the comment she was about to say, settling for a non-committal, 'Oh dear.' She added five birch twigs and a handful of the penny cress and, satisfied with the look, wrapped the bouquet in white tissue paper. Handing it over to Marion, she added, 'Now you see why I don't have a social life. Too much trouble.'

'I envy you sometimes, Daisy. Your own little business. A little flat all to yourself. Time being your own.'

Daisy nodded sagely. 'Debts, business rates soaring, stock prices going through the roof but customers complaining if I add even so much as fifty pence to the flower price. What's not to love about my life?'

'But at least you only have yourself to please,' Marion said, patently not in a mood for empathy. 'No having to impress boring clients and their wives.' She peered at the bouquet. 'Do you think I need roses?'

Daisy reined in her patience. 'Leave it as just the lilies and the greenery. Simple but elegant. Lilies that tall make a statement without having to add much.'

'You know you're so right.' Marion turned the bouquet towards the light from the door to get a better look. Then she put it back on the counter, leaned in and hissed, 'Did you hear what happened?'

Daisy settled in for a gossip. There wasn't much which happened in town that escaped Marion. 'What happened where?'

'Lullbury Bay's crime wave, that's what. All the knitted teddies the Ninja Knitters attached to the railings in the public gardens have been stolen!'

'No!' Daisy was genuinely shocked. 'Not the ones people sponsored to raise money for the RNLI?'

Marion nodded. 'The very same. And,' she paused for dramatic effect, 'there's more.'

'What?'

'Lead stripped off the church roof, that's what. Poor Verity's distraught.'

'Oh no,' Daisy gasped. 'Poor Verity. She must be really upset. That's awful. Things like these never seemed to happen in Lullbury before.'

Marion shrugged. 'Well, they are now. Most crime since Eli and his teenage gang of hoodlums ripped through town vandalising cars.'

'Thanks for reminding me. Aunty Debs has only just got over it.'

A few years previously, Eli Wiscombe had got into some trouble.

'Oh yes, of course. Eli's your cousin, isn't he? I forget how many relatives you have.'

'Think most of the town has Wiscombe blood running through its veins in some form or other.' Daisy tapped her teeth with her Biro thoughtfully. 'It's weird though.'

'What is?'

'Stripping lead off church roofs and stealing knitted teddy bears are two crimes I wouldn't have thought would be done by the same type of criminal. I mean, one's out-and-out crime for gain and the other smacks of petty vandalism.'

'Not your Eli again, sweetie?'

'If it is, he'll have to leave home. Aunty Debs won't give him another chance. She's a founding member of the Knit and Natter Group, she'll be furious if all her hard work has been destroyed by her own son.'

'So, as well as a group of bored kids, do you think we have a gang of real criminals in town?'

'Who knows?'

'It's awful.' Marion got up. She went to go and then turned back. 'Oh, there's some other news. More positive this time.'

'What's that?'

'There's a sold sign on the old restaurant at long last. The one just down the high street. I wonder who's bought it and what they're going to do with it?'

'I wonder.' Daisy suppressed a smile. It looked as though Rick had gone ahead and bought it.

'Well, whoever's bought it, I hope they open a nice clothes shop. We could do with some decent labels in town.'

'What's wrong with Tad's Togs?'

'Oh, darling, purleeze.' Marion flared her nostrils in disgust. 'When I want jeans and yacht shoes, I might lower myself but not until hell freezes over and you know I only wear Gucci.'

Daisy laughed. It was an outright lie. 'In your dreams, Maz.'

Marion ignored the jibe and screwed her eyes up as she tried to read the time on the shop's clock. It was bright pink and each number was a flower, with stems ending in roses for hands. More ornamental than practical, it was difficult to tell the time when the roses and the flower numbers clashed. Daisy held on to it determinedly though.

'Oh gosh, look at the time. Must dash. Toodle-pip, darling.'

'Bye, Marion. Oh wait,' Daisy picked up the flowers, 'don't forget your bouquet.'

Marion took them off her. 'Just goes to show how busy I am. My head's in a whirl. Thank you.' And with that, she swept out, narrowly missing bumping into Jan who was coming in.

'Hi, Mum.'

'Hello, my chickadee. Have you heard the news? Isn't it awful? All that knitting for nothing. Oh – and the old restaurant's been sold.' Jan paused and registered her daughter's knowing expression. 'What?'

'You're too late, Mum. The bush telegraph's just been in.'

'How that Marion Crawford gets to know all the gossip first beats me.'

'Me too. Cup of tea? I've got some chocolate-chip cookies.'

'Now that's the sort of news I like. Lead me to the kettle!'

# Chapter Nineteen

Daisy could hardly believe she'd done it.

It was a gloriously hot sunny day. All morning a stream of happy chattering families had trooped down the steep high street to the beach, wafting coconutty scents of suntan lotion into the shop. She'd decided she wanted a bit of that for herself. Running upstairs and changing quickly into shorts and a crop top, she'd turned the shop sign to Closed and had walked out. In her bag was a fat paperback and a bottle of water. Cramming on her straw hat she slid sunnies onto an already slightly sweaty nose and headed downhill.

She turned right at the cobbled square at the bottom of the high street, sauntered along the promenade, feeling the slidey texture of sand on the concrete beneath her Crocs. The beach was packed; happy squealing children jumped the surf, gulls swooped, chattering overhead and wafts of salty sea, suntan cream and vinegar hit her. She knew it would be quieter on the other side of the harbour so headed there. Everything was a brilliant, sparkling blue. Sea and sky a breath-taking turquoise, the sun beating down hard but with a gentle sea breeze taking the edge off the heat. On Dorset days like these, who needed the Mediterranean? Daisy clambered over the rocks onto the grittier sand past the harbour wall, snaking around tents and family encampments with towels, buckets and spades, picnics and sun umbrellas. Even here it was busy but she spied a quiet patch and set up camp leaning against the wooden groyne. Spreading out her towel, she lathered on some lotion and settled back with her book. Bliss.

In the end she didn't read much, content instead to people-watch and doze under the hot sun. Small children splashing in the shallows and shrieking, babies being held up just above the water to get their first exciting feel of the sea, quiet conversations and babbling laughter, the cackle of gulls overhead and an occasional human yell of indignation as one found its target of chips or ice cream. Some of the angst of the previous week floated away and her shoulders eased. She surrendered to her light covering of gritty sand and began to relax. It was good to reconnect with her hometown and she felt blessed to live in such a beautiful place.

Eventually, the sun lowered, the breeze blew cooler and the families packed away their beach kit, gathered up sticky sandy children and drifted, with sea-wearied legs, home. Daisy shoved her stuff into her bag and headed home too. It had been just what she'd needed, a little naughty time away from work but now she had to get back to some paperwork. Wincing, as the skin on her shoulders felt tight – she must have caught the sun – she trudged up the beach, skirted the harbour and strolled across the open space outside the yacht club. She flirted with the idea of popping into the Sea Spray Café for a snack but contented herself with an ice cream from The Ice Cream Dream kiosk.

An ex-pupil served her and gave her an extra dollop of Extra Chocolatey Chocolate and two flakes. 'Lucky you caught me. Was just about to close up. Been a busy day, like. You enjoy that now, Miss Wiscombe.'

'Thanks, Kyle. I will.' She smiled back at him thinking maybe not all those she taught had been awful. Sauntering slowly back along the prom, licking her ice cream before it melted all over her hand, she bumped into her cousin coming the other way.

'Lucie, hi. You just coming out of work?'

Lucie was an estate agent in the town's only agent in the high street.

'Hey there, Daiz. Yeah. Skived off early. No one serious wants to buy a house in Lullbury in August. Either everyone's on their hols or the grockles come in for a nose, ask a few questions, indulge their fantasy of living by the sea and off they go again. It's a quiet month. I'm meeting Jamie for a drink at the Old Harbour if you want to join?'

The idea of playing gooseberry with Lucie and her husband didn't appeal. 'I would have loved to but I need to get back. Work to do. I took this afternoon off.' She licked at a dribble of ice cream running down her wrist.

'Don't blame you.' Lucie lifted her face to the sun. 'Grab it while you can, I say. I've had no viewings today. Slaved over a hot computer in the office and not seen the light of day. Still, not for much longer.'

'Why's that? Have you got another job?'

Lucie shook her head. 'I've decided I'm going to be a full-time student. My first year's been impossible trying to work and study, even only working part-time at the estate agents. I feel I've missed out on the full student experience. Come October, I'll be a full-time student-union-card-carrying English Literature second-year student.'

Daisy was surprised; she knew Lucie and Jamie didn't have a huge income. 'Good for you. How are you going to manage, for money I mean?'

'Don't you start. I've had Mum going on at me ever since I told her.' She shrugged. 'I'll pick up the odd bar shift or a bit of waitressing. I'll want something to do to keep me occupied when Jamie's on a call or out training.'

'Jamie does a fantastic job volunteering with the RNLI.'

'He does but it's no fun being the one waiting at home when he's out on a shout. I'll need some kind of job to keep me busy to stop me worrying. Study during the day, behind a bar at night. It'll be okay.'

Daisy put her unsticky hand on her arm. 'Nothing dramatic lately?'

Last December the crew had been called out to a stranded yacht during a fierce storm on Christmas Eve. For a while it had been touch and go.

'Thank God, no. Not since that storm.' Lucie shivered. 'Don't want to go through another evening waiting like that. It was a bad night. I didn't think he was coming home. I was so glad I had Honor and Jago's mum to keep me company. We all kept one another busy. Made me realise though, that Jamie's out there doing what he really wants to do, *needs* to do, so thought it was time I did the same.'

'What will you do with your degree?'

Lucie grinned, flicking chestnut hair off her freckled face. 'Haven't got that far yet. Might come picking your brains about teaching. I know it wasn't for you but I might like it.'

'You do that. I think it's a fantastic plan. You've got to chase your dreams.'

'You only live once, don't you?'

Ridiculously, Daisy felt her eyes fill. 'True. Go for it, cuz.'

'I aim to.' Lucie peered at Daisy's back. 'Ooh, Daiz, you want to get some aftersun on those shoulders. They're ever so pink.'

Daisy grimaced. 'Tell me about it. First thing I'll do when I get home.'

Lucie went to go but turned and said, 'Daiz, don't be stranger. Come out one night and celebrate my release from years of glorious servitude at Berry-Francis.'

Daisy giggled. 'You've only been there for ten years.'

'Exactly. And with Ellie Catesby as my boss! I should get a medal for bravery.' Lucie pulled a face. 'Seriously though, be good to have a drink and a catch-up one night. I've hardly seen anything of you lately.'

'I will,' Daisy promised. 'If I don't, I'll see you at Honor and Jago's wedding first.'

They said their goodbyes and Daisy walked slowly along the promenade, deep in thought. She was pleased for Lucie. The girl had a brain and needed to stretch it. Full-time university life would suit her. Someone else who was sorting out her life. Getting her priorities ordered. Maybe she should try harder to do the same? To do that, though, she'd need to decide what her priorities actually were. Shoving the last of her cone into her mouth, by now soggy with chocolate ice cream, she collided with a man coming the other way.

'I'm so sorry,' he said. 'The low sun was in my eyes. I hope I haven't trodden on your toes?'

'Hello, Rick.'

'Daisy! Just the person I most wanted to see!'

# Chapter Twenty

'You wanted to see me?' Daisy was embarrassed. She was conscious she was hardly looking her best, hot and sweaty in scruffy denim cut-offs and a barely there spaghetti-strapped crop top. Their last meeting when she was seen crying her heart out was still fresh in her mind. It would be wonderful if, just once, Rick caught her looking sleek and in control.

'I've just picked up the keys to The Old School Kitchen!'

'That was quick.'

'It went to auction and I was a cash buyer so all the paperwork went through at warp speed.'

'Impressive.' Daisy hitched up her beach bag onto a sore shoulder.

'Been on the beach? Lovely day for it. Wish I'd known, I would have joined you.'

Up to that moment Daisy had been content with her solo trip but his words washed a wave of loneliness over her so acute she thought she'd pass out. She swayed. A family passed by and the teenager bumped into her, making her collide with Rick.

His hands grasped her shoulders. 'Hey, you okay?'

She winced at his touch. 'Too much sun, I think. I spend my days in the shop and when I get the chance, I overdo it.'

'Look, I was heading that way anyway, but why don't I treat you to a cold drink at the Sea Spray? You can cool off a little and rehydrate.'

Daisy nodded. She was light-headed. She'd definitely had too much sun. Refusing to let herself think about any other reason for her sudden dizziness, she allowed him to lead her to the café.

Tracy was about to close but, seeing as it was Daisy, flipped the café's sign to shut and directed them to a table at the back, where it was against a cool wall and out of the direct sun. 'What you wants, maid,' she said in her strong Cornish accent, taking in Daisy's flushed face, 'is a pint of my home-made lemonade, followed by tea, followed by cake.'

A jug of iced lemonade, misty with condensation and two tall glasses filled with ice were swiftly deposited on the table. 'Get that down you, my lovely. I'll be back with the tea and cake d'rec'ly. Don't hurry now. Take your time if you don't mind me tidying up around you.'

'Thanks Tracy.' Daisy took off her straw hat and fanned herself. She already felt much better and a complete fraud. She knew it hadn't been too much sun. Far more likely the close proximity of Rick looking swoon-worthy in a white linen shirt and khaki shorts.

He poured them both lemonade and pushed a glass towards her. 'Sip slowly,' he ordered.

Daisy felt a thrill engulf her. It was nice being the one being looked after, she even quite liked being ordered about. Shocked at her lack of inner feminist – she really didn't recognise herself anymore – she concentrated on drinking. The lemonade slipped down her throat cool and tart. Nectar.

Tracy brought over a tray laden with a giant cerise-pink teapot, two huge mugs and a plate of cakes. 'Ones I haven't sold, so I brought you a selection. They'd only go to waste. I insist on freshly made each day. Been so hot all folks wanted was cold drinks and ice creams. You want to get some cream on them shoulders, our Daisy. They look awful sore.'

'I will. Thanks, Tracy. Didn't realise how thirsty I was. The lemonade hit the spot.'

Tracy nodded sagely. 'Always does. I'll leave you in peace. If you needs me, I'm in the kitchen cleaning up.'

She disappeared through the kitchen swing door and the strains of Bill Withers's 'Lovely Day' could be heard as she switched on Bay Radio.

'One of my father's favourites,' Rick said, as he listened for a moment. He picked up the teapot with difficulty. 'This thing weighs a ton.' He posed. 'Shall I be mother?'

Daisy giggled. 'Think that's a biological impossibility but yes please.'

'Shame, I always wanted children.'

'Do you?' Daisy surveyed him over the rim of her glass. In her experience it was a rare man who admitted to wanting children.

'Oh yes. I'm the youngest of four. All my sisters are much older and so I was spoiled rotten. I'd like a whole brood; it was great growing up in a busy household. What about you?'

'Youngest of three. Older twin brothers.'

'No, I meant, would you like children?'

'I suppose.' Daisy didn't want to get into it. It hurt too much. 'I'd like cake more.'

He passed her the plate to choose. 'Éclair. Victoria sponge. Some kind of flapjack or a chocolate brownie.'

Daisy helped herself to the slice of sponge. They ate in silence. When she got to the chasing-crumbs-around-the-plate stage she sighed and wiped her mouth and sticky fingers with a serviette. She stared at the brown stains, horrified. *Good going, Daisy. You must have had chocolate ice cream all around your mouth. What are you, five?*

Rick watched her through thick dark lashes, his expression

veiled. 'You've missed a bit,' he said, his voice strangely hoarse. He bent and rubbed at the corner of her mouth with his thumb.

Daisy thought her insides would combust. They stared at one another for a long second. He had the deepest, warmest, most chocolatey brown eyes she'd ever seen. A cowlick of thick dark hair flopped over his forehead and she longed to caress it back. She caught the scent of his hot body underlaid with his subtle sandalwood aftershave and felt her eyes cross as she concentrated on his mouth. *What would it be like to kiss him?* Backing off, she stuttered out, 'Thanks. I must look a right mess.'

'You look lovely,' he whispered. 'You always do.' An awkward expression swept over his face and he backed off too. He cleared his throat. Making a deal of pouring more tea, adding milk and stirring it vigorously, he added, 'I wondered if you'd like to come up to The Old School Kitchen with me? Now I've got the keys, I mean. We could have a look around. See the worst. See what I've thrown my money at. I mean, I understand if you're too busy or not feeling up to it...' The sentence trailed off.

'Yes, I'd love to. It's on my way home anyway.'

'Oh yes, of course. As long as you're not too busy,' he repeated.

Daisy was too busy. She had a shedload of paperwork to wade through. Half an hour wouldn't hurt though. She winced. Unlike her shoulders. 'As long as you don't mind a detour via the chemist. I need to buy some aftersun.'

Rick immediately brightened. 'No problem. That would be great.'

He was back to normal. The moment of vividly intense intimacy had fled.

'More tea first?'

Tea was a safe topic. 'More tea first,' she agreed.

❧

Daisy stood behind Rick as he turned the key in the enormous lock and eased open the door to what would become The Old School Kitchen. Trying not to stare, she noticed how his dark wavy hair came to a point just above the collar of his shirt. She was desperate to run her fingers through it, imagining how thick and soft it would feel. Shocked, she felt her hand rise of its own volition and quickly tucked it back into a pocket. She needed to do the same with her feelings for the man. They were getting out of control.

He led her along a short corridor into the main hall. As he'd mentioned previously, it was double height and impressive. 'Well, what do you think?'

Some of the plaster was peeling, the leaded windows were grubby and seagull-stained and the parquet floor was inches thick in dust, revealing where an old carpet had been half ripped up. Motes swam in the soft late-afternoon sunshine.

'It's perfect. Or it will be.' She twisted around. 'Once you get the fireplace uncovered and the floor polished up it's going to be really impressive.'

He grinned boyishly. 'Follow me, let me show you the kitchens.'

They went further along the main corridor towards the back of the building and into a vast commercial kitchen.

'It all needs scrubbing up and checking over, but I don't think I need to do anything more in here. One of the beauties of the place. A new, up-to-catering-standard kitchen would cost a fortune.'

Daisy looked around. The steel work surfaces and huge industrial ovens looked alien to her but then she'd never worked in a commercial kitchen. She imagined, once cleaned up, it would be a good space. 'Wonder if this was the site of the old kitchen when it was a school?' She wrinkled her nose. 'Or did they even have kitchens back then?' She laughed, nervous about being so close to him. 'You can tell I'm a scientist and not a historian.'

Rick shrugged. 'Your guess is as good as mine. Maybe they did towards the end of the century? If I ever get the time, it might be fun to investigate the history of the place.'

'Ooh yes. You could put old photos up on the wall, that would look great, especially if you dig out any ones of ex-pupils, you know, those class pictures.'

Rick shook his head at her, admiringly. 'Fantastic idea.' He bit his lip, on the verge of saying something then briskly said, 'I won't show you the toilets, they're far too depressing. Let's go back into the main hall.' He followed her back along the corridor. 'Hang on, Daisy.' She turned in query. 'You've got cobwebs in your hair.' Reaching up he picked them off. 'There, that's better.' He gazed at her, entranced. 'You didn't flinch. Don't you mind spiders?'

Looking up at him in the half-light she replied, 'No, never been bothered. Besides, the potential of this place is too exciting to get all het up about a few arachnids.'

He gave her a strange half-smile. 'Right. You're quite a girl, you know.'

He was very close. She could see stubble on his jaw and the dark hair beginning at the open neck of his shirt. He was gorgeous. Her breathing became very shallow. 'It has been said,' she answered lightly and turned away, not able to take the intimacy in the enforced close quarters. Once back in the main room she focused on the practical. 'Cream I think for the walls. A warm yellowy cream, like Devon's best clotted variety. Tone down the orange stain on the floor to a cooler hue, black-and-white photographs on the walls, lots of broad-leaved plants, white napkins – real linen.' She clapped her hands. 'Oh, Rick, it'll be gorgeous.' She flinched. 'Ouch.'

'What's wrong?'

'My sunburn. It's really kicking in. I'd better go. Grab a shower and slather on the aftersun.'

'Come here,' he said in an odd voice. With gentle hands, he

NEW BEGINNINGS AT LULLBURY BAY

turned her round so that her back faced him. 'You're not going to reach most of where it's reddest. Pass the tube.'

Daisy's heart tumbled. She reached into her beach bag and brought out the lotion she'd bought on the way. Handing it to him she was mortified to find her hand was shaking. 'You don't have to do this,' she stammered.

'Nonsense. If you don't get enough on, you'll peel. Can't be too careful. I've had enough experience with my sisters to know what I'm doing.'

'Okay.' That was all right, wasn't it? He was treating her as a sister. There was a comical-sounding squirt as he squeezed some out. She giggled nervously.

'Brace yourself, it might feel cold.' He dabbed a little in between her shoulder blades.

He was right, she wouldn't have reached there. 'Ooh.' She squealed as cold lotion hit overheated and tender skin.

'Sorry.' His mouth was very near her ear. She felt his breath stir her hair. 'I'll try not to hurt you.'

Daisy surrendered. She closed her eyes and concentrated on the feel of his strong but gentle fingers massaging. Her whole body quivered, the muscles in her back rippled and undulated. Her breasts under the thin cotton of her crop top grew heavy and her nipples budded and tingled. She longed for his hands to reach round, cup them and pull her into him. Her head seemed too heavy; it flopped down until her chin rested on her chest.

Rick reached under her hair until he found the nape of her neck. He pushed a hand from her neck up into the sensitive part of her head and gathered a handful of hair, holding it out of the way before he stroked more lotion onto her shoulders, his fingers reaching round and caressing her collar blade.

A deep moan escaped. Knees weakened, she fell back into him and his arm came round her waist, his bare arm searing the naked flesh of her midriff, his thumb perilously near a nipple. She couldn't breathe, her entire being centred on his electrifying touch.

'Did I hurt you?' His voice was husky and very close.

The front door opened. A woman's voice with a strong Birmingham accent yelled, 'Rick, are you in here? I've been looking all over town for you. That Ellie at the estate agents said you were headed here. Where the hell are you, babes?'

They wheeled round, guilt etched on their faces.

Rick squeezed the bottle of lotion too hard and some spurted out. It flew in a high arc and landed in a splodge right on the woman's expensive-looking espadrilles.

'Minty!'

# Chapter Twenty-One

'And then what happened?' Mia was agog. She propped her elbows on the shop counter, hands to her cheeks.

Daisy surveyed her audience. Mia had popped by after a shift at the supermarket, Marion had bumped into her on the way and joined her to get all the gossip and her mother had come in with Fleur, having walked the dog along the seafront.

'Yes darling, do tell. This is the most fun I've had since,' Marion paused, 'well since forever actually.'

'I grabbed my things and scarpered.'

'You didn't stay to explain?' Jan asked.

Daisy turned to her mother. 'No, Mum, I didn't hang around to explain. Because there was nothing *to* explain.'

Marion chortled. 'I beg to differ, sweetie. The girlfriend comes in to find her man getting all hot and sticky with another woman and doing some heavy-duty erotic massaging.'

'It was *not* erotic,' Daisy lied. 'Rick was rubbing aftersun in.'

'Because...' Marion pulled a face and tapped lime-green shellacs on her chin. 'Oh yes, you couldn't do that yourself? At home.'

'I'd got burned in an awkward place,' Daisy mumbled.

'I bet.' She giggled lasciviously. 'Did he want you to reciprocate in his *awkward* place?'

'He wasn't sunburned.' Daisy wrinkled her nose, puzzled. 'Oh,' she felt herself blush crimson, 'Maz, get your mind out of the gutter. He was trying to do me a favour.'

'Some favour.'

'What's Minty like?' Mia asked.

'You mean, apart from spitting-feathers mad?' Marion interrupted.

Daisy rounded on her. 'Haven't you got somewhere to be?'

'Nowhere I'd rather be here at this exact moment in time.' Marion perched on the stool. 'Come on, spill the info on the girlfriend.'

'Well.' Daisy paused, thinking back to Minty's look of horror as the woman had stood in the open doorway gawping. She still felt horribly guilty, even as she'd protested, she had nothing to feel guilty about. Well, not much. She had to concede though, Rick's touch on her skin had been anything but brotherly and she could have sworn, from his ragged breathing and his slow languorous fingers, he'd been as turned on as she. 'She's beautiful.'

'So are you.' Mia pointed a drooping stem of pastel-pink gladioli at her.

'I thank you.' Daisy gave the girl a curtsey, holding out her apron.

'Well, you can be when you scrub up.' Marion sniffed.

'And thank *you*, Maz.'

'Was she angry, my lovely?' Jan put in. 'I mean, it's a bit of a daft pickle to get yourself into, isn't it, you loon.'

'I didn't mean to, Mum. Rick and I had been getting on really well, chatting about his new business—'

'What new business?' Marion interrupted sharply. She hated to be the last to know anything.

'He's bought the old restaurant in the high street and he's

going to open a new one there. It's going to be called The Old School Kitchen and specialise in locally sourced seasonal food.'

'Sounds good,' Jan said, as she jiggled the dog in her arms. 'Doesn't it, Fleur, baby?'

'Sounds very *near*,' Marion said meaningfully.

'I doubt he's spent hundreds of thousands on a building just to be close to me,' Daisy said, laughing. 'Get real.'

'He might have done,' Mia said, ever the romantic. 'He might be totes in love with you and it's an excuse to be a few doors away.'

'Always said my daughter's a man magnet.' Jan sniffed proudly.

'You've never said anything of the sort,' Daisy retorted.

'So, let me get this straight,' Marion said, 'you were getting on well, talking business and he offered to rub aftersun in?'

'That's about the sum of it, although it wasn't nearly as sleazy as you make it sound.'

'No, darling, that's not sleazy at all.' Marion laughed and shook her head.

'It wasn't. It really wasn't.' Daisy plonked herself down on the other stool feeling dejected. Marion had made it sound like something it wasn't. It had been a magical moment. Not innocent but not nearly as grubby as in her employee's warped imagination.

'And you say this Minty,' her mother's mouth pursed at the name, 'wasn't angry?'

'Oh no, I never said that. I think she was furious. I ran up the hill to here and I could hear them shouting at one another behind me. I just didn't hang about to get involved.' Daisy scuffed her feet on the floorboards. She ought to cover them in some good quality lino, it would make it easier to clean and mop up spills but she hadn't the money. 'Maybe I should have done?'

'What could you have said that Rick couldn't?' Mia pointed out. 'Probably best to leave them to sort it out.'

'Must have made it look guilty as hell though.'

Mia pulled a face. 'Maybe. But if you weren't doing anything to feel guilty about, don't feel guilty.'

Daisy felt her cheeks burn.

'Look at you,' Marion cried in triumph, pointing a green talon. 'Guilt written all over your face. You've got the hots bad, girl.'

'Oh very grown-up, Maz.' Daisy put her bottle of water against her face to cool it down. Pointless as it had been sitting on the shop counter all day and was lukewarm.

'That's me. You still haven't told us what Minty is like.'

Daisy waved the plastic bottle around helplessly. 'Blonde, beautiful, tall, very slender, immaculately made up.'

'I'm liking the sound of her,' Marion approved. 'Clothes?'

'Yes, she was wearing clothes.' Daisy nodded sagely.

'Daisy!'

'Oh, I don't know. I only caught a glimpse. Linen cut-offs, some kind of black frilly top, off the shoulder.'

Marion sucked in a sharp breath, her eyes flicked from side to side like a bird of prey on the hunt. 'Valentino, new season. Bound to be. Shoes?'

'Someone missed their vocation.' Jan chuckled. 'Specialise in pulling nails, do you, love?'

'What?'

'Should have been around during the Nazi interrogations, my lovely. You'd have been in your element.'

Marion drew herself up. 'Are you calling me a Nazi?'

'No, love. I'm not calling you anything.' Jan beat a hasty retreat. 'Best get little Fleur back. Have a nice time tonight, my chickadee. And leave the aftersun at home this time.'

'Bye, Mum.'

Marion turned from staring at Jan's receding figure and rounded on Daisy. She pounced. 'What's happening tonight?'

Mia answered on Daisy's behalf before she had the chance to speak. 'Well, in an effort to get herself some kind of love life, a proper one this time, without sneaky lotion sessions and hovering girlfriends, our esteemed boss is going out on a date tonight!'

Pete took her to The Station House, a new cocktail bar which had just opened in the abandoned railway station on the edge of town. It was a balmy still evening so they decided on a table outside.

'I haven't been here before,' Daisy said as they were shown to their table on what was once the platform. 'Isn't it fun? You were lucky to get a booking, especially at this time of year.' Their table was situated in front of a railway carriage painted a glossy maroon and cream and proclaiming the sign, *Eat, Drink and Go Nowhere!*

Pete went a bit pink under his suntan. 'I know the owner, Caroline. She did me a favour. Thought it would be good to go somewhere other than The Toad for once and I have to confess I avoid the seafront in August. Gets too busy for me.'

'Know what you mean.' Daisy looked around her. The ex-station house obviously housed the bar, from which the sound of happy early evening chatter and the clink of glasses floated out. It was busy outside too, with all the other tables taken or reserved. The sky flamed flamingo pink and fairy lights strung between poles marking out the outside seating area glowed. She approved of the planting scheme with structural New Zealand flax and palm trees. With the warm weather it felt almost Mediterranean and made a welcome change from the seafront pubs which could get crowded and sandy on a summer's evening.

'Good evening.' The young miniskirted waitress did a double take as she clocked the pair of them. 'Hello, Mr Fletcher!'

Pete's face crimsoned even more. 'Hi, Eleanor.'

'Mum mentioned you might be coming in tonight. Hope you have a good time.'

'I'm sure we will. Eleanor is Caroline the owner's daughter and big sister to Cora who was in my class this year,' he explained to Daisy.

'And you were her favourite teacher ever.'

He laughed. 'I'm sure. Until she gets her new one in September.'

'Maybe, but you're a big act to follow.'

'Wow. Thank you, Eleanor. You working here for the summer?'

Eleanor nodded vigorously. 'Off to uni in October. Can't wait.' She glanced behind her as the sound of revelry coming from the bar increased. 'I'd best do the spiel and get back otherwise Mum will be on my case.' She took a breath and gabbled out, 'Welcome to The Station House. Our snacking plates are listed on the chalkboard and here's our drinks menu.' She placed two enormous, laminated cards on the table. 'Special craft ales tonight are Old Stoker, Railway Porter and Get Steamin' and, if you want the most alcohol for your money, I can recommend the Brighton Belleini cocktail. I'll be back in a mo to take your order. Cheers, guys.'

'Thanks, Eleanor.'

'This is so great,' Daisy said, genuinely. 'Had I known how nice it was I would have tried it out sooner.'

'Eleanor and her family haven't long developed it,' Pete clarified, his eyes scanning the menu. 'Think they're going to fit the railway carriage out as a restaurant eventually but they're only doing snacks at the moment. Is that all right?'

He looked so anxious, Daisy was quick to reassure him. 'Absolutely. I'm going for the Brief Encounter cheese and salami board and a Bellini, seeing as it was recommended.' She perused the menu, checking her decision. 'Yes, definitely the Bellini. What about you?'

'I'm a bit of a real ale fan so I'll have the Old Stoker. Only the one though, seeing as I drove.'

Eleanor returned and took their order and an awkward silence dropped.

'I'm sorry I–'

'How was Crete–' they said in unison.

'Sorry.' Pete's face flushed again. He pushed his specs up his nose.

'What were you about to say?'

'I'm sorry I didn't get back to you sooner.'

'That's all right. Mia said you'd been to Crete. Did you have a good holiday? I've never been.'

'Oh you should. Marvellous place. Lots of ruins, Knossos and such. And the walk through the Samaria Gorge, although if I'm honest it was far too hot to do much other than lie on the beach.'

'Sounds perfect after a busy school year.'

'It was, it really was.'

They were interrupted by Eleanor bringing their food and drinks.

'Delicious.' Daisy speared a sliver of salami. 'Look, I've far too much here, would you like to share? I hadn't realised it would come with bread too.'

She pushed the platter into the middle of the table and then froze as a familiar voice with a strong Birmingham accent could be heard.

'Oh honestly, babes, dunno why you wanted to come here. They don't even do proper food.'

Rick and Minty passed their table. An overpowering cloud of Opium perfume floated with them.

Rick stopped. 'Hi, Daisy.'

'Rick, hi.' She felt his eyes flicker from her to Pete. As he didn't move on, she introduced him. 'This is Pete Fletcher. He's a teacher at the primary school.'

Minty thrust a possessive arm through Rick's, tugging him closer to her.

'Good to meet you, Pete. And this is Minty.'

Minty glared. 'We've met. Sort of. When you got my boyfriend to rub cream onto your back. How's the sunburn?'

'It's much better, thanks.' Daisy refused to feel guilty but cringed inside.

Minty tugged on Rick's arm. 'Come on, kiddo. We've got things to talk about.'

'Have a nice evening.'

'Oh we will.' Minty waggled her head. 'You can be sure of that.' She strutted off on a pair of sky-high white stilettoes.

Rick gave Daisy a long penetrating look and followed. Thankfully, they disappeared into the bar.

Daisy stared after them. They made an odd couple, not seeming at all compatible. Seeing Rick had brought back the physical reaction she'd had when he'd massaged the aftersun into her back. She'd tried hard to persuade herself it had all been innocent. She'd tried hard at forgetting how it had made her knees buckle and her heart race. Her heart had skipped into a tango at seeing him again. Dressed formally in black shirt and trousers, he'd looked pale and exhausted. She'd wanted to scoop him up, give him a cuddle and let him pour out his worries. It looked as if he had a few. Aware her feelings for him had shifted into new depths she forced a shrug and turned back to Pete, aware he'd been saying something. 'Sorry, what did you say?'

'I said, have you tried the Cornish Yarg cheese? It's really tasty.'

Feeling a rush of gratitude that he hadn't asked her to explain, she smiled at him warmly. 'I haven't but I will. Now, tell me all about Crete.'

# Chapter Twenty-Two

As part of her promise to herself to create a better work-life balance, Daisy took to strolling along the promenade at daybreak to the harbour and back. Used to early starts anyway, getting up an hour earlier in the summer was a joy when the town was still sleepy and the sunrise painted everything pink. Apart from one or two dog walkers, there were few people about and she relished the peace and solitude.

As she walked along today, with the sea calm and still and quietly murmuring to her left, the sun tickled the back of her head promising another hot day to come. It had been an incredible summer so far. A heatwave had broken through the cold rainy spring with endless hot sunny days with warm balmy nights. Profits were slightly down but trade always dropped off in the summer months. If she could secure WebFlorist status she was sure it would treble trade at least – she had a lot riding on that decision. Besides, come autumn, people's thoughts would turn to decorating their homes once more with fresh flowers. Daisy deliberately closed her mind off to worrying about the shop. Instead, she reflected on the date with Pete.

She could hardly call it a date. They'd got on. She'd even shared the story of the embarrassing aftersun incident as a way of explaining Minty's frostiness. Luckily, Rick and Minty hadn't stayed long. Daisy had seen them leaving only about thirty minutes after they'd arrived. Once they'd gone she'd been able to relax. Pete had seen the funny side and they'd gone on to talk Greece, teaching, his plans for the long summer holidays and that they'd see each other at Jago and Honor's wedding. Daisy would hardly miss him, Pete explained, as he and Ben Townham would be ushers.

He was nice. Really nice. Friendly and uncomplicated. He'd make someone a fantastic boyfriend and partner. But not her. Daisy didn't think she'd ever feel the spark that she needed. She'd made a good friend but she knew – they both sensed it – it was never going to develop into a romantic relationship.

A man walking a bouncy spaniel passed by going the other way along the promenade. He said good morning. It made her think of Austin and how much he must be missing Gretel and their walks. Lots of customers came into the shop with their dogs and Daisy didn't mind one bit. Her crushing work life meant she had no time to own one herself, but she liked other people's. She made a mental memo to get in a jar of dog treats to sit on the counter. A vision of 'Walter's' gloriously lush lawn rose in her imagination and, for a second, she pictured herself there, playing with a spaniel puppy. She wondered if 'Walter' had ever had a dog? The garden of the house in Withycombe Lane was perfect for one. They were still no closer to finding out who 'Walter' was and it was all very frustrating.

Her attention was caught by two people walking along the far end of the harbour wall. A middle-aged man with a shock of silver hair blowing in the breeze with a little brown-and-white Cavalier spaniel who looked just like Fleur. The man was tall and distinguished-looking in jeans and a loose-fitting jacket. He pulled the woman to him for a long affectionate hug, and they shared a playful kiss, laughing as the dog jumped up at them, pawing for attention. Daisy stopped dead. Seeing a middle-aged couple enjoying a dog walk on the harbour wasn't unusual. But the woman in the bright-pink jumper and cream linen trousers was her mother.

Daisy turned on her heel, nearly bumping into a woman coming the other way. Her feet slipped on the sandy concrete in her haste to get away and she nearly fell. Ignoring the woman's concern she stumbled back along the prom, head down to avoid the low sun. What was her mum doing kissing a strange man? And, if she had a boyfriend, why hadn't she told her?

For nigh on seventeen years she and her mum had been a unit. A close mutually dependent unit. Following the sudden shocking death of her father it had been just her and Jan against the world. They'd moved into the little cottage her mother still lived in, not needing the space or expense of the family home. Jan had seen her through the first grim years when everything had seemed grey and hopeless; the last thing Daisy had wanted to do was study for A-levels and university. It was another reason she'd slept-walked into teaching. She knew her dad would have been proud to see her in a respected, solid career, plus following the career's advice at school had seemed the path of least resistance; she hadn't wanted to cause her mother further anguish by being difficult. She didn't think she and Jan had any secrets from one another.

Daisy thought back to the last proper conversation she'd had with her mum. They'd talked about her father. She wrinkled her nose trying to remember. Had Jan been attempting to say something then but, as usual, she'd been panicking over getting flowers ready and delivered. Could it be they were drifting apart? Was the unit not as tight? She hadn't even shared her angst over Rick. As far as her mother was concerned, he was a nice chap who'd taken her to lunch once.

'I should make more time for her,' she muttered to herself as she navigated a mum and dad swinging their little girl between them. Her own parents used to do that with her on this very spot, Daisy remembered with a pang. When was the last time she'd taken her mother out for a meal? She'd not even bothered for Mothering Sunday. And when you were a florist for a living, an enormous bunch of flowers didn't seem quite as special. Maybe she should take her out to The Station House? It had been good fun. A girly night out with cocktails and a taxi home so they could sample a few sounded just the thing to bond again. Then Mum could tell her all about this mysterious man. He looked nice, Daisy admitted to herself cautiously. She examined her feelings. Did she mind her mother seeing someone? She couldn't decide. When it was theoretical she'd been all for it but now it looked to be a reality, her emotions were all over the place.

Daisy was still preoccupied when Marion reported for work three hours later. Going on autopilot she'd changed the water in all the flower buckets, put out the lavender bushes, flipped the shop sign to Open and boiled the kettle, leaving it steaming noisily to itself, forgotten.

Marion found her sitting at the counter, staring into space, a neglected pile of unprepared midnight sky agapanthus in front. 'So, sweetie, how did the date go? All well with the gorgeous Peter?' She disappeared into the office and made tea. 'Not that he's all that gorgeous but looks aren't everything and he seems steady.'

Daisy vaguely registered her chatting nonsense.

She returned with two mugs. 'And steady is good. My Barry's steady.' She plonked them down on the counter. 'Or I think he is. Don't see enough of him these days to remember. Hello, darling, earth to Daisy. Phone's ringing.'

'Let it go to answerphone. Thanks.' Daisy sipped her tea and winced. 'It's hot.'

'Usually is when it's just been made. What *is* going on with you this morning?' The ringing phone stopped and Daisy's quiet voice on the answering phone clicked in. 'Not rushing to answer the phone the minute it rings?' Marion placed a hand on Daisy's forehead. 'Are you coming down with something? Oh!' She removed the hand and clasped her throat. 'It's Peter. You've fallen in love. I knew it would happen to you at some point. No one can be that hard-hearted and anti-romance for real.'

Daisy shook her head.

'Did he do something?' Marion got serious. 'He didn't hurt you? Oh, sweetie, he didn't get all steamy and heavy and try it on? He doesn't look the sort but you never can tell. Slip something in your drink?' Her eyes widened dramatically. 'My Brit tells me these awful stories about what goes on in clubs these days. Spiked drinks and all sorts. She worries me something awful does my Brittany, but she can look after herself. Very savvy is Brit. Whereas you, sweetie, you're such an innocent in the world. I know you make yourself out to be all cynical and–'

'Maz, stop talking.'

Marion subsided onto the stool. Daisy rarely used that tone and when she did it was serious.

'Mum's seeing someone.'

Marion heaved a sigh of relief. 'Oh, is that all? Thank goodness. Thought something awful had happened.'

'It has. After all this time Mum has found herself a boyfriend.'

'Might just be a friend.'

'Looked more than that from where I was standing. They looked very relaxed with one another.'

'Friends with benefits?' Marion sipped her tea thoughtfully.

Daisy shuddered. 'Don't put that image in my head.'

'Oh, come on, Daisy. Your mum's only what, sixty? She's still got life left in her.'

'As I said, don't put that image in my head.'

'What's got you all riled up? Colin is a nice enough bloke.'

A pause dropped. Daisy's mouth fell open. 'You *knew*?'

'Whoopsie.' Marion blushed as crimson as her most recent manicure.

'You did know!'

Marion put up her hands in defeat. 'Look, I only know what I've seen. Colin is a neighbour three doors down. Got chatting one day when he was mowing his front lawn, lovely garden he's got, works ever so hard in it–'

'Marion!'

'Okay. Okay. Told me he'd started seeing someone called Jan. Jan Wiscombe and did I know her.'

Daisy pointed a finger. 'Stay. Right. There.' Jogging across the shop floor she went into the back room, collected the packet of digestives and sat back down. 'Spill. Tell me everything.'

Marion shifted uncomfortably. 'Shouldn't you be talking to your mum about all this? Feels like telling tales in school.'

'I will talk to Mum but I need to know what you know.'

Marion eyed the biscuits. 'I shouldn't, but what with all the stress you're putting me under.' Picking one up she crunched into it with her perfect veneers. 'What do you want to know?'

'Full name.'

'Colin Bryce.'

'Occupation?'

'Retired.'

'From what?'

'Oh really, Daisy!'

'From what, Maz?'

Marion wrinkled her nose as far as it could, Botox permitting. 'Some kind of engineering firm, I think. He owned it and has passed it on to his daughter.' She looked vague. Marion didn't do engineering firms.

'So solvent then?'

Marion became more animated. 'Oh yes, I'd say very. He's got one of the five-beds. They're enormous. Drives a very nice BMW too.'

'Why does he need such a big house?'

'How would I know? He likes space? Probably so the grand-children can stay. He's got three he said. They live up country in the Midlands somewhere.'

'Why's he moved here?'

'Daisy darling, why does anyone move here? It's a nice place to live.'

'Married? Divorced?'

'I think he said his wife had died.' Marion was visibly wilting under the verbal assault.

'Oh.'

'That enough gossip for you? Honestly, don't ever tell Jan I was telling you all this. She doesn't like me much as it is.'

'Nonsense. Mum's very fond of you. You just rub each other up the wrong way occasionally.'

'Is that what it is?' Marion said drily, taking another digestive. 'I'm going to have to eat nothing but salad after all these biscuits.'

'You've only had two.'

'Darling, I only have to look at a carb before putting on three inches around the waist.' Pointing a half-eaten biscuit she added, 'You just wait until you get to my age.'

'I'm not far off it,' Daisy said gloomily. 'And still manless. Not that I mind,' she said hastily. Shuffling some discarded ribbon boxes around randomly, she added, 'I'm perfectly content.'

'If you say so. Of course you can exist without a man. God knows I do most of the time as Barry's away so much.' She eyed Daisy with a twinkle. 'Much more fun with them around though. And I reckon your mum has found that out.'

Daisy slumped over the counter, laying her head on her hands. 'I just don't know how I feel about it,' she wailed.

'Jealous? Left out? Furious she didn't tell you?'

'Yeah. Maybe. Possibly yes to all the above.'

'It may have escaped your attention, sweetie, but your mother is a grown-up. She's entitled to a private life.'

'No she's not. She's my mum!'

'What do you tell us when we get on your case about your love life, or the lack thereof?'

'I tell you all to back off.'

Marion took another biscuit. 'There you go.' She brandished it in triumph but there was an unusual gentleness in her tone.

Daisy's bottom lip quivered. 'It's coming up to the anniversary of Dad's death. End of the month.'

'Oh, my darling, I'm sorry.' Marion reached out again. 'Maybe that's another reason why your mum didn't tell you. Delicate time and all, even after all these years.'

'Possibly. Perhaps she thinks I'd mind?'

'Do you?'

'I don't know.' Daisy's face contorted with conflicting emotions. 'I don't think so. I mean, I want her to be happy. But I'm a bit worried he's stringing her along, after her money, messing her about.'

'From what I can see he's a really nice guy. Loves his family, his little dog, said he wants to become part of the community. Don't think he'll be after her money, he's loaded. As for messing her about, well none of us know that, do we? Look at you and your Neville.'

'Exactly.' Daisy sighed. 'I suppose I'll have to just wait until she tells me all about him herself.'

'And maybe get out on a few more dates yourself?'

Daisy swilled the tepid dregs of her tea moodily. 'Not sure there's anyone out there for me.'

'Rubbish. Every pot has its lid. Or every shoe has its foot, or something like that. You know Mia's started going out with someone, don't you, although how she finds the time with all her jobs, I don't know.'

'Is it Ben from school?'

'Yes.' Marion looked vaguely affronted that it wasn't news. 'How did you guess?'

'She went all pink and girly when he walked into church for Gretel's memorial service. Of course!' Daisy exclaimed suddenly. 'Fleur! Colin is the friend Mum is walking her for. I should have guessed something was going on when she went all soppy over her. Dogs!'

'Dogs indeed,' Marion replied crisply. 'Can't stand the smelly hairy things myself.' She peered into the now empty biscuit packet, having demolished most of them. She crumpled it up. 'You've eaten all of these, Daisy. Will have to get you to my gym.'

'Or maybe I should get a dog? Get talking to a handsome fellow dog walker who just happens to be single? And you, cheeky cow, I only had three, that was a full packet! First job of the morning. Off you go, replenish supplies and while you're at it, get a couple of Belgian buns from Bella's. Extra icing on mine. I need sugar. I'm in shock.'

Marion huffed but collected her purse and went.

Daisy watched her teeter out. Sky-high scarlet stilettoes this morning. Daisy had no idea how she wore them all day. She pinned her best professional smile on her face as Aggie and Austin came in. These two, Mia and Ben and her mother and her mystery man. Even Marion and Barry. Everyone was coupled up. Except her. Perhaps she should get a dog after all. At the rate she was going, it would be the only way she'd ever be assured of unconditional love. That and a wet nose. Bay Radio blasted out 'Who Let the Dogs Out' to underscore the point.

# Chapter Twenty-Three

It had been the final meeting with Honor that had Daisy decided. The bride-to-be had come in with her mother to finalise the last-minute details about the wedding flowers and to arrange for when Daisy could get into the church and marquee to arrange the flowers for there. Honor was looking tired and harassed. It was as close to a celebrity wedding as Lullbury Bay could get and the town was making the most of it. Despite Honor's obvious exhaustion, though, her happy glow shone through. It bubbled up and out and infected Marion, Mia and herself. They'd all ended up in giggles. True, the laughter bordered on the hysterical, but it turned out to be a happy chaotic appointment.

Daisy admired Honor. She also saw herself in her. A fellow professional, Honor had suffered her own fair share of heartbreak and, up to meeting Jago, had devoted herself to her career. She now seemed to be happily managing teaching and a full life outside the classroom. If Honor could do it, Daisy was willing to give it a go. It was simply a case of finding the right man to help force through that balance. It was such a shame Jago and Honor only had sisters between them. With genes like theirs, any single male relative would be a contender on her dating wish list.

Daisy was determined to avoid any whiff of self-pity, although confessed to the odd misery fest when having time to indulge in a quart of chocolate ice cream and a romcom or two. She was a logical person who had diagnosed a problem in her life, so she would seek a solution. The scientist in her was coming to the fore. Surely, if she went on enough dates, met enough men, she'd find one who met her criteria. She'd decided under forty-five, working and a sense of humour was the absolute minimum. As it looked as if Rick and Minty were still definitely an item, she resolutely banished the other factors on her tick list: thick dark hair, warm brown eyes permanently on the edge of humour and a pair of firm thighs encased in snug chinos. After all, you had to compromise on something.

Glen was one of Barry's business contacts. In the area for meetings, he was at a loose end in the evenings and Marion had suggested they all meet up for a drink. All very casual but Daisy had her sussed. In the spirit of new adventure, she'd said yes. After all, what could she lose?

It had begun fairly well, despite Barry not turning up, citing a mysterious but important business call. Marion, having heard how good The Station House was, had suggested meeting there. As they sat at the exact same table she'd shared with Pete, Daisy couldn't quite meet Eleanor's eyes as she once again went through the welcome spiel.

'Well, this is pleasant, isn't it?' Marion proclaimed, over her cranberry mocktail.

Ever since biscuit-gate she'd been on a health kick involving consuming little but water, cucumber and celery. Daisy had spotted her stuffing a Gladwin's pasty into her mouth yesterday but decided to pick her battle and ignored it.

'I'm so sorry my husband couldn't make it, he's such a busy bee. He'll hopefully pop by later and say hello.'

'And I'm sorry he couldn't make it, Mrs Crawford,' Glen said. 'And it's very good of you to take pity on me and entertain me.'

'Oh, sweetie, it's Marion please.' Maz giggled. 'Do tell us about yourself, Glen. What do you do for a living? I'm always so vague about what pies my Barry has his fingers in.'

As he explained his role in buying menswear for a major department store chain, Daisy surreptitiously studied him. About her age, maybe a few years older, he had hair that nice shade of light brown that went blond in the sun. His job explained his immaculate linen shirt, skinny jeans, no socks and loafers look. He had a pleasant voice too, accent-less and deep. Daisy couldn't fault him so far. He was drinking a lite beer as he was driving so no woebegone drunken lurches onto the table in store. If she was lucky. She just hoped he wasn't into lawn-mowers.

Marion's phone trilled out 'I'm a Barbie Girl'. 'Oh, do excuse me, I must take this.' She left the table, wobbling on six-inch platform espadrilles.

'Where are you based, Glen?' Daisy sipped her Off the Rails cocktail, it seemed to be a version of a Pina Colada and was strong and scarily drinkable. Picking out a pineapple ring, she crunched into it. Juice dribbled deliciously down her chin. She caught it on a finger and sucked it without thinking.

'Not far from Woking. It's a great place to live. I can get into London fairly quickly and the motorway network isn't too far away. Makes one's working life easy.'

'Do you like to go into London often?'

'I do. I like to get to the theatre as often as I can. Do you go much?'

'It's tricky, living in Lullbury Bay. Even if I had the time. There's a good theatre in Exeter and one in Yeovil but it's not a big theatre scene around here.'

'But you have other attractions. I have to confess I love having an excuse to come to Dorset. Fresh sea air, the slower pace of life. The lack of pressure. I find it relaxing.'

Daisy wasn't sure about the slower pace of life or lack of pressure; in her experience, neither was true. 'I suppose you must.'

'I'm looking into buying a little place so I can have a base here.'

Daisy didn't think it was the moment to launch into her theory of how second homeowners were pricing out the locals, especially the young, so remained silent.

Glen went on to tell her all about the rooftop cocktail bar he'd tried on his last visit into London and Daisy's heart began to sink. She wasn't sure they had anything much in common. She couldn't remember the last time she'd been to the theatre and a cocktail here at The Station House was about as sophisticated as she got. She was relieved when Marion returned.

'I'm so sorry, my darlings. That was Barry on the phone. Some emergency with the youngest. He's backpacking around Thailand,' she explained to Glen, 'and we're rather worried about him.' Marion fluttered her eyelashes and Daisy didn't believe a word. 'I have to return to *mi casa* and try to FaceTime with him. I'm so sorry to cut short the evening but have fun, you young things. Toodle-pip.'

It was amazing how quickly Marion could travel on those heels when she had to.

Daisy coughed with embarrassment.

Eleanor reappeared. 'Can I get you guys anything else?' She scooped up Marion's discarded glass. 'More drinks? A snacking platter?'

'We can go if you'd prefer?' Daisy tried not to sound too hopeful.

'Oh no.' Glen shook his head vigorously. 'Evening's only just begun. Let's stay and have another drink.' He snapped his fingers at Eleanor. 'What have you to eat?'

Eleanor raised her eyebrows, ignored his rudeness, and listed the options, Daisy died a little inside. Jan always insisted how men treated waiting staff told you a lot about them.

He ordered two more drinks and a cold meats and cheese plate and began telling her about the last play he'd seen at the National. As she listened, she realised he hadn't really asked her much about herself. In fact, his question about whether she went to the theatre aside, he hadn't asked her *anything* about herself.

She concentrated on drinking, and eating her body weight in Somerset Brie and, after his lengthy and detailed critique of the second half of *The Crucible*, excused herself to visit the loo. In the Ladies she banged her head repeatedly against the door of the cubicle in frustration. Was it so hard to find a man? She wasn't asking for drop-dead gorgeous. She'd turn her nose up at a millionaire. All she wanted was an ordinary bloke with whom she shared some common ground, and who liked her. Was it too much to ask? It obviously was. 'Last time, Marion. This is positively the last time. I. Am. Not. Going. On. Any. Other. Blind. Dates!'

'You okay in there?' A woman rapped on the door.

'I'm fine.' Daisy flushed the loo. 'Just coming out.' As she washed her hands she stared at her reflection in the mirror. She didn't think she was bad-looking. Black hair, so dark it had blue lights, she'd been told her navy-blue eyes were her best feature, not a stick-thin figure but toned through carting flower trays around and trim enough as she never had enough time to eat. She had a brain too. All right, she lacked Minty's on-trend grooming and Marion's high-maintenance veneer but if you were going for the girl-next-door look she wasn't that bad. Was she? Why was it so hard to meet someone? She ran through this summer's dates. Brett had been hung up on his ex, Pete was going to be a lovely friend, and she didn't even want to get started on Mr Liar who'd disappeared. Rick's face swam into her vision. If only he had a twin! An unattached one with exactly the same personality. Sighing and reaching for a towel, she resigned herself to going back to Glen and giving him another chance.

Pushing through the scrum in the bar, she found herself pressed against a man. She'd know that lemony aftershave anywhere.

'Rick!'

'Daisy!' His arms came around her to steady them against the crush. 'Hello. I bumped into Marion earlier. She explained you were all here but she had to go. Said you were on a date.' He frowned. 'Thought it was odd, you being on a date with Marion tagging along but it's really none of my business I suppose.'

Daisy had had enough. Why couldn't Rick be the man she was spending the evening with? Instead, he popped up where she least expected it and flirted like mad even though he was most definitely not single. Well, maybe flirting didn't quite describe it but there were vibes. Heavy duty vibes of attraction. On both sides. Fury, fuelled by the potent cocktails she'd been drinking, combined with sheer frustration, boiled over. 'You know, it really isn't.'

He reeled back. 'No. Quite right. I'll leave you to enjoy your evening then. Bye, Daisy.' He said it softly, his voice almost inaudible over Bananarama on the sound system pointing out it was a 'Cruel Summer'. 'Hope he deserves you.'

As Daisy marched back to the table, Glen was on his phone.

He clicked it off quickly as he looked up and saw her. 'Maisie, hi. Back already.'

'It's Daisy and yes it would appear I am.' Daisy couldn't shake off her anger. Rick really needed to examine his behaviour. It wasn't fair. And she needed to stop herself obsessing with him and move on. Especially if he was going to be living and working in the same town. Time to move on from Rick blinkin'... She didn't even know his surname! That's how little she knew about him. She had only the haziest idea where he was from, London at a guess, and no idea what he was called. How stupid. How on earth had she developed such strong feelings for a man she hardly knew? With difficulty she tuned back into Glen. From nowhere he'd produced a thin leather document case. 'Sorry, what did you say?'

'I said I've been having a dabble at playwriting myself.' He gave a half smug, half proud smirk and opened the case. Her heart plummeted. His phone pinged again and a shifty look crept over his face. 'Sorry, I need to take this. Hi, yes,' he glanced at Daisy guiltily, 'yeah, I'm kinda in the middle of something here at the moment. Okay. Ring you back later. Sorry.' He clicked off the phone again but left it on the table, precisely in line with his placemat.

'Work?'

'Um. Sort of.' He gestured to the case. 'I'd love to read some of it to you. I can do all the voices. I loved drama at school.' Without waiting for her answer, he launched in.

Thirty minutes later and very aware of the faces of those on nearby tables, some perplexed, some sympathetic and some outright mocking, she'd drunk her third cocktail, sucked out all the alcohol from the fruit and eaten the orange and lemon slices, rind included, from sheer boredom. She couldn't take anymore. The play wasn't too bad, she supposed. Something about a man trapped in a lucrative career but yearning to express his creative side in the theatre – no guesses as to where the inspiration had come from – but it just wasn't the time and place. It was downright embarrassing, especially when Glen had affected a high-pitched voice to portray the love interest.

Had he mistaken her for some kind of literary expert, or someone in the publishing business? Or even someone who *cared*? She thought back. She was pretty clear she hadn't given that impression. It wasn't often she had time to read anything more taxing than *The Lullbury Bay Echo*. She was sure Glen hadn't actually asked her what she did for a living, or if he had, he hadn't shown the slightest interest. Why did he think she'd want to hear him act out his play? No, he'd simply assumed she'd be gagging to hear his masterpiece. The arrogance of the man!

She longed for a conversation. A proper one. One where the person with you paid attention to what you had to say and answered back. Glen hadn't once shown the slightest interest in her, hadn't asked one question. Well, he couldn't. Not when he was preoccupied by acting his socks off portraying the angst-ridden protagonist and the pneumatic blonde heroine. She groaned inside. 'I'll go and find Eleanor, shall I,' she asked in desperation, as eventually, he paused for breath. 'Maybe get the bill.'

'Oh. Right.' Glen looked surprised at the suggestion. 'Maybe another drink first? I've got loads more to read out, another two acts. You know, I'm having such a good time, Maisie. You're a brilliant listener.'

Shoving her chair back so forcefully it screeched on the slabs, she gritted her teeth. 'Thanks. If only you were a brilliant conversationalist,' she muttered under her breath. Heading back to the bar she found Eleanor, paid the bill and ordered a taxi.

'How was the date?' Eleanor asked. 'Receipt?'

Daisy nodded. 'Fine if you count having a play read out to you. An extremely mediocre play.' As she said it, she still couldn't believe it had happened.

'No!' Eleanor pulled a horrified face. 'Bummer.' She tore off the receipt and handed it over. Leaning closer, she whispered, 'If you want my opinion, he looks a right wanker. I so nearly told him where to go when he clicked his fingers at me.' She shrugged. 'But, you know, customer's always right. You want me to tell him you've gone? You can hide in the Ladies until your cab turns up.'

'No. I've had that done to me. It's not nice. I at least owe him a goodbye. But thanks for the offer. And the drinks and the food were lovely. If I ever find a man worth bringing here, I'll be back.'

'You do that.' Eleanor winked. 'You can even have your regular table.'

Daisy mooched back outside. The place wasn't as busy now and she could see Glen was, yet again, on his phone.

As she got nearer, she overheard him say, 'She's called Maisie.' He giggled. 'No, I know. She's not even that pretty. What? Oh, no more than a six.'

Her mouth dropped open in horror. She froze, wanting to eavesdrop some more. Fury rose in her like bile.

'Don't think she's ever met a playwright before. Looked a bit starstruck to be honest. Yeah, real local yokel. Think I'm in with a chance though. Anything's better than a boring night on my own in a hotel room. Yeah, mate. Any port in a storm. Ooh, hang on. She's back. Maisie, hi.'

Daisy sucked in her anger, felt an icy calm descend and straightened her shoulders. 'Yes, *Ben*, I'm back. I've paid the bill. I've ordered a taxi. I really wouldn't want to put you to the bother of taking me home. I'm sure it's out of your way. And there's no chance I'd ever go into any hotel room with you. In your dreams, sunshine. Besides, I really don't want to risk having to listen to any more of your play. I may not go to the theatre very often, I may not have time to read much, being a local yokel. Both of which you'd know, by the way, if you'd bothered to get your head from out of your own arse for one second and pay the slightest bit of attention to me. But even I know it's the biggest load of self-indulgent clap-trap I've ever heard. Take some advice, *Len*. Stick to the day job because you haven't a hope in hell of making it on stage.'

She drew herself up, vaguely aware someone on one of the other tables was applauding. 'And, for one last time, it's Daisy. D-A-I-S-Y. Like the flower. Great name for a florist. So lots of people tell me. That is, the ones who actually ask me what I do and are interested enough to enquire. Not a difficult name to remember. Have a nice life, *Den*. Without me being in it.' Feeling a weight lift, she turned on her heel and marched off into the night.

# Chapter Twenty-Four

I t was the morning of the WebFlorist inspection. The day had not begun well. Daisy was so jittery she'd drunk three enormous mugs of strong coffee already. Up most of the night going over and over the paperwork had meant she'd overslept.

'Calm down, darling,' Marion said as she prudently took away the fourth mug of coffee Daisy had poured.

'Calm down? Calm down! I've been working towards this for the best part of the year. With footfall customers dropping off it could be the saving of the shop.' Daisy glared at her. 'And your job!' She jabbed a finger at the older woman. 'And I still haven't forgiven you for Glen-gate.'

Marion winced and handed back the mug. 'Perhaps you need this after all. I can't say how sorry I am about how it worked out.'

'Or didn't.'

'Or didn't. I had no idea he'd be like that, sweetie.' She rubbed Daisy's arm. 'You deserve someone so much better than him.'

'Or any of the other dates I've been on this summer.' Daisy swallowed half her coffee in one and grimaced. It was lukewarm. 'That's it, Maz. I've sworn off men. From now on I'm concentrating on the business. I don't need a man in my life and I don't want one.'

A masculine-sounding clearing of the throat behind them in the main shop alerted them to the WebFlorist inspector's arrival.

Daisy froze, her mouth open, mug poised mid-air. 'Is that him?' she hissed.

Marion peered out and nodded. 'Looks like you might have to put your anti-man stance on hold, sweetie. Sounds like our inspector definitely has the X-whatsit chromosomes.' She grinned. 'Still, there's an upside.'

'Which is?'

'Shake your hair back, thrust your chest out and smile. Use what God's given you to win him over.' She turned Daisy round and towards the door of the office. 'Teeth and tits, darling, teeth and tits.'

'Maz, that is the single most terrible thing I've ever heard,' Daisy grumbled, flicking her fringe out of her eyes and pinning on a professional smile. 'It all depends on the paperwork being correct.'

'Every little helps. I'll put on the posh coffee, shall I? And dig out Bella's home-made hazelnut-and-choc-chip cookies?'

Daisy took in a deep breath, channelling some of the fearlessness she'd had when dealing with Glen. 'Good plan. And it's XY chromosomes. XX are female.'

'I forgot you were a biology teacher once. Go and flash your XX tits and teeth credentials then, sweetie, and good luck. You can do it.'

It turned out Daisy could do it. Trevor Jarrett was a genial but thorough man in his forties who drank their coffee, exclaimed over the quality of the biscuits, studied the online evidence, examined their stock and didn't miss a trick. It helped that he was tall and good-looking and utterly charming so it was hardly a hardship having to be in his company. While Marion served in the shop, Daisy took him through her application.

After two intense hours after which Daisy thought her eyes needed uncrossing from concentrating so hard, Trevor declared it all looked in order and, as far as he was concerned, she had WebFlorist accreditation. He said this as they walked back onto the shop floor and Daisy was so relieved she flung her arms around him and hugged him hard. It was unfortunate timing then that Rick chose that exact moment to walk in.

He stood for a second staring aghast at the scene before Marion pounced. 'Hi, Rick, can I help you with anything?'

'I wanted a quick word with Daisy, if that's possible.'

Marion grimaced. 'She's a bit busy at the moment, darling. Can you come back later? Did you want any flowers while you were here?'

'No. I'll pass, thanks. Don't need any.' Rick's eyes were glued to the sight of Daisy and the man embracing. 'I'll maybe come by later.'

'You do that.' Marion ushered him out and greeted Brenda Pearce as she came in. 'Must dash. Customer.'

'I'm sorry. I can see you're busy.' Turning on his heel, he left.

Marion shrugged and began the long process of serving Brenda.

Daisy made the executive decision to shut up shop completely at lunchtime. Jan popped by, bringing some of Bella's coronation chicken sandwiches and some fresh cream doughnuts in celebration so the three women took everything out into the garden, spread a blanket on the grass and set up a picnic.

After eating, Daisy fell back in the hot sunshine, closed her eyes and lay spreadeagled to the sky. 'That's such a relief to get it all over.'

'Are you sure he said everything was in order?' her mother asked. A pesky seagull marched stiff-legged over, bent a beady yellow eye towards the remnants of the food and flew off as she shooed him away.

'Yes,' Daisy replied sleepily, one hand over her eyes. 'Said the accreditation certificate would be on its way with all the terms and conditions early next week. As soon as I've signed to agree them, we can start WebFlorist sales. Then when people search on the site, our name will come up as their local florist. We'll reach a much bigger potential client base.'

'Well done, my chickadee. I'm so proud of you. That's a real step forward.'

'It is. It'll make a real difference.'

The women stayed silent for a while, enjoying the distant sounds of the sea and happy squealing children drifting up from the beach on the breeze.

'No Fleur today?' Marion asked innocently.

Daisy opened one eye and glared at her mother. 'Yes, Mum. You got something to tell us?'

'I don't know what you mean.'

Daisy sat up. 'Oh come on, Mum. You've been spotted. Cavorting about town with a handsome silver fox. Fleur belongs to him, doesn't she?'

'Well yes,' Jan replied stiffly. 'I've been walking her for Colin when he can't. As I said, I'm doing a friend a favour.'

'From what I could see when you and Colin were on the harbour, walking his dog wasn't the only favour you were doing him.'

'Daisy! I don't know what you're implying.'

'Then tell us what's going on!'

Marion made a strangled sound. 'Would you like me to leave you two to it?'

'No stay, Maz. I need a witness.' Daisy flapped a hand.

'Oh really, Daisy, do stop being melodramatic. Colin and I are just friends. We like each other's company, enjoy walking the dog, the odd meal out, a drink in The Old Harbour when we can squeeze in–'

'And a kiss and a cuddle on the harbour,' Daisy interjected.

Jan blushed crimson.

'So, are you going out with him?' she demanded.

'I wouldn't put it like that–'

'Mum!'

Jan gave an enormous sigh and brushed crumbs off her jeans, refusing to answer.

'Well?'

'I've been on my own for a long time, Daisy.'

'I know.' Daisy hugged her knees. 'But you haven't really been alone. You had me and the twins. Not to mention the enormous Lullbury Bay Wiscombe clan.'

'You know what I mean.'

Marion began to stir, obviously uncomfortable. 'Look I'll leave you to it. I'll open up the shop, shall I?'

'No leave it,' Daisy answered. 'Won't hurt to close for an afternoon. There's a bottle of fizz in the fridge, Maz. We'll have to drink it out of tumblers but break it out. We can celebrate properly. I've drunk far too much coffee and tea today. Prosecco would make a nice change.'

'Prosecco, the very thought.' Marion shuddered. 'And in tumblers.' She clambered to her feet and shook her head. 'If only you'd said, I could have brought proper flutes from home.' Glancing from mother to daughter she added, 'I'll do the washing up while I'm there too, shall I?' There was no answer so she huffed off.

Once she'd gone, Jan asked, 'Do you mind, chickadee?'

Daisy buried her face in her knees to give herself time to answer. Eventually she looked up. 'I don't know, Mum. It's a big thing to adjust to.'

Jan pursed her lips and looked down. She picked at a loose thread in her jeans.

'Are those new? Pastel-pink jeans are a bit of a departure for you.'

'Yes. Bought them last week. Fancied a change.'

'They suit you.' Daisy studied her mother properly for the first time in probably years. Instead of the woman who had brought them all up, single-handedly after the death of her husband, who had worked full time and steered three traumatised young people through the difficult years of early adulthood, she saw a woman. Heading for her sixties, a figure kept trim through Pilates and walking and generally keeping on the go, silver hair cut in a pixie style which suited her good bone structure, a neat white shirt teamed with her new jeans.

For the first time Daisy saw her as a woman rather than simply her mother. And she saw what Marion had hinted at; that her mother was a woman in her own right and was entitled to friends and a private life of her own, separate from that of the role of mother. What's more, she had suffered the death of not only her husband, but her only sister too. She must have been lonely. 'So, tell me about him,' she said reluctantly, concentrating on plucking dandelions from the neglected lawn. 'Where did you meet and is he nice to you?'

Jan explained she'd met Colin in the Sea Spray Café. 'He'd ordered a slice of lemon drizzle and so had I and there was only one left so we ended up sharing. We had an enormous pot of tea, a couple of scones as well, had a mild disagreement about which to put on first, jam or cream and spent the rest of the time talking. Tracy had to remind us she was shutting up as we hadn't noticed the time. He insisted on paying for the lot and we carried on talking as we walked back to his car.' Jan paused. 'In answer to your question, he's extremely nice. Nice is a good word for him,' she glanced at her daughter, 'although I'm sure you think that's boring.'

Daisy thought of the dates she'd been on recently. Had any of the men one iota of niceness she would have forgiven them a lot.

'Actually, Mum, I don't. I think nice as a value is much under-rated. Is he nice *to you*?'

'Very.' Jan smiled. 'He's the first man I've looked at since your dad. He's different of course. He's a very different kind of man but he's at a very different stage of life. So am I, I suppose.'

'How does it feel?' Daisy asked curiously.

'Weird. Scary. Exciting. A little guilt-inducing.' Jan sighed. 'I've been on my own and been happy on my own. I came to terms with your dad's death a long time ago and I never thought I'd meet another man who I could see myself with. But, you know, I had a wonderful man in my life with your dad. I was so lucky to love and be loved. When I got over the worst of the grief,' she gave Daisy another quick look, 'I'll never stop missing your dad, you know that, but when I found my peace with the grief, I sort of hoped another love would come along. When you've loved so happily once, it leaves you optimistic that it can happen again. Like having children, I suppose. You worry, having had one, that you'll never find enough love for a second but your heart expands. My love for your dad, and the grief, is still in my heart but Colin's squeezed in there too now.'

'It sounds serious.'

'We're taking it slowly. Seeing where it goes. He's just as sensitive about how his family feels as I am.'

'Oh, Mum, why didn't you tell me? You know I only want you to be happy.'

'I'm sorry, Daisy. I should have. It was wrong of me. But you always seem to have so much on your plate, I didn't want to add worrying about me to the list.'

Daisy reached out a hand. 'I'll always worry about you.'

'Well don't. I'm perfectly happy.'

'So when do I get to meet this Colin?'

'Soon. Would you like that?'

'Of course!'

'And we'll take your dad some flowers soon. Just you and I. Up to the cemetery. To mark the anniversary. Just because I'm with Colin now doesn't mean I've forgotten your dad. I've just tucked the grief aside to make room for some affection from someone new. It doesn't mean I love your dad any less or miss him any less either. The heart's got a remarkable capacity to expand and feel all sorts of complicated emotions and all at the same time.'

'Deal. And I understand,' Daisy added, tears clogging the back of her throat. 'I'll make the biggest bouquet I can. All of your favourites; roses, lilies, gerbera, some gyp. How does that sound?'

'That would be lovely, chickadee. I'll have a think about what went in my bridal bouquet.' Jan pressed her lips together, also on the edge of tears. 'It would be a nice gesture, wouldn't it?'

'It would.'

They sat in silence for a moment, digesting all that had been said.

Daisy threw an uneaten sandwich crust at the gull which had returned, looking at once optimistic and vaguely threatening. It was a herring gull, a huge snowy white and pale-grey bird, majestic in its own way. She stared at it, thinking. 'Mum,' she said eventually, just as Marion staggered back under the weight of a tray bearing the bottle of Prosecco, three clinking glasses and the inevitable packet of biscuits.

'Yes, chick?'

'If you get married again, I'm first in line to do the flowers, right?' She was trying to lighten the conversation, hide the hurt in her heart. It was a big thing to think of her mother with another man.

It made Jan laugh. She threw a handful of grass at her daughter.

'Who's getting married?' Marion put the tray down.

'Digestives, Maz? With Prosecco?' Daisy feigned outrage.

'What could I do, darling? Not a cracker or a smidgen of cheese in there. Digestive biscuits to go with the fizz, the sunshine, and the mother and daughter reunion.' She narrowed her eyes at them as she sank onto the blanket. 'You have made up? Or have I to do what I used to with Brit and Cassius and make you hug it out?'

'We hadn't argued,' Daisy replied, 'but yes, we've talked things through and we're all good. Now, you going to open that bottle before it warms up?'

'With these nails, sweetie?' Marion spread her fingers and admired her latest shellacs, a silvery blue in colour. 'Not on your nelly. You know, Jan, with your new relationship status, you could really do with getting on Aggie's *sex for the silver-haired* blog. You'd pick up lots of great lifestyle hints.'

'Marion!' Mother and daughter exclaimed in unison.

'Just saying.' She handed the bottle to Daisy. 'Use it or lose it, I always say.'

This was too much. 'Maz, I do not want to discuss my mother's sex life. I do not even want to think about my mother *having* a sex life.' To shut her up Daisy added, 'Now let's start celebrating.' She opened the bottle with a satisfyingly loud pop causing raucous laughter and cheers.

The celebrations were so noisy they didn't hear the shop door being rattled as Rick tried it, putting up a hand to shade his eyes and peer in to see if anyone was around. Receiving no answer, he turned and, with defeated shoulders, walked away.

# Chapter Twenty-Five

The day of Jago and Honor's wedding dawned cool and clear with the sort of watery turquoise sky that would deepen to a hot August blue later.

It was all hands to the deck. Jan and Marion had headed over to sort last-minute details in the marquee at Cheney House and Daisy and Mia had let themselves into a serenely quiet church to arrange the flowers. With the hot weather and the shortage of cool storage space, a lot of the hard work had necessarily had to be last minute. The pew-end posies, of white freesias, lavender and silvery eucalyptus had been made at five that morning.

'Tie them at the end of each pew like this, with a loop of pink ribbon,' Daisy explained. 'Make sure you use enough to create an impressive bow.'

'The freesias scent everything. They're gorgeous.' Mia gazed around the ancient space with its stout walls and glowing stained-glass windows. They'd put the lights on but it didn't quite reach into the furthermost corners where shadows and memories lingered. 'It's such an atmospheric place,' she whispered, as if not daring to disturb the ghosts.

Daisy straightened from where she'd been tying on a bouquet.

The last time she'd been in here with Mia was for Gretel's memorial service. A weird but surprisingly poignant affair. It was where they'd held her father's funeral service too but that seemed a long time ago now. For a second, the picture of her mother sitting on the front pew flanked by Luke and Drew, uncomfortable in their unfamiliar formal suits, flashed into her mind. It hadn't been Verity who had conducted the service and Daisy wished it had been. She would have done a far better job than the vicar who led it. Verity's predecessor had been going through the motions for a long time before he retired.

With a pang Daisy realised she was missing her father. Maybe it was because it was the seventeenth anniversary coming up or maybe it was Jan's revelation that she had a new relationship. Daisy wasn't particularly religious, except for attending the Lullbury Bay Christmas service, which was a town fixture and kicked off the festive season every year, but she sensed something or someone in the atmosphere here today. She sent up a little prayer to her dad, added a request that all would go well today – for everyone involved – and prayed that this Colin bloke would treat her mum well. 'So many important rituals, weddings, christenings, funerals. Some of the high emotion must soak into the fabric of the building,' she replied, eventually.

'I think it does.' Mia was wide-eyed. 'I'm not sure if I believe in anything but at times like these I definitely feel something's with us. Do you believe, Daisy?'

'I'm a scientist. I need proof something exists.' Even as she said it, Daisy felt something shift behind her. The hint of a dry chuckle. Turning quickly, she didn't know whether she was relieved or unnerved to find no one there. The sooner the church filled up with people the better. It was seriously creeping her out.

'Ben's a Christian. I'm not sure how I feel about that.'

She tuned back into what Mia was saying. 'Is it getting serious between you two?'

'I don't know. Too soon to tell but he's older than me.' Mia frowned, making her nose ring glint in the early morning light streaming through the leaded windows. 'We're at different stages of life. He's well established in his career, I haven't even begun mine. I'm not sure we're on the same page. You know?'

Daisy thought about what her mother had said about Colin. 'Is he nice? And is he nice to you?'

Mia smiled, happiness shining through. It lit up her face. 'He is. He's lovely.' She gave a short laugh. 'A few years ago I would have got all cool and snotty about describing a boy as nice and liking him for it. Now I'm older I can see how, well, *nice* it is.'

'The wisdom of great age,' Daisy teased gently. 'Mum said the same thing about Colin. That's this bloke she's just started seeing. Said how nice he is. Said the word and the quality is underrated. If Ben's nice to you I think you can probably work through the rest of your issues.'

'I worry I'm not good enough for him though. He's really clever and,' Mia screwed up her face again, 'turns out he's actually quite posh. His mum and dad have this stonking great pile over Somerset way. I'm from a single-parent family who lives in social housing.'

Daisy put the bouquet down that she was holding. The long-forgotten teacher in her yearned to care for the pastoral needs of her pupil. Going to Mia, she took the girl's hands. 'Look at me.' Mia stared at her trustingly. 'You are bright, clever, hard-working, kind and thoughtful. If I had a son and he brought you home to meet me, I would be over the moon.'

'Even with purple hair and a nose ring?'

'Even with multicoloured hair and three hundred nose rings!' She pulled her in for a hug. 'Any mother would be proud you were going out with her son.' Then putting her at arm's length she added, 'And don't you go changing. Never change for a man.' She glanced at Mia's hair. 'Keep the hair dye, don't take out the nose ring and be yourself. Any man who can't accept you for who you are isn't worth having.'

Mia's eyes shone with unshed tears. 'Aw thanks, Daisy. That means a lot coming from you.' She sniffed hard. 'Ben doesn't want me to change, he likes me just the way I am. It's just I'm not sure I do.'

'Then, at the risk of channelling lifestyle guru Aggie's blog, work on liking yourself. Because there's a lot to like.' She gave the girl another quick hug. As she was doing so the thought occurred that she ought to do the same. Like herself more. It would make life much easier if she accepted herself for who and what she was. As the emotion was teetering out of control, she moved away from Mia and asked briskly, 'Now, tell me, what do freesias symbolise?' She knew perfectly well but wanted to get the conversation back on an even keel.

Mia rolled her eyes. 'Don't you know? They stand for innocence, purity and trust. Perfect wedding flowers.'

Daisy laughed. 'I knew there was a reason I use them in wedding arrangements so often. And the white ones?'

'Fidelity.' Mia sighed with the rightness of it all.

The scent of the freesias misted up and filled the church.

'What could be better?' Daisy beamed at her. 'Told you. Such a clever girl. Now, come on, we'd better get cracking, or the guests will start arriving with the place half dressed.'

The ushers and one or two extremely early guests arrived, along with a pink-faced Verity. Mia slid off to talk to Ben with the excuse of helping him sort the piles of service sheets. After a final tweak to the two huge flower arrangements placed either side of the altar, Daisy made her way to the back of the church. She waved to Pete, looking immaculately smart in his morning suit, and said a quick hello to Verity. She'd wanted to pump her for information about who 'Walter' might be but the vicar mouthed back, 'So sorry. Running late,' and promptly ran into the vestry. As Daisy was dressed in her *Va Va Bloom!* work uniform and felt out of place, she found a pew right at the back, somewhere inconspicuous.

Surveying all her hard work she thought it was perfect. The flower arrangements were of the palest of pink roses combined with ones the colour of clotted cream, delicate freesias and sprigs of lavender, with snowball-globe chrysanthemums, pastel-pink peonies and soft silver-dollar eucalyptus greenery to add volume. Classy but quietly dramatic. Along the aisle the pew-end flowers added prettiness to what was already a magnificent church interior. It was everything she'd planned: subtly romantic and sweetly fragrant.

She watched contentedly as the church came to life. The organist took his place and began playing a quiet medley, groomsmen directed guests to their seats who then promptly got back up to greet relatives and friends, and a much calmer-looking Verity mingled and chatted. The volume of noise increased as the church filled up, perfume and aftershave mingling headily with the scent from the flowers and the faint whiff of musky damp from the old walls. And then Jago and best man Jamie entered. Daisy knew through her cousin Lucie that the two men had bonded through their RNLI volunteering; there would be a good smattering of RNLI volunteers in the congregation today. Jago twitched nervously at his cufflinks but looked piratically handsome in his grey-jacketed morning suit, his earring glinting in the lights. Verity gave him a hug and what looked like some reassuring words.

Most of the town seemed to have been invited, Daisy thought. The large Wiscombe family, with Lucie giving her a wave, the Catesbys from the animal sanctuary, Tracy from the Sea Spray café, Bee and Bella, Sid from the farm shop, Aggie and Austin, Brenda Pearce and her husband and a gaggle of staff from St Winifred's Primary School.

Daisy's phone vibrated. A message from Marion at the marquee: *Things all set here. Looking perfect. Will drop Jan off for the big event.* Daisy sighed in relief. She'd wanted to oversee the reception-venue flowers herself but had had to delegate, with Jan and Marion offering as a favour. Maybe, with WebFlorist status now secured, it was time to take on another member of staff? She couldn't be in two places at once. Switching her phone off, it wouldn't do for it to go off during the ceremony, she stowed it in her breast pocket. Marion must have broken all land speed records as, ten minutes later, Mia slid onto the pew bringing Jan with her.

'She just made it,' Mia whispered. 'Seconds before the bride arrived. Marion said hi but is off home now.'

Daisy nodded. It had been good of Marion to work an extra morning. She saw her mum fish out a tissue and smiled; she always cried at weddings. At a signal from Verity, Jago stood up, Jamie at his side. A sense of expectation rippled through the church. Everyone stopped gossiping, sat up a bit straighter and primped themselves for the main event. One or two kept glancing backwards to see if they could get the first glimpse of the bride. Honor's mum, resplendent in pale grey and an impressive hat made of pale-pink feathers, took her place at the front of the church. Verity stood at the altar ready to receive the bridal party and the organ music swelled to a crescendo.

'Ooh, and here we go,' Jan said. 'I suppose as soon as the happy couple go off to sign the register, we can leave. We need to get back up to Cheney House before anyone else.'

'Oh, we can't leave before the end,' Daisy whispered back, leaning forward past Mia and looking cagey. 'I've a feeling they've got something special organised for when Honor and Jago leave the church.' Mia gave her a conspiratorial look.

'Everything's looking beautiful up at the marquee anyway,' Jan hissed over the organ music. 'We can relax a bit and enjoy the wedding. They'll be having photos done outside the church for ages. Suppose it'll give us plenty of time to get to Cheney House before them.'

Daisy sat back, unable to answer as a blast from the organ

playing the first notes of 'The Arrival of the Queen of Sheba' announced the bride and they all had to stand up.

The congregation held its collective breath as Honor walked along the nave on the arm of her father. One or two sniffs could be heard. With her honey-gold hair and cornflower-blue eyes she was a stunning woman and made a beautiful bride. Wearing a simple satin ballgown with a lace bodice and the merest hint of sparkle, she was enchanting. It was more than that though, the town was deeply fond of their deputy headmistress and the little church swelled with love for one of their own.

Daisy sighed in relief that the bouquets she'd dropped off at eight that morning had survived the heat and looked pristine.

Bridesmaids Lexi and Sarika, teachers from school, followed, with Honor's older sister as matron of honour and then in bounced a beaming Merryn, Jago's irrepressible little sister. She caused one or two murmurs as she held, on a pale-pink plaited satin lead, Ivy the Pengethleys' black-and-white rescue spaniel. More sniffs were audible as Honor reached Jago and everyone saw the love light in his eyes as he gazed down at her. Thankfully Ivy, and a fidgety Merryn, went to sit with Avril, Jago's mum.

'Please be seated,' Verity said and the congregation, with a rustle of silk dresses and programmes of service settled back in their pews. 'Thank you all for joining Honor, Jago and their families on this gloriously sunny Dorset day for this happiest of events. Just one or two housekeeping notices and then we can get this wonderful couple married.' Verity stared over her specs and raised her brows comically. 'And go somewhere a little warmer for a glass of fizz.' There were one or two nervous titters as those guests unused to Verity's humour didn't know if it was allowed to laugh in church. 'We welcome most warmly babies and children,' she paused, 'and even *dogs* into St Winifred's but church services can sometimes seem dull, even the ones I lead, for little ones and those with four paws and a tail, so we respectfully ask that they be quiet during the solemn part when the bride and groom take their vows.'

She glared in comic fashion at some children. 'However, I demand you children in the second pew there make as much noise as possible when singing the hymns. We want to raise the roof today.'

The vicar was a beloved figure in the Lullbury Bay community and this caused a few giggles. 'A gentle reminder to turn all phones off or on to silent please. That is unless you are an RNLI volunteer. If we have a shout we'll probably have a mass exodus as we have so many of them here. Including the groom.' More laughter. 'In which case, we'd better get Jago married to Honor before he disappears! Let us stand for our first hymn, "Give Me Joy In My Heart".'

The service was as beautiful as the couple getting married. Blythe, Honor's sister, read from Corinthians, the babies mostly stayed quiet, no one objected when Verity reached that horribly awkward part in the ceremony, the couple declared their vows with clear voices and enthusiasm and the kiss as husband and wife was greeted with cheers and applause. It was just the right balance of warmth, humour, worship and solemnity.

*It was all perfect,* thought Daisy. *I'd like to get married in exactly the same way, one day.* She, Jan and Mia sneaked out just after the main bridal party and followed them to be greeted by a uniformed guard of honour of RNLI volunteers. Once everyone was out of church and the formal photographs had been taken, Jamie ushered the guests onto either side of the wide path which led to the church. They soon saw why.

A Land Rover Defender chugged up, towing a trailer holding the new RNLI lifeboat. The one named in memory of Jago's father.

'Hop aboard the *Kenan Pengethley*, newlyweds,' Jamie commanded. 'We're taking you to the harbour and you can cast your bouquet onto the water.'

Beside her Daisy heard Jan gasp. 'Oh my. They've found a way of including Jago's dad in the celebrations.' She turned to her daughter. 'Did you know anything about this?'

179

'Of course I did. There's a replica bride's bouquet in the vestry so Honor can throw the first onto the sea and still have one featured in the photographs at Cheney House.' Daisy smiled, feeling her throat thicken with tears. 'Judging from the look on Jago's face though, I don't think he had a scoobie.'

'Clever girl,' her mother approved.

The rest of her words were drowned out by cheers as the new Mr and Mrs Pengethley climbed aboard the lifeboat. Honor, giggling, and a little hampered by her beautiful dress, was gallantly helped by her husband. Once perched on the bench seats, Jago pulled his wife to him and kissed her passionately. The guests surged forward and threw confetti so the sky was full of gently swirling dried rose petals. Then the Land Rover was expertly backed onto the road, the happy couple waving and laughing, and headed to the harbour.

'Oh that was all so lovely.' Jan sniffed. 'What a wonderful service.' She blew her nose on a tissue. 'I suppose we'd better get ourselves up to Cheney House then, hadn't we?' She turned to Daisy and hugged her arm. 'One day, chickadee, I'd really love to see you get married like that. You'd be just as beautiful a bride. And the flowers would be wonderful!'

Daisy pulled a face. She heard the wistfulness in her mother's voice and tried not to get resentful or defensive; she knew Jan would love to see at least one of her offspring married. 'I'll try my best, Mum, but I've got to find myself a groom first and, funnily enough, they seem to be evading me. Maybe if your Colin has a younger brother, you could introduce me!'

# Chapter Twenty-Six

After Honor and Jago's wedding Daisy felt scratchy and unsettled. The aftermath of the pressure of a big job, she supposed. It had gone like clockwork, and she'd received endless compliments for the church and the reception flowers. The marquee at Cheney House, decorated in the same frothy pink and cream roses, peonies, lavender, freesias, snowy chrysanthemums and silvery eucalyptus had looked and smelled heavenly. She, Jan and Mia stayed for a quick glass of fizz and had then left them all to it.

Walk-in trade had dropped off. Although the month of August seemed to have gone on for about a year, it was now hurtling to its summer bank holiday and everyone was squeezing in last moments of leisure until the rush back to school. Daisy had no more weddings to cater for until late September and, for once, she had little to do and was bored. She wandered outside, a pair of secateurs in her hand. The Stranglers belted out 'Peaches' from Bay Radio from the shop's interior and, looking around the deserted high street, it looked as if that's where everyone was – down on the beach. A pall of heat hung over the street, shop doors yawned open in a desperate bid to get some air circulating and windows glinted in the hard sun. Even the summer bunting strung across looked a little weary. The promenade, beaches and harbour would be packed; Daisy didn't begrudge anyone seeking a sea breeze and cooling dip in the bay. She might pop down herself when Jakob had gone.

As she snipped at one of the lavender bushes on either side of the shop door her thoughts drifted to sunny golden sunflowers and raffia, clashing tangerine and Schiaparelli-pink gerberas. She'd loved the classy subtlety of the flowers she'd done for Honor but, now summer was in its dog days, she longed for the vibrancy autumn brought. For the excuse to use hot pink and yellow together with orange ribbon to bind. And then it would be Christmas which was always full on in Lullbury Bay. Daisy loved the buzz tourists brought to the town but when they went home and Lullbury Bay embraced its own with Christmas craft fayres, carol concerts and the legendary best decorated beach hut competition, she relished living in a little seaside town all the more. A walk along a storm-battered seafront with towering waves and a face numb from icy sea spray followed by hot chocolate and marshmallows was her idea of heaven. And, as a florist, it meant holly and ivy and Christmas wreaths. The prickly holly wrecked her hands every year but she loved making them and they sold like some of Bella's hot cakes. Maybe she should think about classy white wreaths this year too? Dried baby's breath. Would that work? Might sell well, along with her usual holly and mistletoe bunches at the annual craft fayre.

Autumn first though. Calling through to Jakob, who was inside the shop unpacking a box of agapanthus he'd just delivered, she asked him to bring over some yellow and bronze chrysanthemums on his next trip. Maybe some statuesque strelitzia too. The Bird of Paradise flowers would go down well with Maz's crowd. The wealthy women in the big houses in the new development liked statement flowers: big and bold. There was no answer so she assumed he had disappeared into the office to sort the paperwork.

The hot sun prickling on the back of her neck reminded her she was still in summer and cosy autumn was some way off. Trying not to lapse into nostalgia for a home-made steak-and-ale pie in front of a roaring fire in The Ship, she flicked sweat off her nose and concentrated on the task in hand.

'Daisy?'

The voice was familiar. An echo from her past and one she'd strived to forget. She whirled round, pruning shears in hand to come face to face with Neville. 'What are you doing here?'

Her ex stood on the pavement. Her first thought was that he'd aged. And hadn't aged well. It must be at least five years, if not more, since she'd seen him last. She flash-backed to the Monday lunchtime in the staff room when a concerned colleague had mentioned seeing Neville with another woman at a party. And that they were clearly being referred to as a married couple. With a sickening lurch things had begun to slot into place: why he was so often unavailable at weekends, his insistence on pubs and restaurants a ridiculous forty mile drive away, his demanding ageing parents who, allegedly, would never spend Christmas and New Year or his birthday without him.

Even the weekend before Neville had claimed his mother had wanted him there for all of Saturday and Sunday to help clear a garden shed. Daisy, irritated at the prospect of yet another weekend alone, had offered to go along to help but had been rebuffed. And now she knew the reason why. Neville may well have difficult parents to whom he was overly attached but the real reason why she saw so little of him at certain times was that he was married.

She'd rushed into the staff toilets and had been thoroughly and comprehensively sick. Shaking off the kind enquiries and suggestions from her colleagues to go home ill, she'd staggered through the teaching afternoon like a zombie, her mind whirring, not focusing on the role of leaf stomata in gas exchange. Biology with a tricky Year Eight set had passed in a blur; the children seemed to recognise she was in a mood to take no nonsense. As soon as the teaching day was over Daisy had phoned Neville and confronted him. The meeting on a bench in the public gardens overlooking the harbour – she refused to have him in her flat and it had become abundantly clear why they couldn't meet at his house – had been brief. She'd been ferociously angry; he'd been pleading and tearful. It had been awful.

'It's good to see you again, Daisy.'

Daisy couldn't say the same. Had Neville always had that paunch? Had he always worn his hair in that greasy comb-over? Had his voice always had that whiny nasal quality? Looking at him in his baggy surfer shorts and Hawaiian shirt she couldn't see why she'd wasted two years of her life on him. Had she really been so desperate to not be alone that she'd put up with *that*?

'Again, what are you doing here? I thought you and Fran had moved away.' She added the name of his wife deliberately.

'Fran wanted a day on the beach. Too hot for me, you know I always burn so I thought I'd have a look round town. Bit dead though.'

'It's over thirty Celsius. No one in their right mind shops on a day as hot as this.'

Neville shuffled his feet in his battered leather flip-flops. 'Yeah. You're right. Thought I'd come and check you out. See if you're still here selling flowers. See if it all worked out for you.'

'I'm still a florist. And it's worked out very well for me, thank you. You still married? How's that working out for *you*?'

He shuffled his feet again. To Daisy's disgust she saw he hadn't bothered to cut his toenails and they were long and yellow. A shiver of revulsion ripped through her. She'd never, ever been shallow enough to dismiss someone on the grounds of their appearance, but the older Neville really was unpleasant-looking.

'Oh, okay. Fran wants kids but I don't know.' He shrugged carelessly.

'You're lucky to still have her after what you did.'

His face flushed an unbecoming maroon. 'She never got me like you did, Daiz. She never understood me properly. I've never had the connection I had with you with anyone else.'

With a flash of insight Daisy saw what was happening. She had no idea whether Fran had known about her but could imagine Neville coming clean in a fit of abject confession thinking it was the right thing to do, unloading his guilt, making himself feel better and destroying his wife's life in the process. It looked as though Neville and Fran had worked through their problems and now poor Fran was thinking of children. Neville, panicking about the next stage in a committed relationship, had made an excuse to wander into town and look up his old girlfriend.

Daisy felt a wave of nausea wash over her. 'I'd say, after your behaviour, you're very fortunate to still have any woman in your life, let alone one who wants your children.' She looked in loathing at a stain on his shirt, half hidden by the vivid pattern. The crusted red might be ketchup. Neville had always been fond of a burger. She couldn't believe she'd let this man anywhere near her. Surely he hadn't been this repulsive when they'd been in a relationship? She wouldn't even give him the time of day now. On top of what she knew of his personality he was greasily sweaty and, her nostrils flared, he smelled. Not of body odour but more of clothes that hadn't dried quickly enough.

'Yeah well,' he let the sentence hang, looking hopeful.

'What *are* you doing here? Really?'

'Thought we could go for a quick drink, or a coffee for old times' sake.' He nodded to the shop behind her. 'Maybe you could make me a coffee here?' He inched nearer, looming over her, waggling his eyebrows in a pathetic parody of suggestiveness. 'You know, do a bit of catching up, for old times' sake.'

The cheek of the man! 'That would suit you, wouldn't it? Well out of the way of prying eyes just in case Fran decides to wander up into town after you.' Daisy stepped back and blocked the doorway. She tried not to brandish the secateurs; he didn't deserve that.

Yet. Having Neville in the space she'd so carefully constructed, that was hers and hers alone and of which she was inordinately proud, felt like a violation. 'No.' She laughed at the ludicrousness of the situation. 'We're done, Neville. We were done years ago. And we were certainly done on the day I discovered you were married. Go away. I never want to see you again. Go back to your poor wife waiting so patiently down on the beach. Or I'll–'

'Or you'll what?'

Was she imagining it, or was he *swaggering?* 'Or I'll march right on down to the beach and tell her what you've just done. That you haven't changed and don't seem to have any intention of doing so.' Too late Daisy missed the change in his mood. She'd forgotten Neville didn't like being thwarted.

'You bitch. You always were a sanctimonious cow.' He took a step nearer.

Daisy gasped in shock. Then she laughed again, but this time from fear. 'You what? You come up here seeking me out after however many years and think we can simply carry on from where we left off? You've got another thing coming.' She raised her secateurs. 'Go away, Neville.'

Jakob, hearing raised voices, came and stood behind her in the shop doorway. 'Is there a problem here?' he asked in his soft Dutch accent.

'Oh, so that's it, is it,' Neville said nastily. 'Moved on, have you?'

Had he always been this thick? Suspecting Neville would more easily take on board another man being around than her being happily single, Daisy launched into a lie. 'Of course I've moved on. It's been five years! Everything's fine, Jakob. I'm just trying to convince this idiot to go back to his wife and do the right thing.' She let Jakob put a comforting arm around her shoulders. He really was a good friend.

None of them noticed Rick march up the high street alerted by the shouting.

'Go back to Fran, Neville. I never want to see you again.' Daisy didn't mean to wave the secateurs in his face but they were getting heavy and making her wrist ache. She only meant to swap hands.

Neville raised his fist. 'I'll have you for assault. I'll get the police onto you, you see if I don't!'

'Oh please,' Daisy bit out. 'I haven't touched you. Go away and leave me alone! I might have been stupid enough to go out with you when I was young and lacking in self-confidence, but I've grown up a lot over the last five years, Neville. I'm a strong, independent, successful businesswoman, why would I have anything to do with someone like you?' For a moment Daisy thought she'd gone too far. Neville's face flushed puce; he was on the edge of losing it. She'd forgotten his temper too.

'You heard what Daisy said. Please be so good as to leave.' Jakob stepped towards Neville, still hugging Daisy to him.

Neville did a strange shrugging, wiggling motion with his shoulders. 'You threatened me with those,' he pointed loosely at the secateurs, 'things.'

'I did no such thing. For the last time, go away or I'll report *you* for harassment.' Out of the corner of her eye she spotted Rick looking pinched with concern.

'Assault, that's what it is. And it'll be my word against yours.' He still sounded threatening but some of the fire had gone from his words now he was faced with six foot three of blond Dutchman and a glowering Rick.

'Are you all right, Daisy?' Rick asked. 'Do you need any help?' He glared at Neville. 'I'm happy to be a witness to the fact you haven't touched this man.'

'I will be, also,' added Jakob.

'I'll say this for the last time,' Daisy said to Neville. 'Go away or I'll call the police.'

Neville looked at a well-muscled and fit-looking Rick, to Jakob, still with a protective arm around Daisy, threw up his hands in angry defeat and marched off down the hill. At least he would have done. Just outside The Old School Kitchen one of his leather flip-flops came off and he had to stop and adjust it.

Daisy, Rick and Jakob watched his hobbling progress until he'd turned into the cobbled square which led to the promenade and was safely out of sight. For the first time in their encounter Daisy wondered if Neville had been entirely sober. Surely he hadn't always been quite so awful and aggressive? She felt a pang of concern for Fran.

Rick rubbed a puzzled hand across the back of his neck. 'Are you sure you're all right, Daisy?' he repeated. 'What was that all about?'

Now it was all over, adrenaline leaked out. Daisy's knees began to wobble, and she was very glad of Jakob's arm holding her strong. She stared at Rick, pride not allowing her to cry in front of him again. 'I'm fine, Rick. It was all something and nothing.'

'Are you sure? You're ashen.'

'I said I'm fine,' she bit out, frustration and reaction setting in. 'And I am. Besides, it's none of your business.'

'No, I don't suppose it is.' His voice was thin with sadness. 'Look, is there a chance we could talk? Not now obviously–'

Daisy couldn't take anymore. Her eyes filled with tears and Rick's image, in his pale-green polo shirt and khaki shorts blurred. Another man who had a partner he seemed happy to cheat on. 'Not now, Rick.' She turned away. 'Maybe not ever.'

'Come, come, I'll make tea,' Jakob said and led her inside. He shut the shop door firmly in Rick's face.

# Chapter Twenty-Seven

Jan's bouquet
*Red roses – Rosa spp.*
*Love, passion, romance, eternal and long-lasting love.*
*Poppy – Papaver spp.*
*Eternal sleep.*
*Calla Lily – Zantedeschia aethiopica*
*Rebirth, new beginnings.*

Just at the end of the August Bank Holiday when the hot summer was turning dry and dusty and leaves began curling down into crispy heaps, Daisy and Jan visited Rod's grave to lay a bouquet.

Jan had wanted red roses but also some calla lilies. Daisy hadn't liked the red and white combination; the lilies always reminded her of her father's funeral, but she had wanted to please her mother more. She'd added some white gerbera, and vibrant scarlet papery poppies to represent her dad's birth month of August. Feathery ferns and glossy bay laurel gave the bouquet a rich opulent look.

Jan arranged the flowers in the holder while Daisy found the watering can and filled the receptacle. The gerberas wouldn't last long but the roses were in bud and would slowly bloom. She left her mum to her thoughts at the graveside and found the bench she had sat on when talking to Rick. She felt uneasy about how rude she'd been to him when he'd tried to help her with Neville, but she had been so overwhelmed with the situation she hadn't been able to think clearly.

'I ought to pop down to The Old School Kitchen and say sorry,' she addressed the blackbird hopping about at her feet, its golden-ringed eye cocked hopefully. Its response was to cackle a warning. 'Yes, maybe you're right. What good would it do? I'm not in control of my feelings enough to be allowed anywhere near Rick and not pine after him. And that's not going to do me any good, is it? He's with Minty and I have to accept the fact. Maybe he ought to accept that too. He's not a single man.' The blackbird took off, flying low over the hedge and disappeared, leaving her alone with her thoughts.

Immediately after the strange and disturbing confrontation with Neville the week before, Jakob had taken her into the office, sat her down, made her sweet tea and fed her biscuits, insisting it was good for shock. Watching him while he fussed around her, she thought how easy it would be if she could fall in love with him. Tall and loose-limbed with dark-blond hair and grass-green eyes and that seductive Dutch accent he should be easy to love. But her heart remained stubbornly and irrevocably in love with Rick. She'd banged the mug down onto the table, spilling her tea. She loved Rick! The insight had come as such a shock she began to tremble anew, worrying Jakob so much he sat down next to her and enfolded her in his arms, shushing her like a baby. He really was a lovely man. Like a big brother. But, now her heart had been captured by Rick, it seemed she couldn't see any other man in any other way. But Rick was attached. No good could come of that so it looked as if she was destined for a life alone, suffering unrequited love. And it wouldn't do to encourage Jakob if she loved Rick; it wasn't fair. So she needed strategies to get over a man she couldn't have.

She'd come a long way in a few years. The encounter with Neville had shaken her but it had also reminded her of the person she had once been. Bumbling along in a career she wasn't any good at and wasn't suited to. Why had she thought that, just because she excelled at science and especially biology at school and university, she'd be any good at teaching it? She hadn't been too awful with the more able students and had even quite enjoyed their bright-eyed curiosity and willingness to learn but her classroom management skills had been awful. The less confident she felt in the classroom, the worse her discipline got. And the grinding paperwork; the endless marking and lesson planning. She had her fair share of bureaucracy and boxes to tick as a business owner but at least whatever she did, it was for her profit and in her interests – and it was up to her how hard she worked. Yes, she'd made the right decision to change career, difficult though it was at times.

She thought back to how she'd felt when first opening the shop. A mixture of terror and exhilaration. But mostly terror. Funnily enough, she realised, although she still worried, she was far more confident about it all now. A few years' experience under her belt made all the difference. And she loved what she did; that helped too. Things had been so hectic she'd hardly had time to reflect on how she'd grown as a businesswoman. The difficulties and problems would surely be there but it occurred to her, now, she would never want to do anything else. And if she could survive the awful time when everything was locked down because of Covid and she'd had to take all orders over the phone and deliver them personally, doing endless hours and working alone, surely she could survive anything?

The new beginning she'd put in place so tentatively long ago, the hard work of an evening class in floristry when she was still teaching, had all been worth it. She'd triumphed! And look how far she'd come, WebFlorist status successfully negotiated, expansion plans coming together. She didn't often analyse, didn't often have time for reflection but the insight into how far she'd come made her sit up proud. She was doing pretty damn well! Giving herself a metaphorical pat on the back, she made a promise to remember this moment. And with a dry laugh, she felt she might owe it all to Neville. Him turning up at the shop so bizarrely had put a lot of things into focus.

Straightening her shoulders, she closed her eyes, lifted her face to the sunshine and took a moment to listen to the birds. Perhaps another new beginning would be to give herself a little more, no a *lot* more credit. She heard a flurry of wings and opened her eyes to see the blackbird had returned. It hopped about then stopped, one head sideways to the ground.

'Oh, so you're back. I still haven't anything for you to eat, I'm afraid but I promise the next time I pop by I'll bring you some birdseed.' The bird gave her an old-fashioned look as if not believing a word. Daisy considered herself a scientist but the thought the blackbird might just carry a message from her dad crossed her mind. Or was it robins which were supposed to appear when passed loved ones were near? 'Love you, Dad. Always will,' she whispered. 'And thanks for reminding me to be proud of myself. I promise I'll do better in the future.'

The bird flew off again at the sound of feet on the gravel. The bench sank a little to her right as Jan joined her. Her mother looked calm but there was no mistaking the red puffiness around her eyes.

'Enjoying the peace and quiet, chickadee?' she asked, taking out a tissue and blowing her nose.

'I am. I don't often get a moment to myself. I've been talking to a blackbird.'

'Was it a good listener?'

'Surprisingly, yes.'

'I've a little robin who comes to call at the cottage. Often talk to him too. Good listeners, birds. What did you talk about? The unsolved mystery that is Walter and his monthly order?'

Daisy smiled at her mother's mention of the robin. If it was her dad, he'd been busy. 'No, even he didn't have a clue who Walter is. He was all about the worms and why I didn't have any crumbs. I told him I was quite proud of what I've achieved with the shop and he agreed.'

Jan chuckled. 'Have you only just realised that?'

'Weirdly, yes.'

'And what's brought all this on?'

'Oh, Neville happened by the shop.'

'Neville? Oh, chick, I thought he'd been consigned to history.'

'So did I. It's just that nobody had told Neville. He wanted a coffee with me, God knows why. Then he got a bit angsty when I told him to bugger off.'

'No!' Jan took her hand. 'Oh, my lovely, he didn't get nasty, did he?' Her voice was warm with concern, she'd never liked Neville. 'What happened?'

'Just that really, I told him to go, he got all whiney and sulky, annoyingly didn't take any notice of me so Jakob had to step in.' Daisy decided not to mention Rick. Talking about Rick was all too confusing. 'What is it about men who take on board what other men say but won't listen to women?'

Jan huffed. 'Might have something to do with Jakob having height and muscle. Neville always struck me as having the potential of being a bully come half a chance. Thank goodness you weren't on your own. Are you sure you're all right?'

'I'm fine but yes I was glad of Jakob. Neville eventually took the hint and trotted off back to his wife.'

'Awful man.' Jan shuddered.

'I know. I can't think what I saw in him.'

Jan was silent for a moment. Daisy sensed she was building up to saying something.

'Daisy, I know it comes across as if I nag at you to find a man but I'd far rather you were alone and happy than with someone like that and miserable. You do know that, don't you?'

Daisy turned to her. 'Oh, me too, Mum, me too. And yes, I take all the teasing on board but I do know that.'

'But why did it make you think about how well you're doing with the shop?'

'Oh, I don't know really. It got me thinking about how if Neville asked me out now I wouldn't give him the time of day. I'm such a different person now.'

'I never understood why you did in the first place.'

Daisy sighed. 'Oh, Mum, I was so unhappy teaching, so mixed up and confused as to who I was and what I wanted out of life, I think he caught me at a vulnerable moment. And then I suppose it was so nice to have someone around, to have someone else to take to parties and go to the cinema with, that sort of thing, I just carried on.'

'And you wouldn't do that now?'

'No. Definitely not. Think I'm more confident. Think I've finally gained some self-esteem. It took Neville turning up to make me realise how different I am to the person he knew back then. I'm definitely more sure of what I want.' *It's just that I can't have it.* Daisy left the last sentence in her head. 'I think it's finally dawning on me that if a bloke comes along and wants to be with me that would be fine but, equally, I'm more than okay on my own.'

'I think what you've achieved is wonderful,' her mother said unexpectedly. 'And I know I don't say things like that very often. With the shop, I mean.'

Daisy felt a lump lodge in her throat. 'Thanks, Mum, that means so much.'

'Well, you have, Daisy. You've worked so hard and it's been a tough few years for any business let alone a small one that's not long been established. Lots of people tell me how lovely your flowers are, you know, and how long they last. Even Brenda Pearce is complimentary.'

'So she should be, she always gets them at a discount!' Daisy said, with a twist of the lips. 'Still, I don't mind too much, she's one of my best, most regular customers. She could easily buy them from the supermarket probably even cheaper but she always comes to me. Thanks, Mum,' she repeated. 'It feels good to hear you're proud of me.'

Jan sniffed. 'Well, as I said, I don't praise you nearly enough. It can't have been easy, going into something as hard as teaching having not long lost your father.'

'It wasn't easy for any of us, Mum, especially you. And you did an amazing job with us all after Dad died. You held us all together. Along with help from the Wiscombe clan.' Daisy took her mother's hand. 'What's brought all this on? You usually run a mile before talking about feelings.'

'Suppose I've got used to bottling them up, controlling them. I had to keep a brave face on for you and the twins. Coming here, seventeen years after your dad died, it's made me rethink a lot of things.'

'A cemetery's a good place to think things through.'

'True. And this is a nice one. You could end up somewhere a lot worse. I knelt by Rod's grave and thought of all the times I didn't tell him how proud I was of him, of working so hard to look after us all.'

Daisy put her arm around her mother and hugged her close. 'I'm sure he knew.'

'That's just it, I'm not sure he ever did. I took him for granted, I think. In fact, he spent so much time at work, I often used to get a bit jealous of the time it took away from me.'

'You were both so young. Dad was young when he died. You probably thought you had loads of time to say the things you wanted.'

'Possibly. But I'll say to you what I wanted to say to him.'

'What's that, Mum?'

'That I couldn't have wanted a better daughter than you, my

chickadee. When you went into teaching I mistakenly thought it was the perfect job for you. A career for life. Secure, good prospects. Your dad would have thoroughly approved of it too. So when you told me about wanting to start up a florist's shop, I have to confess I thought you were throwing your qualifications away. And then I saw how hard you were working, just like your dad, putting in all the hours, not having time for a social life, or much of one. I worried you'd end up like him. Worked into an early grave.'

Daisy hugged her mother closer. 'None of us knew about his heart condition, Mum. We didn't know, couldn't have foreseen he'd keel over from that massive heart attack. He was never even ill apart from the odd cold. The heart attack could have happened had he been a lazy so-and-so.'

'And there speaks my scientific daughter.'

'Well, it's true,' Daisy protested. 'How could any of us have known?'

Jan shrugged off her daughter's arm and twisted to face her. She took her hands. 'So I'll say I'm incredibly proud of you, for being brave and hard-working, but I'll also say this; don't let your job be your life. Or it'll end up being your grave too.'

Daisy wasn't sure what to say. Without Rick, all she had left was her career. Perhaps this was what was behind her mother's teasing banter about finding a boyfriend? It was less to do with grandchildren and more to do with preventing her daughter becoming a workaholic.

'I promise, Mum. I promise.' Daisy scrubbed at her face, as tears were beginning to fall.

'Here.' Jan fished in her pocket and brought out a little packet of tissues. She peeled one off and handed it over.

For a long time, mother and daughter sat in silence gazing over the serried graves, the smooth lush grass, the leaves circling down from the sycamore trees. The blackbird landed yet again, eyed them and took off.

'I'll say one thing for that bird, I admire its optimism,' Daisy said, breaking the quiet.

Her mother laughed. 'However misplaced. Must remember to bring a few biscuit crumbs next time. That's if Marion ever leaves us any digestives. For someone permanently on a diet, she doesn't half get through them.'

'Think she's trapped in the indulge and flagellation cycle.' Daisy changed the subject abruptly. She needed to know. 'I suppose it's not the day for the question but how's it going with Colin?'

'I suppose it might not be the right day, chick, but seeing as you've asked the question, I'll answer it. It's going slowly. I haven't met his family yet, although they know about me. Hoping to meet them soon at a family barbecue. Be nice if you could come along and give me some moral support.' Jan snorted. 'I'm ridiculously nervous about it. We're taking our time over everything. Just enjoying getting to know one another.'

'Sorry. Crass time to ask you.'

'Maybe, but I can see why you've mentioned him. I've actually just told Rod about Colin.' Jan wrinkled her nose, a mannerism Daisy recognised as having inherited. 'Weirdly, I think they would have got on, although they're very different.'

'You're right, that is a weird thought. I suppose they have you in common. Ah but, Mum, how could Colin's family not like you? Reckon they'll see he's very lucky to have someone like you around. And of course I'll come with you to the barbecue. Not sure how comfortable I'll be but I'll be there for you.'

'As I've said before, just because I'm getting fond of Colin doesn't push the love I have for your father out of my heart. The heart's a wonderfully expanding muscle, Daisy. It enlarges to love more people. It's just like having children.' Jan chuckled. 'And I should know, I've had three. I love your brothers but I loved you too when you came along.' Jan sucked in a deep breath and then went on with difficulty. 'And, something else, whatever happens with me and Colin I'll always put you and your brothers first.'

'I know. I love you, Mum. We're not the sort of family who do emotion very well, are we? But I do.' Then Daisy flung her arms around her mother and hugged her close so she wouldn't see the tears streaming down her face.

# Chapter Twenty-Eight

September's bouquet
*Pink carnations – Dianthus caryophyllus*
*I'll never forget you.*
*Heliotrope – Heliotropium spp.*
*Devotion.*
*Sweet Peas – Lathyrus odoratus*
*Love, devotion and blissful pleasures.*

As Daisy drove to deliver September's flowers to Walter's house she was thoughtful.

The emotional day with her mother had made her take stock. She was genuinely pleased her mother was moving on, even though she still felt odd about it. Even a little lonely. Despite Jan's words, she was sure she would have to learn to share her mother with someone else. Since her brothers had moved abroad some six years before, it had been just the two of them. Despite her misgivings, she'd met Colin, along with her mother and little Fleur in tow. They'd decided to meet up for a quick coffee in the sun sitting outside the Sea Spray Café. Less pressure than being stuck having a three-course meal enduring tongue-tied small talk.

Colin had been, thankfully, lovely. Obviously nervous, he'd chatted about how much he loved living in Lullbury Bay and about his new role as a volunteer with the League of Friends for the cottage hospital. He was obviously and genuinely fond of Jan. Daisy had stayed for nearly an hour, fussed over the spaniel when the conversation lulled and promised she'd attend the barbeque Colin had planned when his family next visited. She'd felt a twang of disloyalty to her father that she'd liked him so much but raised her face to the sun as she strolled back through the tourists and up the hill to the shop and forced the ridiculous notion out of her head. At least Colin seemed a decent sort. More importantly, her mother was happy. The happiest she'd seen her in seventeen years. It was a new beginning and it was suiting her.

As well as meeting up with Jan and Colin, she'd spent the week keeping busy, studying the flower catalogues, reading the book she'd borrowed from the library on the language of flowers, getting builders round for quotes for a conservatory and spending an hour at a car showroom eyeing up new vans and feeling horribly guilty about Primrose. Freaking out about the amounts of money involved. She wasn't sure she could afford any of it but it kept her thoughts from straying to Rick.

She also felt guilty about Jakob. After he'd returned to the Netherlands, he'd, very unusually, rung her several times. She only saw him as a friend and didn't think anything would change that. After he'd suggested she take some time out and go over to stay with him, they'd had an awkward conversation about staying friends and that it was all she wanted. She couldn't shake the irony that a perfectly nice, decent, extremely attractive man had come into her life just as she had become besotted with another. Poor Jakob. There was nothing she could do to change her feelings towards him, however, and he deserved someone who could love him as he wanted. He was too lovely a man not to have that. As, she reminded herself, was she!

Now, as she headed out of town, she pressed determined lips

together. Sod 'em. Men. The lot of them. She'd concentrate on building her business, enjoying life, making more of a work-life balance, maybe even take that trip to Thailand she'd always promised herself but had never got round to. She didn't need another person, be it her mother, Marion and certainly not Rick to make her whole. She didn't need a man, thank you very much. She was doing very well all on her lonesome. She gave herself another metaphorical pat on the back. Less a road to Damascus moment, more of a random occurrence on the Lullbury bypass, but she'd take it.

Somehow the decision, no matter how muddled and half thought through, cheered her. It was like shedding a skin she'd been inhabiting for too long. She seemed to have spent the summer being angry: at men, about her life, about anything. And mostly the fury had been directed at herself. The letting go of the angst made her shoulders ease and her heart lighten.

Now she felt fresh and sparkling and ready to face whatever life might bring her. The future spread in front her, inviting and hopeful. She was doing okay, and she was doing it on her own!

The van protested as she crunched the gears. 'Sorry, Primrose, I do apologise. Wasn't paying attention.' Daisy concentrated on turning right onto the busy road which led west. She tried not to look at the cemetery and remember the weirdly happy hour she'd spent with Rick. He'd been so understanding. So comforting. Being a good friend, she tried to convince herself. Maybe if she could work through the agonising sexual attraction, that intense connection she always felt for him whenever she saw him, even whenever she thought of him, he'd end up being a good friend. Just like Jakob.

As she settled into slow progress along the A-road, heavy with traffic, singing along to 'Here Comes the Sun', her thoughts drifted again, this time to making a business plan. A conservatory or a garden makeover? She glanced at Primrose's decrepit dashboard; a new van ought to be a priority. Even though WebFlorist status had only been granted in August, it had already boosted trade. She was at that awkward stage of not being quite ready to take on another member of full-time staff although it was beginning to feel as if it was necessary; there was only so long she could rely on Jan's goodwill and now she had Colin in tow she wasn't sure how much more free time her mother would have. It was unfair too; her mother deserved a life of her own. Maybe then, she should scrap any other plans and hire an assistant. Maybe Mia would be interested in more hours? The girl loved her work at the school but she might be willing to give up her supermarket job.

She was still mulling it all over as she pulled onto Walter's drive, the green Ford Focus in its usual position. Going to the back of the van, she was busy leaning in to take out September's bouquet and didn't notice the white Transit on the track behind her, half hidden by a Devon bank smothered in pink herb-Robert and parked up next to the gate at the end of the garden.

Walter's flowers this month were an eclectic bunch but hadn't been difficult to source. Carnations, no colour specified so Daisy had chosen baby pink, heliotrope and fragrant sweet peas. Mia had assured her the choice was a good sign as together they represented love, devotion and blissful pleasure. Daisy had added some blushing pink-and-white alstroemerias as the bouquet had looked a little thin and ordinary and was pleased with the country garden vibe. Pastel-pink and olive-green ribbons to match added just the right casual touch. She inhaled the honied scent of the sweet peas as she took the bouquet from its holder and smiled. Looked as if Walter had made up for whatever he'd done. She wondered again what the story behind the flowers was.

Sighing with resignation that, with just one more month's worth of flowers to go, she was unlikely to ever find out, she turned and nearly dropped the bouquet as she spotted the French doors to the house were wide open. Instinct silenced her and a prickle of unease made the hairs on the back of her neck rise. Spotting the white Transit van made her gasp silently. Her suspicions raised, she thought rapidly. Tiptoeing back to the van, she put the flowers back in their holder, slid her mobile out of her shorts pocket and held it with her finger poised ready to key in 999.

Ducking around the corner of the porch she waited. It could all be entirely innocent of course but Mia's dire warnings of thefts of lead from the church roof fell heavily into her mind. Hadn't Marion said something about dodgy characters in a white Transit, or was that Mia too? She'd always thought Walter's house was vulnerable, being empty and isolated, and there were probably all sorts of valuable architectural goodies on an Arts and Crafts house like this one. But what could she do? She was on her own. Her heart thumped. What if there were two or more of them? Hearing footsteps crunch along the path from the house to the track her breath hitched in terror. Primrose! Bright yellow and a dead give-away that someone else was here. She could only hope the over-grown laurel hedge which screened the drive from the house hid her van. Screwing up her eyes, she peered around the corner to see most of a man putting something into the back of the Transit. She wasn't going to let him get away with it. Poor Walter!

Without thinking it through and keeping her phone in one hand, she scanned around, her eyes lighting on a length of decora-tive tile edging. Picking it up, she ran over the lawn towards the man yelling, 'I've called the police. Told them there's a burglary in process. They're on the way. You put down whatever of Walter's you've got. And do it now!'

The man backed out from the rear of the van. There was some-thing very familiar about the khaki shorts he wore and even more so about his thick dark hair.

'Rick!'

He backed away, hands in the air, eyes wide in shock. 'Daisy. For the love of God, you frightened the life out of me!' His eyes slid to the length of tiled edging she brandished in her hand. 'And I know you're annoyed with me but are you really going to hit me with that thing?'

Daisy let it slip soundlessly from her fingers. Luckily it fell on the lawn and bounced without breaking. She felt her mouth drop open. 'What are you doing here? You can't be the burglar.'

'No, I'm not a burglar.' Rick thrust a perplexed hand through his hair making it flop over his face. 'Whyever would you think so?'

'Because this is Walter's house,' Daisy blurted out and then realised how stupid she sounded.

'Walter? Walter who?'

'Walter's the man I bring flowers for every month. I've been doing it since May. I drop them off on the porch and at some point he must collect them. I've never seen anyone here; the house is always empty.'

'This house doesn't belong to a Walter.'

'How do you know that?'

'Because it's Keith Hamilton's house.'

'Keith?' Daisy squeaked. 'But who's Walter?'

Rick sighed the sigh of the long suffering. 'Let's go into the house, Daisy. I could really do with a cold drink and I think we need to talk. I've been trying to talk to you for the last four weeks. I've absolutely no idea who your Walter is. And I know this is Keith Hamilton's house because he's my dad!'

# Chapter Twenty-Nine

Rick collected the bouquet and put it in the bucket of water which was waiting, then led her into the kitchen. 'Don't want them to keel over.'

'It'll be me who'll keel over in a minute unless you explain what's going on.' Daisy couldn't help but be irritated. It was like doing a jigsaw and finding out halfway through that most of the pieces were from a completely different one. Discombobulated was the word which sprang to mind. She'd never had recourse to use it before ever in her life but it described her current state of mind perfectly.

The kitchen was larger inside than could be spied through the porch. It was L-shaped and housed a battered pine table and dresser in the long part of the L. Rick poured them both pints of weak lemon squash in glasses full of jangly ice cubes. He sat down at the table so Daisy followed. Her nerves felt just as jangly but it was clear Rick wasn't quite ready to talk. He drank half his pint down in one go, his throat working. Now she had time to study him properly, he looked flushed with a sheen of sweat gleaming on the dark hairs revealed by the vee of his polo shirt.

It was cool in the kitchen, away from the window. A shabby

chintz-covered armchair nestled by a radiator, an old-fashioned radio on the shelf above. In the winter it would be cosy.

Eventually Rick sat back, eyed her narrowly and said, 'What do you want to know?'

'Is Walter really Keith?'

Rick scrubbed an exhausted hand over his eyes. 'I really don't know who this Walter is,' he said heavily, 'but I can assure you Keith Thomas Hamilton is my father and has never, to my knowledge, been known by any other name.'

'Then who's Walter?'

'Daisy, I've no idea. Who do *you* think he is? My parents bought this house about fifteen years ago. Dad had to be in the Midlands for work but they used it as a holiday home and came to live here permanently when Dad retired.'

'Some holiday home.'

Rick mustered a smile. 'I suppose. We lived in a flat in Birmingham provided by the company. It was nice but a flat nonetheless. I'd left home by the time they could live here properly. I never really got to know the place. But, I'm pretty sure someone called Walter never lived here. Mum and Dad bought it off the Forbrights. Adam and Audrey I think they were called. Nice couple. They came to the funeral.'

'Funeral?'

'Yes. My mum passed away earlier this year. In March.'

'In March,' Daisy repeated, light beginning to glimmer. She recollected her manners. 'I'm so sorry about your mum. Is that why you were in the cemetery that day?'

'Yes.'

She reached out a hand. 'You were so understanding. I wondered if you'd lost someone.'

'Yes.' Rick heaved a deep breath. 'Mum went after a quick illness. It's the one consolation we all have. That she didn't suffer too much. I know seventy-five isn't young but it doesn't seem all that old either.' He gestured wearily towards the garden. 'Not when she had all this to enjoy. That and her grandchildren too.'

'You've got children?' Daisy asked, startled. Somehow Minty hadn't looked the maternal type.

Rick gave a short laugh. 'Not me. Not yet. My sisters have all got one each. Keeps them busy.'

'Oh yes, I remember you mentioned them once.'

'Annie, that's the eldest. Then Di, then Izzy and then me. Only boy and the youngest.'

'And spoiled rotten,' Daisy said fondly.

'Yeah.' Rick made a face. 'Probably. With them having young children it's difficult for them to get down here to see Dad so I've done the bulk of it.' He paused. 'And there were other attractions in the area for me.'

'Setting up the restaurant.'

He gave her an oblique look. 'That was part of it.'

'We had a letter from a Mr Hamilton sent to the shop. Asking for flowers to be delivered here from May until October. No reason. And there was never anyone here whenever I brought them over. It's caused quite a stir amongst us all.' That was putting it mildly. They'd built it up to be a mystery it quite clearly wasn't.

'Dad became ill and had to go into a nursing home soon after Mum's death. They were devoted to one another, and it hit him hard. The flowers idea had been cooked up between him and Mum before she died and he was determined to see it through. Only then *he* became ill. That's why he couldn't be here to receive the flowers. He was desperate to have some flowers taken to the grave so got me to help him set it all up. He got a bit obsessed with having his orders followed exactly so I began calling in here to collect the flowers, check they were the ones he'd ordered, and then take them over to the cemetery. I'd take a photo to show him and it seemed to soothe him.'

Rick faltered, on the edge of giving in to his own grief. 'I suppose it was his way of trying to get through the first stages of grieving for Mum. When he fell ill it turned out he needed more care than any of us were in a position to provide so a nursing home seemed the best solution. He won't be there forever, just until he feels strong enough to come home. And, at least, when he does, I'll be living here too. It's the ideal base for me to launch the restaurant. Popping in once a month was a good excuse to keep an eye on the place too, start his car so the battery didn't go flat, mow the lawn, that sort of thing. Why did you want to call the police on me?'

Daisy was still processing all the information Rick had given her and was startled by the abrupt question. 'What?'

'When you came at me with the ornamental tiling thing you said you'd called the police.'

'Oh sorry. I hadn't. I was just bluffing. There's been a spate of thefts in the area. Lead from the church roof, that kind of thing. I thought you were the culprit.'

'I'm not the lead-stealing type.' It was said with a glimmer of humour.

'No, of course you're not. It's just there's been reports of some blokes in a white Transit looking shifty and I thought they were here.'

'And you were ready to tackle a criminal all on your own? Bit daft, Daisy. I could've turned violent.'

'Yeah, I suppose it was. I've grown very fond of this house over the past few months.' She blushed. 'I'd hate anything to happen to it while Walter was away. I've grown rather fond of him too.'

'That was amazingly brave.' He fixed her with a burning look.

The words made Daisy feel hot. A charged pulse passed between them.

'One thing that's really puzzling me. Why did you think it was a Walter who was the customer?'

Daisy blushed. 'We got a bit carried away in the shop with the romance of it all. We thought Walter was possibly a grieving widower.'

'Definitely a grieving widower involved but not Walter. What made you decide on that name?'

'The letter was signed by a Mr W Hamilton. We decided on Walter and it stuck. So this became Walter's house, and I delivered Walter's flowers here.' It was sounding more daft the more Daisy explained.

'The Mr W Hamilton is me and I'm definitely not a Walter. Not even in the slightest.'

'But you're Rick,' Daisy said stupidly.

'Rick for short. My real name is Warwick.' His lips twisted. 'I've never liked it, to be honest. I was named after a great-uncle.' He rubbed a tired hand over his face. 'Not sure why I signed myself off with a W that day. Grief and stress telling, I should imagine.'

Rick was really Warwick. Not a manly strong Richard but a town in the Midlands. Daisy rolled the thought around. Did she care? To her amazement she didn't in the slightest. Her feelings for Rick trumped any daft prejudice over what he was called. 'At least it's not Warren,' and, too late, realised she'd said it out loud.

'Warren?' He scowled. 'That's a rabbit's name.'

'Exactly!' She beamed at him.

'I can't believe you didn't put me and the flower order together.'

'And I can't believe you never mentioned I was the florist your father had his order with.'

Rick grinned. 'To be honest, I've had so much on my plate I've only just put the two things together.' He frowned, knitting his brows delightfully. 'I knew there was something familiar about the name of your business when you gave me your card.' He thrust a hand through his hair. 'It's been a hell of a whirlwind of a few months and I just haven't been thinking straight about some things.'

'Well, we never discussed anything like that,' she pointed out reasonably.

'We didn't. We always had other things to talk about.' He gave her a warm smile which made her toes curl up in her Crocs.

'And, of course, I thought you lived in London.'

'London,' Rick said, startled. 'Why?'

'You support Spurs.'

'Oh, I see. Sort of. You know you don't have to be local to support your chosen football team?'

'Haven't a clue.' She shrugged. 'I remember telling you I don't know anything about football.'

'We need to put that right. How do you fancy the next home game at White Hart Lane?'

'I have no idea where that is.'

Rick laughed.

'Oh, and another thing,' Daisy exclaimed, remembering. 'The report in the paper said Mrs Hamilton, your mum, had left a widower and a daughter. There was no mention of any other children.'

Rick grimaced. 'God, don't ever tell my sisters, they'll be livid.' He finished his squash. 'Not the first time a newspaper got something wrong but to miss three children off entirely is a little remiss.'

'So, if you don't live in London, where do you live?'

'Here now, mostly, but I used to live in Birmingham.'

'Ah,' Daisy exclaimed on a long breath. 'That explains the mailbox letter heading. You can see why all of it added up but didn't obviously point to you.'

'I can.' Rick smiled a little. 'That was Minty's. She had some headed notepaper hanging around in her flat. She's a PA to a marketing company based in there.'

'Oh. Minty.' Daisy's heart plummeted. It was all very well deciding she was just fine and dandy on her own but to be reminded why she couldn't ever have Rick still hurt.

Rick reached over and took Daisy's hand. 'And Minty,' he said on a heavy sigh, 'is who I've desperately been trying to get you alone to discuss.'

# Chapter Thirty

'There is no Minty and me. We split up.' Rick sat back and eased his shoulders. 'In fact, we split just before the evening in The Station House. When we bumped into you and your... boyfriend?'

Daisy gasped, trying to take in what he was saying. 'Not a boyfriend. Pete's another friend,' she explained hastily. It was important he knew that.

Rick's shoulders sank. He closed his eyes for a second. 'Thank goodness for that. Minty was staying here,' he went on more briskly, 'and we went out to thrash some things through. I was in between flats and had stayed at hers in Brum for a couple of months. We had to sort out what I owed for bills, when to pick up my gear. All that tedious stuff. The atmosphere here had got heavy so we went out to get something to eat somewhere more neutral.'

Daisy remained silent, her heart soaring at the thought of Rick being single and fancy free.

'We'd gone out, off and on, for a few years but we'd definitely been drifting apart. We wanted different things, different lives,' he continued. 'She's happy to stay in the city and I wanted out. It was the source of all those arguments we had, the ones I had to buy flowers for afterwards.' He smiled softly. 'Although I don't begrudge the last peace offering bouquet I bought as it brought me to you. The more time I spent in Lullbury Bay, the more certain I was that I wanted to make my life here.' He paused and Daisy could see him thinking. 'It actually ended up being as amicable as these things can be. We had a good talk, probably talked more, and more honestly than we'd done in months. She knows she could never be happy with a restaurateur in a small town in Dorset and I was tired of the clubs and cocktails life in Brum.'

'I'm sorry,' Daisy said, not meaning a word and feeling horribly guilty.

He gave her a quick look, raising a brow. 'Are you? I'm not. Since I've been in Lullbury Bay things have become so much clearer. I know what I want for the first time in years.' He blew out a breath. 'Minty and I were happy together for a while, especially in the early days, but all the time I was with her I never looked to the future. Do you know what I mean?'

Daisy nodded.

'I hope that doesn't make me sound callous. I enjoyed going out with her, she's great fun but I never saw my relationship with her as the one I'd always be in. Everything was kept strictly in the moment. For both of us.' He pressed his lips together to suppress the emotion. 'I had an excellent role model of marriage from my parents. I suppose I wanted, *I hoped*, to replicate that with my own marriage and knew with Minty it was never going to happen. And I knew she felt the same. We never discussed the future any further than the next week and it suited us both. At the time. As soon as I began bringing up what I might want for the future the cracks began to show.'

'She was very proprietorial when I saw you at The Station House,' Daisy pointed out. 'She called you her boyfriend.'

'She did. It was still all a bit raw at that point.'

'And she was furious when she caught you rubbing suntan lotion into my back.'

'True, and I don't blame her, do you?'

Daisy shook her head. 'It was all completely innocent but I felt incredibly guilty afterwards.'

He gave her another hungry look. 'It wasn't innocent, Daisy. Not for me. I wanted you so badly at that moment. Had you been willing I'd have taken you there and then, on that dusty floor.'

Daisy's throat closed. 'Oh.' It was all she could manage. She reached for her glass of squash with a trembling hand and spilled some. 'Sorry.' Using the hem of her polo shirt she wiped it up.

'Sorry for turning me on or sorry for making a mess?' Rick's eyes creased up with amusement.

'Don't laugh at me.'

'I wouldn't dream of it.' He reached out and took her hand.

'I couldn't blame Minty for being angry.' Daisy's words were coming out all hiccough-y. 'I mean, it looked awful. Her walking in on us like that. You were her boyfriend, after all.'

Rick shook his head. 'No, I wasn't. Not by that point. We'd had the talk and had agreed the best thing to do, if my life was going to be down here and she was staying in Brum, was to split up. She was hurt and upset. Injured pride, I suppose. She's a really good person. I hope we'll be friends one day.' He pulled a face, wrinkling his nose. 'I hadn't wanted her to walk in on something like that though. I didn't – I don't want to hurt her. She accused me of moving on, of having someone else all the time I was seeing her and lying to her. All sorts.' He rubbed his face again, looking exhausted. 'It took some working out. I couldn't justifiably claim I was innocently rubbing in aftersun because, for me, it was anything but innocent and she's known me long enough to know if I was lying. The upside is she also knows when I'm being honest and straight with her. I explained I had feelings for you. Strong feelings. But I hadn't acted on them while I was still in a relationship with her. Once she'd calmed down she realised it was the truth.' He gave a short laugh. 'Even asked all about you.'

'Oh,' Daisy repeated.

'Do you know the moment when I knew how much I loved you?'

Daisy's mouth fell open. Part of her brain registered how unattractive it must look. Most of her clung on to the words Rick had just uttered. He loved her? He loved her! 'When?' she spluttered. *Get a grip, Daisy!*

'When you got all excited about seeing the restaurant premises. So excited you didn't mind a few cobwebs and spiders.' His tone changed. 'I admire so much about you, Daisy. Swapping careers because you accepted teaching wasn't for you and being brave enough to do something about it.'

He admired her! Perhaps she'd misheard that he loved her? She answered with the flippant, 'Being a failed teacher, you mean.'

Rick twisted towards her and took both her hands in his. 'But that's not it. It's not about failure. It's about acknowledging your strengths lay in another direction and having the bravery to step outside your comfort zone and do something about it.'

'It wasn't very comfortable trying to teach and knowing you weren't very good at it.' Daisy's mouth twisted. 'Those young people deserved someone who was fully committed to their education.'

'But that's just what I mean.' Rick warmed to his theme. 'You could easily have stayed in your job, enjoying the security, coasting until you retired, but you didn't. You got out and tried something new. It's incredibly brave. Setting up a business on your own is amazingly courageous. I mean, yeah I think you're hot as hell too–'

'You do?' Daisy asked, delighted.

'Have you looked in the mirror lately? You're gorgeous, Daisy. But my attraction to you is more than that, it's based on something deeper. I admire who you are and what you've achieved. The last few years haven't been easy for any business, but especially the face-to-face service industries. I'd like to spend time with you, learn from you, develop some of your resilience.'

Was this how others saw her? Despite her recent acknowledgement to herself that she was doing okay, Daisy was so used to being filled with wracking self-doubt and worry she couldn't adjust her mindset to step outside and see herself as others did. As Rick did. 'Thank you,' she managed. It felt a totally inadequate response to his outpouring of words. Of love. It seemed he did actually love her! She screwed up her face in puzzlement. 'I still don't get what the spiders and cobwebs have to do with anything though.'

Rick groaned and took her gently by the shoulders. 'Can we forget about insects?'

'Arachnids,' Daisy said, on a giggle, ever the scientist.

'Insects. Arachnids. Whatever. Can I just kiss you instead?'

Daisy reached up and ran her fingers through his dark hair, sighing a little that she was doing something she'd yearned to do for so long. It felt as thick and lustrous as she'd always imagined. Tugging him to her not nearly so gently, she whispered, 'No, I don't think that would be at all acceptable. I rather think *I'll* kiss *you.*'

# Chapter Thirty-One

The kiss was all Daisy had dreamed of. And more. Rick's lips were firm and warm and exciting. When he reached around to the back of her neck and pulled her in for even more, the situation was in danger of getting out of hand. After a long, utterly delicious interlude they broke apart and stared at each other, panting.

'Oh,' Daisy said yet again.

'Oh indeed.' Rick shook his head a little. 'I've wanted to do that ever since the first time I came into your shop and we had that surreal conversation about red and white flowers and Tottenham Hotspur.'

Daisy giggled, her breath out of control. She tried to calm the situation down. 'We called your Mr Spurs for a while until Marion wheedled out what your name was.'

He grinned ruefully. 'If only I'd introduced myself by my full name none of the misunderstandings would have happened.'

'There weren't any really.' She shrugged. 'I think Marion and Mia, and me and Mum got carried away with the romance of the story of Walter's flowers.' She pulled a face. 'What can I say? There's only so much excitement to be had in a small town like Lullbury Bay.' She kissed him again, not able to resist. 'But I'm awfully glad you're not my customer and you're not called Walter.'

Rick grinned and kissed her back. 'You wait until we tell Dad. He'll be tickled pink he was the object of so much gossip. It'll make his day.'

'Is there a story behind his choice of flowers? Mia, who's really into the language of flowers, the *Lingua Flora,* I think she calls it, is convinced there is.'

Rick nodded. 'There is but maybe we can get Dad to tell it himself? He'd love that. There's a garden party soon up at Dolphin View which is the nursing home he's in. Maybe we can get him to tell it then?'

Daisy loved the way Rick was bracketing them together. 'Sounds like a plan and I'd love to meet Walter, I mean Keith, at last. He really knows his flowers!'

'Consider it done.' Rick took her hands again and kissed the palm of one. He licked her wrist and it turned her insides liquid.

'I think you'd better stop that. I won't be responsible for my actions,' she said, her voice hitching and her eyes going slightly cross-eyed with lust.

He grinned wolfishly. 'I can't help it.' He groaned feelingly. 'Oh, Daisy, I've wanted to touch you for months.' He lifted her hand to his mouth again. 'To kiss you, to caress you. You've been driving me crazy. But I wasn't sure how you felt about me. And, of course, I had Minty to consider; I wasn't a free man until I'd sorted things with her and had an honest conversation. I knew I was falling for you but couldn't do anything about it. I was wracked with guilt over Minty.' He screwed his eyes shut and shook his head. 'I felt awful.'

Daisy thought back to what her mother had said about the heart's capacity to hold many and conflicting emotions and understood. 'I hope Minty's okay.'

'So do I.' Rick sucked in a deep breath. 'I'd do anything to avoid hurting her. But I couldn't carry on as normal knowing I had feelings for someone else. It just wasn't fair. Neither would it be fair asking Minty to change her life so drastically and come and live in Lullbury Bay. Not that she was prepared to. I think she understood. We'd,' he paused and gave Daisy a flickering glance, 'we'd been rubbing along, hardly seeing one another as it was. We'd already lapsed into friends territory. Minty needs to be free to find someone who can love her on her own terms. She deserves that.'

They sat holding hands, mulling over what had been said. The only sound punctuating the silence was the steady ticking of a clock somewhere and a sparrow twittering in the guttering outside.

'And then, once we split and I was desperate to talk to you, I couldn't get near you. Every time I bumped into you, or sought you out, you had a man in tow.' He raised one eyebrow quizzically. 'You're a popular woman, Daisy. Who are all these men?' He looked stricken for a second. 'Oh God, you're not going out with anyone are you?'

Daisy shook her head, basking in his view of her being popular. Again, it was so far from her own self-image as to be laughable. 'I'm glad you think I've got men buzzing round me. One day I'll tell you the truth about all of that.' She put her head on one side, unable to resist flirting. 'You could have rung me.'

'Yes, I could have but what I wanted to say needed to be said in person. And every time I've come near you recently, you seemed so angry with me, so I lost all confidence. It was eating me up. The tall guy at your shop. He looked very protective when that other bloke was giving you some aggro.'

'That's Jakob. He supplies me with flowers from the Netherlands. And he's lovely and yes, he is protective but he's just a friend. An old friend and a valued business acquaintance. He was helping me deal with Neville. He's an ex-boyfriend. Well,' Daisy admitted, '*the* ex-boyfriend. We went out back when I was still teaching. I found out, too late, he was married.' She pursed her lips. 'It was,' she added, haltingly, 'a difficult time.'

'I can imagine.'

Time to come clean. She wasn't proud of this but it had to be said. 'So when you explained how Minty wasn't interested in your restaurant plans, in my head I heard the phrase, "my girlfriend doesn't understand me". It's what Neville said about his wife when I discovered he was married. It's why I was angry with *you*. I thought you were another player.'

'Ah.' The word came out on a long breath. He sat back. 'Now I understand.' He shook his head. 'I can guarantee I'm no player. I'm strictly a one-woman man. It's just I had to end a relationship before I could be honest with you about my feelings. And then, once I was single, I couldn't get anywhere near you! It's been torture. And I can see, now, why it's been awful for you. My poor Daisy.'

'You can say that again. One day I'll tell you all about the blind dates I've had to endure this summer in order to try to forget about you.'

'You like me then?' His lip curled.

Daisy slapped his arm playfully. 'Don't look so smug. Yes I like you. I was attracted the very first time you came into the shop and ordered Minty's flowers.'

'What did it? The air of hopeless confusion when surrounded by all those things on stalks that smell?'

'If that's my stock you're talking about, think again. I've got WebFlorist status now, you know.'

'Have you now?'

'You have no idea what that means, do you?'

He kissed her nose. 'None whatsoever but if it helps your business then I'm very glad.' He frowned suddenly. 'I came into the shop and saw you hugging some random dressed in a grey suit. Another man!'

'Was he mid-forties-ish and dark-haired?' Daisy asked, giggling.

'He was!'

'That was the WebFlorist inspector. He'd just awarded me

status and I was so relieved, I hugged him.' Daisy thought back, unable to resist teasing. 'He smelled delicious I seem to recall.'

'Minx.' Rick pulled her to him for a kiss that left her breathless.

She slid her hands up his chest enjoying the feel of his bunched muscles. 'Why didn't you stay in the shop so I could explain? We had a little celebration afterwards. You could have joined in.'

'Marion booted me out. She shut the door in my face.' He nibbled Daisy's earlobe. 'You taste good. All hot and salty.'

'I'll have to have stern words with her about turning customers away. Although sales have already rocketed,' she panted. 'I'm considering taking Mia on as assistant manager.' *Why am I gibbering on about work when this delicious man is turning me insane with lust?*

'That's good,' Rick murmured, patently only half listening. He nuzzled at the opening of her polo shirt and licked her collarbone. Cupping her breast, he teased the nipple. It sprang into life and made Daisy's head loll back on a neck weakened by liquid desire.

'It'll mean,' Daisy whimpered, trying to focus, 'that I'll have more free time.' She pulled his face to hers and kissed him, opening and deepening the kiss until they broke apart, blurry-eyed and breathing hard. 'Ooh. You're awfully good at this.'

'I could say the same and we haven't even got started yet.' Rick gazed at her, another feverish burning look from his liquid brown eyes. 'I'm so very attracted to you.' Tucking a strand of her hair tenderly behind her ear he added, 'I want you to know that I'm serious about you. About us. I want to build a life with you, Daisy, if we can squeeze one in, in between running two businesses. I want to work with you, make love with you, sleep with you.' He slid a hand under her shirt finding hot skin and making her gasp. 'I love you, Daisy.' He captured her mouth again. 'I love you very much. Shall we take this upstairs?' he whispered, the sound vibrating through her. 'I need you so very badly.'

'Oh,' Daisy breathed, fearing she'd combust. It had never ever been like this with anyone else. For a second she wavered. She and Rick barely knew one another; they'd not even gone out on a date. Were they rushing things? A compressed horror show of the dates she'd been on that summer flashed through her mind. If she was meant to go through that farce in order to get to this moment, she'd do it all over again. *What are you thinking, you stupid girl? You've paid your dues and earned this.* 'Oh,' she said yet again. 'Yes please!'

Daisy came to, several hours later, tangled in a cool white cotton sheet. It was the only thing she had on, under it she wore only skin. Judging from the light outside and the blackbird singing, it was getting late. She and Rick had slept the afternoon away. She glanced over. Not that much sleeping had been involved. Holding her breath, she slid over onto her side, not wanting to wake him, wanting to indulge in being able to gaze greedily at him.

Rick was fast asleep, lying on his front, a lock of glossy hair flopping over his forehead. His face was resting on one hand and he was frowning slightly, as if concentrating very hard on something. His back was toned, his lateral muscles defined and lightly tanned. Daisy was ridiculously turned on by the thick growth of dark hair in his armpit; his body was so excitingly different to hers. He had a tiny freckle on one shoulder blade which she delicately traced with a feathery touch. Half of her wanted to wake him but she resisted, preferring to study him instead.

Beyonce's 'Crazy in Love' thrummed through her brain, so loud she almost thought Bay Radio was playing somewhere in the house below. How ironic, that as soon as she had recognised her own true worth and decided being on her own was enough, this had happened. But maybe the saying that you had to love yourself first before being able to love anyone else was true. It had been amazing. *Rick* had been amazing. If she had only this afternoon of stolen bliss, if nothing more came of them, then she'd die happy. Little shivers of arousal stole through her as she remembered how cherished he'd made her feel.

He stretched, rubbed his nose and woke up. Seeing her staring at him, he smiled sleepily. 'Hello, gorgeous Daisy.' He pulled her down for a kiss, grinning crookedly. 'I just can't seem to get enough of you...'

Afterwards they lay together, limbs entwined. Daisy lay against Rick, his arm heavy over her middle. She stroked the dark hair on his forearm. 'I haven't been very nice to you lately.'

He kissed her hair. 'You've just been very nice to me.'

She giggled. 'That's not what I meant. I meant before.' She sobered. 'When you tried to help at the shop with Neville. When I bumped into you in the bar at The Station House. I was really cross with you.'

He kissed her again and snuggled her in closer. 'You've had a lot going on. And, as far as you were concerned, I was the Big Bad. Forget it.' He laughed and the vibrations echoed deliciously through her body. 'What you need is a great big bunch of flowers. Does anyone buy you any?'

'No,' Daisy answered sadly. 'I spend my life selling flowers to other people. For their hot dates. For their celebrations, weddings, christenings. Funerals even. And I've not once received one. Suppose it's a bit like coals to Newcastle as my mum would say.'

'Well, we'll have to remedy that.' Rick pulled her in even closer and they lay in a companionable silence for a moment listening to the blackbird rev up outside. It was very peaceful.

Daisy looked around the room, lazily taking in the details. King-sized bed, a faded paisley rug on the floorboards, clotted-cream-painted walls up to the dado rail and soft white from then on upwards. Small-paned windows with stained-glass panels reflected soft crimson, gold and emerald onto the white bedding. From her vantage point she could just see the corner of the turret.

It was like being in her own personal fairy tale and, for once in her life, she felt like a princess. The golden-tinted late-afternoon light streaming in through the windows made an abstract flower pattern, she mused sleepily. She jerked upright. 'Flowers!'

'Yes, I'll get you the biggest bouquet I can find,' Rick murmured. 'Just tell me your favourites and consider it done.'

'No! I've still got your dad's bouquet on the porch. It's been so sunny they'll be fried. I'd hate them to be spoiled and your dad disappointed.'

Rick pulled her back to him. 'Then we'll take them together. Could you bear for our first date to be to a cemetery?'

Daisy smiled at him ruefully. 'I'm very fond of the cemetery. It's where my dad is and it's where you were so kind to me after you discovered me weeping and looking puffy-eyed. I must have looked a right mess. At the time I compared myself horribly to Minty, imagining her all cool and sophisticated.'

'Which she can be,' Rick admitted. He feathered a touch down her cheek. 'My heart went out to you that day,' he said tenderly. 'You were so distraught, I wanted to gather you up and make your pain disappear.'

Daisy swallowed tears. 'Oh, Rick, what have I done to deserve you?'

He smiled pure love. 'I don't know but don't worry, I'm not going anywhere.'

# Chapter Thirty-Two

D aisy tripped down the steps to open up the shop the following morning, her happy feet dancing a tune, high on adrenaline and endorphins. She unlocked the door, singing, 'Oh, What a Beautiful Mornin'' It was. There was a clear Dorset-blue sky and a breeze swept up the high street whipping up the sharp tang of fresh salt from the beach and the promise of autumn. She shivered but not from the cold. In her mind's eye she pictured Rick and herself cosied up in front of a roaring fire, snuggled under a blanket. Sometimes a pang of melancholy stabbed when the busy summer season passed, the tourists went home, and the days shortened but today all she felt was euphoria.

Still humming to herself she went through to the back room and flicked the kettle on. It steamed to a boil ignored as she opened the back door and stared out dreamily at a dew-laden garden laced with swirling tendrils of early morning sea mist.

She and Rick had thrown their clothes on, rescued the bouquet from the porch; thankfully it hadn't drooped in the hot afternoon sun too much, and had driven Primrose to the cemetery. She'd checked on her father's grave, tidied it up a little and thrown away the roses and lilies she and Jan had left there in August, then they'd placed Keith's flowers against his wife's headstone. Rick had taken a photograph to show to his father and they'd sat on their bench – Daisy now thought of it as *theirs,* enjoying the soft sounds and scents of the early evening. Even the blackbird reappeared which made her smile.

Making love with Rick had been stupendous but sitting there quietly and companionably with him had possibly been even better. More solid somehow. The promise of a lasting relationship had hung in the gentle damp air. Somehow she knew they would build on the heady physical passion they felt for one another and grow it into a life together. Daisy had no illusions. It would be tricky, with them both running businesses, but she was certain it would work. Weird that such a profound moment could happen in a cemetery but, somehow, she felt the presence of her father and Rick's mother giving them their blessing.

She'd never been happier and when Rick turned to her with tears in his eyes and declared the same, she wanted to bottle the moment, to preserve it forever. Afterwards, he'd gone to visit his father and she'd returned to her flat, dizzy with it all. Half of her wanted to share the news immediately, the selfish part wanted to hug the delicious secret to herself for a little while longer.

Hearing the shop door bang open and the familiar tap-tap of Marion's stilettoes on the wooden floor brought her down to earth with a thud.

'Have you heard? They've only gone and caught those good-for-nothings who were stealing stuff off buildings. Your Colin, or should I say, your *mum's* Colin spotted a suspicious white Transit lurking round the back of the cottage hospital and reported it to 101. Turned out a van with the same reg had been seen in Bridport just before some ornamental gates got nicked. Three blokes arrested in Yeovil, stuff stashed in the back of the van recovered, although I don't think poor Verity's ever going to get her church lead back. Colin's a local hero!'

Marion came to the door of the office. She leaned against the jamb. 'And, not only that but the mystery of the Ninja Knitters' vandalism has been solved.' She giggled. 'You'll never guess who it was.' As Daisy didn't answer, she rattled on. 'It was only that Colonel Smythe chap. Knew he had a thing about the yarn bombing but honestly, taking it all off was a bit much. The man's unhinged. They found it all in his garage apparently. He's been taken into the police station and cautioned.' She giggled again. 'It's all over the socials. This town's never had so much excitement going on.'

Marion examined her nails, holding out her hand and admiring the violent fuchsia pink. 'Still, at least we can sleep safe in our beds tonight knowing our lead piping won't be stolen and our knitted graffiti won't be ruined.' As Daisy chuckled, she added, 'What? What have I said? What's funny about sleeping safely in our beds? You know, I might even be tempted to go back to the Knit and Natter Group. I tried it a couple of times but it was too much like hard work. Thought you'd be pleased. Daisy,' she accused, 'you haven't said a word since I got here. Ooh, is there tea in the pot?' She picked up the still-empty teapot, lifted the lid and peered in. 'Daisy, you haven't even made the tea yet! What's going on? Did you oversleep? I've told you a million times you work far too hard. Get some work-life balance. Get yourself a man. *Now* what have I said?'

Daisy couldn't help it. She turned and faced Marion, a grin splitting her face. 'I've hardly had the chance to get a word in. You been on those spinach-and-banana smoothies again?'

Marion studied her suspiciously, narrowing her eyes. 'You look different.' She held the girl by the shoulders and scrutinised her face. 'You look happy. Cheerful. Contented. Strangely relaxed.' She let go and gasped. 'You got laid!'

Daisy busied herself making tea, letting her hair flop over her burning face. Switching on the radio, Donna Summer's 'I Feel Love' blasted out at top volume. She hastily switched it off again; she was overheated enough. 'Do you have to be so crude, Maz.

Honestly, sometimes I think you're more juvenile than your Brittany.'

Marion perched on the edge of the rickety table putting it in danger of collapse. 'I've had to put up with her nonsense for weeks now.' She sighed. 'Still no sign of her getting anything remotely resembling a job. She seems to harbour ambitions, if you can call them that, to become an influencer and is auditioning for *Love Island*, *Bake Off* and *Britain's Got Talent* depending on which day of the week it is. Or hour. She changes her mind like the wind.'

'Has she got any talents?'

'Only for spending her father's money.'

*Like mother, like daughter.* Daisy kept the thought inside, too charitable and too in love with the world to make a bitchy comment.

'Oh!' Marion clapped, making Daisy jump. 'I see what you're doing.' She waggled a fuschia-pink talon. 'I know what you're up to, Daisy Wiscombe! You're deliberately changing the subject. Well, I'm cleverer than that. Pour the tea, break out the digestives, spill the goss. And I mean all of it!'

'I've a florist's to run, Maz. I can't spend all morning gossiping.'

Marion's eyes went huge. 'Why? How much sex have you had?'

This made Daisy laugh. She gave in. 'Okay. A quick mug of tea and I'll give you two biscuits' worth of news.'

As Daisy filled her in, Marion ate the digestives deliberately slowly, her eyes getting even bigger with each nibble. 'I knew it,' she proclaimed. 'I knew he had the hots for you!'

'Don't be ridiculous, Maz. The last time we discussed him you were more fascinated by Minty's wardrobe.'

'Minty? Who's Minty? She's toast, darling.' Marion took Daisy's hand. 'Still, sweetie, I'm so pleased you and Mr Spurs have got together. It's brilliant news. We must go out as a foursome, I know Barry will have a lot in common with him.'

*Not ruddy likely.*

'A foursome with who?' They hadn't heard Jan come in, trailing Mia in her wake.

Marion gabbled it out before Daisy had a chance to explain. 'Your daughter has only gone and bagged the most delicious man.' Before Jan could reply she turned to Daisy and exclaimed, 'The restaurant! Does it mean we can eat for free?'

'No it doesn't.' Daisy laughed. 'Marion, you're dreadful. At least let me tell my own mother my news.' At her crestfallen face, she softened. 'I'll make sure you're all invited to the opening night though.'

'That's what I like. The promise of a party.' Marion tapped a nail across her teeth and got out her phone. Scrolling through it, she murmured, 'Must begin planning my outfit.'

'Have I missed a year's worth of news or something?' Jan asked and flopped down. She poured herself a mug of tea. 'What's going on?'

Mia flicked the kettle on to boil again and hunted through the cupboards for a Very Berry teabag. 'Don't know what's happening but I need to know, like *now*.'

Daisy gave up on the idea of getting any work done and resigned herself to repeating the story of how she and Rick had got together. She left out one or two details, seeing as the audience included her mother.

'Oh, I'm so pleased for you, my chickadee. It's so good to see you happy,' Jan said, giving her daughter a hug.

'Good going, Daisy. He's hot,' said Mia. 'Sex on legs that one.' She wolf-whistled and they all laughed.

Daisy stared at her aghast. 'And there's me thinking of making you assistant manager and giving you more hours and a pay rise.'

'Do you mean it, Daisy?' Mia's eyes shone.

'If you'd like it, yes. I'm planning on having a better work-life balance from now on, so I need someone trustworthy and reliable in the shop.'

'Charming,' Marion put in, her eyes not leaving her phone screen. 'You never asked me.'

This made them all laugh again.

She looked up. 'What? What have I said?'

'Want to work Saturdays, Maz?' Daisy asked, serenely.

'Not a chance, sweetie.'

Daisy winked at Mia. 'Done deal. Will you be able to drop your hours at the supermarket?'

Mia nodded her head eagerly. 'I'll give them notice asap. Thanks, Daisy. It means a lot, you showing me this trust.' She blushed. 'I won't let you down, I promise. You have no idea what this means to me.'

'I think I do.' Daisy patted her hand and then gave in and gave her a great big hug. 'Oh, and I haven't told you all the most exciting part. I know who Walter is and he's not called Walter at all. His name's Keith and he's Rick's dad!'

# Chapter Thirty-Three

D aisy strolled hand in hand with Rick across the undulating lawn in front of Dolphin View Nursing Home. A white Georgian country house, it commanded one of the best positions in Lullbury Bay and she could easily see how its name had come about. The grass sloped gently downwards towards the chalk cliffs which stood proud and resolute above the western beach. Below them the sea was a deep purply-blue, with flashes of white whipped up by a soft breeze. Fluffy clouds scurried across the sky and the horizon melded into the water out in the bay; the perfect spot for dolphin watching. It was a peerless September day. Still warm but with an edge of coolness to mellow the heat. You couldn't hope for better for a garden party.

Daisy was feeling anxious. Rick was leading her through the crowds of guests to the sunny patio where his father sat under the shade of an enormous sun umbrella. She was meeting him for the first time and wanted to make a good impression. As it was a full-on garden party, she'd dressed with unusual care. A broad-brimmed straw hat topped a pretty blue-and-white floral-patterned sundress. She didn't often wear anything with quite so much material billowing around her legs and had become self-conscious when Rick had collected her. His burning kiss and, 'Boy oh boy' comment had brought blushes to her cheeks and she'd made a memo to wear something other than her *Va Va Bloom!* uniform more often.

She'd hauled herself into his white Transit, glad she'd stuck to white trainers. Turned out the glamorous soft-top sports car belonged to Minty. Daisy didn't mind; she knew the van would be of far more practical use when it came to setting up the restaurant. Now, as she strolled over the grass, she was even more glad of practical shoes; the uneven turf would have been impossible in high heels.

Rick turned to her, his expression concealed behind sunglasses. He looked edible in a pale-green shirt which showed off his darkly handsome looks, and his usual chinos. He raised her hand in a sun-tanned one of his own and kissed it. 'Nervous?'

She nodded.

'Don't be. He'll love you.' He kissed her lightly on the nose. 'As do I.'

'It's just that I want to make a good impression.'

'I did too, when I met Jan.'

'She thinks you're the bees' knees. She liked you even before she knew you were my boyfriend and that was from one glance from the shop's office! Less pressure there. And, not only have I got to meet Keith, I've to run the gauntlet of all your sisters at some point.'

'True.' Rick nodded sagely. 'But don't worry, they'll only make you do a four-page questionnaire and put you through a three-hour physical examination. Nothing onerous or demanding.'

Daisy was so caught up in her nerves she missed the joke. She slapped him playfully on the arm. 'Very funny. I don't think.'

'Hey, come on, I had to pass muster with Marion and Mia too!'

She gave him a disbelieving look. 'Marion?' Peering at him over the top of her sunglasses, she looked him up and down and added, 'Do you wear trousers? Are you male?'

'After what we got up to last night, if you haven't sussed I'm male yet, I'm seriously doubting your biology qualifications, Daisy.' He raised an eyebrow suggestively.

She blushed even harder. 'Don't make me think about sex at a time like this,' she hissed, not quite quietly enough.

A passing woman bent over a triangular walker struggling in the opposite direction heard them. She stopped, struggling for breath and winked at them. 'If I had a bonny lad like Rick on me arm, I'd think about sex all the time! Have you got an older brother, my 'andsome?' she cackled in a pronounced Dorset burr. 'A much older one?'

'Sadly not,' Rick replied on a grin. 'Only sisters. And you know my heart belongs to you and you alone, Doreen. I couldn't bear to share you with any older brother. How are you?' He left Daisy, went to the woman and kissed her on the cheek. 'Are you all right? Can you manage? Are you going far?'

'I'll manage just fine now I've had a kiss off you, my gorgeous boy. Just off to grab a cuppa and a slice of lemon drizzle. Make sure you get some, it's the best cake they do here.' She smacked her lips together. 'Delicious, it is. Made my day, you have, young Rick, with that kiss. Give my regards to your dad. He's on the patio with his fans all round him.' She shook her head and laughed again.

'I will.'

'Those for me?' Doreen asked, pointing at the bunch of creamy yellow and gold flowers Daisy had brought for Keith. Sunflowers, and cream and bronze chrysanthemums. The colours of the best kind of mellow autumn day.

'I'm sorry, they're not. I've brought them for Rick's dad.' Daisy felt horribly guilty. She eased a sunflower out of the tissue paper and handed it over. 'I promise the next time I come I'll bring you some. What are your favourites?'

Doreen took it with glee and stuck it in her hair at a jaunty angle. 'Not fussed, my lovely. When you get to my age any bouquet that's not going on your coffin is a bonus.'

Daisy smiled. *What a character.*

'You take care now.' Rick gave Doreen a gentle hug. 'We'll come to see you soon.'

The old woman didn't hear, she was concentrating on pushing the walker uphill towards the vast conservatory from where the teas were being served.

Daisy went to Rick and hugged his arm to her. Her heart had swelled watching the encounter. 'That was so lovely of you.'

'What was?'

'Making such a fuss over her.'

'Doreen? She's a fascinating character. Become a friend. She's ninety-nine, can you believe? Completely indomitable. Worked in munitions during the war and a shocking flirt. Has some eye-opening stories. I've become very fond of her as I've spent so much time up here visiting Dad.'

*How could he be so nice?* As she'd said to her mother, it was a much underrated and undervalued quality. Once more she counted her blessings that she had a man like Rick in her life. 'If I didn't love you before, I love you all the more now.'

He stopped dead and stared at her, wonderingly. 'That's the first time you've said it.'

Daisy frowned. 'What?'

'That you love me.'

Daisy's throat closed with emotion. 'Is it?' She gazed up at him. 'I do, you know. I have done for a long time, but I didn't think you were free. I had to fight against it for so long I think I've forgotten to tell you. I had to really battle my feelings. I think that's another reason why I kept being so horrible to you. Self-defence, I suppose.'

He cupped a hand around the back of her neck and brought her close. 'Promise you'll never stop saying it.'

She grinned back, giddy on love. 'I promise. Now, come on, let's get to your dad. I'm dying to hear all about the story behind the flowers.'

# Chapter Thirty-Four

I t turned out the group of 'fans' seated around Keith consisted
of Mia and her boyfriend Ben, Marion, Jan and Colin. They'd
brought along Fleur and Keith sat in splendour as the guest of
honour, holding court with the little spaniel on his lap. A table
laden with tea things and an enormous cake had been placed next
to them.

'Rick, dear boy, come and join the party.' Keith waved them
over. 'And this must be Daisy.'

Daisy went nearer. Fleur slipped off Keith's lap as he grasped
one of Daisy's hands in his. 'Dear girl, I cannot tell you how much
your flowers have meant to me. Rick sent me a photo every month
so I could see them on my darling Susan's grave. They were perfect.
Simply perfect.'

'And I can't tell you how thrilled I am at meeting you at long
last. I didn't think I'd ever get to meet my mysterious Mr Hamilton
and I'm so glad you liked the flowers. It's such a pleasure to finally
meet you.' She beamed at the man, an older and frailer version of
his son. So this was 'Walter', the man who had ordered all those
wonderfully meaningful bouquets accompanied by the snatches of
poignant poetry. Her nerves fled as she gazed at his uncomplicated

cheerful face. His hands were bony and gnarled but he still had a full head of thick hair which waved at the front in the same cowlick Rick was always flicking back. This is what Rick would look like when he was in his eighties. It gave Daisy a warm, solid swell of happiness that, with any luck, she'd be around to grow old with him. 'These are for you.' She handed the sunflower bouquet over.

'My darling girl, how wonderful. Bold and cheerful. Thank you.' Keith summoned a passing nurse, handing them to her. 'Karen, be a dear and put these in water, would you? I'd be most grateful.'

Karen dimpled. 'For you, Keith, anything.'

'What a girl,' he said to her departing back. 'So obliging. They really do look after me here. Now, sit down, sit down and we can have tea and cake. They make a wonderful lemon drizzle here.'

'So I've heard,' Daisy replied and slid into a very upright striped deckchair. 'Lemon drizzle's my absolute favourite.'

'Best cake in the world.' Keith rubbed his hands together and winked. 'I knew you'd be the girl for my Warwick.'

'I'm confused,' Mia said. 'Exactly who is Warwick?' She took the cup Jan passed to her.

'That's Rick's real name,' Daisy explained. 'He's our Mr W Hamilton.'

'I thought that was Walter?' Mia's nose ring jiggled as she screwed up her face trying to make sense of it all.

Rick groaned. 'I can see I'm going to have to change my name.' He sat down at Daisy's feet and leaned against her knees.

'Oh no you don't,' Daisy warned. 'Or it'll be divorce before we've even got married.'

Marion spluttered into her Earl Grey. 'Married? You're getting married?'

'Oh absolutely,' Daisy said blithely. 'I haven't asked Rick yet, but he'd better marry me.'

Rick also spluttered into his tea and then grinned up at her broadly. 'You're on.'

'Well, I'm short of a few wedding bookings so I need the business.'

Marion looked aghast. 'Darling, I've heard more romantic proposals.'

'She's getting on a bit,' Jan giggled, 'so she can't waste time. And I need my grandchildren.'

Colin and Ben looked faintly alarmed, wondering if the banter was in jest or whether they needed to rescue their fellow male.

'Again, you're on. Jan, how many would you like?' Rick asked, apparently not in need of any rescue attempt.

'Oh, at least three.'

'The more the merrier,' Keith added. 'Grandchildren are a blessing you can't have too many of.'

'I completely agree, Keith,' Jan added, 'although my three offspring have been slow off the starting blocks in that department.'

'We obviously need to team up and encourage them, Jan, my dear.'

Rick groaned. 'Looks like the parents are already in collusion.'

'Of course!' His father twinkled. 'Now we have Daisy in the fold, Jan is family too. And Colin as well.' He took an enormous bite of his cake and chewed, looking pleased with himself.

'Well, maybe we'll start at one grandchild and work up,' Daisy murmured, smiling into her delicate bone-china cup.

'Whatever, whatever,' Keith cheered. 'Splendid. It's all splendid. Congratulations to you both. I couldn't be happier. Welcome to the family, Daisy.'

'I haven't a clue what's going on,' Ben said.

'Nor me,' said a confused-looking Colin.

Fleur barked in agreement.

'Have some cake,' Jan offered and handed the bemused men generous slices of lemon drizzle.

'Could we gloss over the proposal or non-proposal or whatever that was and get Keith to tell us the story behind the flowers,' Mia suggested. 'I'm dying to hear the story and it's why we're all here.'

'Ah, darling girl,' Keith said, balancing his plate on his knee perilously close to Fleur's quivering nose. He clasped Mia's hand. 'You remind me so much of my dear Susan. To the point and fascinated by the language of flowers. We had a little chat, Mia and I, before the rest of you arrived,' he explained to the others. He studied her nose ring. 'My Susan always had an independent sense of style too. What is it you want to know?'

Mia came to sit at his feet, cuddling Fleur and keeping her from eating something she shouldn't. 'I had to explain to Daisy and Maz all about how the Victorians understood the language of flowers, the *Lingua Flora*. Can you imagine, Keith, Daisy's been selling flowers for five years and had no idea of their meaning.'

'Oi! It's not too late to retract that offer of promotion,' Daisy said, poking her with her foot.

'Well, it's a long-lost skill,' Keith put in, attempting to be diplomatic. 'Not many do know these days. It was a hobby of my dear late wife's. She was always the more creative one.' He pulled a face. 'I was all facts and figures. She had a beautiful garden in the house she grew up in as a child. Her father grew runner beans, strawberries, raspberries.' He laughed, remembering. 'Nothing can beat the taste of a fresh pea picked out of the pod or of a raw rhubarb stick dipped in sugar. Her dad grew flowers too. Lovely geraniums, dahlias and cornflowers. When we married and took the flat I don't think Susan really ever settled. She missed the garden too much.'

'It was a nice flat, Dad,' Rick said.

'It was, son, but your mother never got over the lack of a garden. But then we became busy raising the family. All girls, and then Rick came along. Think Susan was too busy coping with all the children to miss not having a garden.'

'How many girls were there?' Mia asked, deftly catching a paper serviette which attempted to fly off in the September breeze.

'Three. Anne, then Diana and Isabel, and little Rick here came along as an afterthought.'

'Wow. Four children. No wonder you were busy.'

'We were and wouldn't have had it any other way. Luckily the flat was in one of those mansion-house blocks. Built in the thirties, you know, and roomy. And by the time Rick came along, Anne had left home so he could have her bedroom. Diana and Isabel never minded sharing, thankfully.'

'And Susan always loved flowers?'

Keith patted Mia's hand. 'She did. She loved them. I'd buy her some every week. Fresh flowers, the biggest bunch I could find. She always put them in her mother's best crystal vase on the dining-room table.'

'And it survived four children?' Jan asked, laughing disbelievingly.

'Three. It lasted three children. The girls all knew if they broke that vase there'd be hell to pay.' He bent forward and ruffled Rick's hair. 'It took a four-year-old boy on a trike to bang against the table and over the vase went, water and lilies everywhere.'

'I don't remember that!' Rick's eyes went huge.

'Yes well, I think your mother tried hard to forget too.' The group laughed. 'But it got us thinking about the future and where we wanted to be. So, we started saving every penny we could and eventually bought Beech Tree House. Helped, of course, that the flat came with my job which meant no mortgage.'

'That's the lovely Arts and Crafts one I've been dropping the flowers off at, isn't it?' Daisy asked. 'It's beautiful. I can quite see why you fell in love with it. I have too, although I've always called it Walter's House.' At Keith's confused expression, she explained again about the mix-up, although she knew Rick had already told him.

Keith roared. 'Ah yes, I remember now. Fancy me being a

Walter, or, for that matter, Warwick being a Walter. See the problems you cause by not using your given name, son!'

'I know, I know.' Rick held his cup up to Jan for a refill. 'I've just never really liked it but maybe I should suck it up and in penance for breaking Mum's beloved vase, revert to Warwick.'

'What does Daisy think?' Marion asked, looking sly. She crumbled a fragment of cake on a plate. 'She's got a thing about names.'

Daisy caressed Rick's shoulder. 'I don't really care what your name is. I'll just call you darling.'

Marion made gagging motions and swapped an amazed look with Jan. 'She's gone over to the other side, Jan.'

'My little girl has finally seen the light and discovered romance.' Jan gave a mock sigh and clasped her hands together.

'I'm still confused,' Colin put in.

'Can we get back to Keith's story please,' Mia pleaded impatiently. 'It's just getting to the interesting bit. So you bought Beech Tree House?'

'We did, child.' Keith smiled at her. 'Had our holidays and weekends there. Did it up little by little. Was a right old mess when we got hold of it. Susan tended the garden and then when I retired, we came down here to live in it permanently. Happiest few years of our lives.'

'It's just such a shame you and Mum didn't have more time together, Dad.'

'It is but what we had we made the most of.' A tremor of pain crossed Keith's voice. 'Your mother picked up her old hobby. She took flower arranging classes and researched the language of flowers on the internet. Then, one evening, she came into the kitchen where I was reading in my favourite chair and said she had something serious to talk about.'

'Oh, Dad, did she know she was ill?'

Daisy put a comforting hand on Rick's shoulder.

'No, no, I don't think so. Not then. It was just something she felt very strongly about. Said she'd been to enough funerals to know how she didn't want hers to be! Had all the prayers and hymns sorted, what readings she wanted and what music. That was another of her passions,' he explained to Mia. 'She loved classical music.'

'She was always playing Sibelius,' Rick murmured.

Daisy tightened her hold on his shoulder, feeling him vibrate with grief. He reached up and put his hand over hers.

Keith nodded. 'We looked it all through and I said, in the unlikely event of her going first, I would put flowers on her grave every week just as I'd bought them every week when we were first married. I promised her.' He paused for a second, emotion overcoming him, then cleared his throat and continued, laughing gruffly. 'Susan, in typical Susan style said what a load of nonsense as she wouldn't be around to enjoy them! So we compromised. I insisted on a bouquet every month for the first six months and she said she'd pick the type of flowers she wanted. She wanted very particular ones. Insisted on them.'

'Because they tell a story!' Mia exclaimed.

Keith nodded again. 'Indeed. Clever girl!'

There was a pause while Jan passed him a fresh cup of tea. 'So where did you two meet?' she asked.

'Yes, I'm interested in this,' Rick said. 'I don't think I know where you and Mum met.'

Keith sipped his tea and pursed his lips. 'Not that exciting really, I suppose. We met at work like a lot of folk do or did.' Keith cast an amused glance at Mia. 'I understand you young people all meet online these days.'

Marion huffed and nibbled a corner of her cake.

Mia blushed. 'Not always. Me and Ben met at work too.' She gave Ben a loving look and he smiled back.

Keith patted her hand again. 'Wonderful! Well, Susan and I bumped into one another at work, even though we were in completely different departments. I was more often found on the shop floor overseeing the manufacturing and Susan was in the offices. Secretary to the big man, she was, up to when we married. I spotted her across the canteen floor.' He chuckled. 'Not the most romantic of settings but as soon as I saw her I knew she was the one for me. Not very tall but curves like a queen and a head of thick glossy dark hair.' He ruffled Rick's. 'You've inherited it, son, and her brown eyes. I could have drowned in Susan's eyes.' He shook his head, tutting fondly at the memory, his own rheumy eyes growing misty. 'Pretty little thing she was. And sharp as a pin. Couldn't get anything past my Susan. I know because I tried. Tried a few lines on her in the canteen and she wasn't having any of them.' He chuckled.

'So what did you do?' Mia asked.

'What did I do? Asked her to the work's social, that's what I did. Swept her off her feet with my foxtrot. We started courting and, well, one thing led to another.'

'So May's flowers are all about that time?' Mia said. 'You had lilac. It means love's first emotions.'

'That's right. We got serious, were properly walking out,' Keith added.

'June's flowers. Tulips. Love's passion.' Mia sighed at the romance of it all. 'Totes emosh.'

'I had no idea flowers meant things like this,' Ben said. 'I'm going to have to be careful when I give you any, Mia.'

Mia grinned at him. 'You have no idea!' She twisted back to Keith and frowned up at him. 'So something must have gone wrong because for July you chose red geraniums and they mean an apology.'

Keith rubbed his temple.

'Are you getting tired, Dad?' Rick asked. 'We can always finish this another day.'

'No. No. It's not that. I'm just thinking what a fool I was.' Keith sighed deeply. 'I wasted so much time when I could have been with my Susan.' At their expectant hush he carried on. 'I had the chance to work in Canada, you see.'

'I never knew that,' Rick exclaimed.

'Yes, went over there for eighteen months. The longest your mother and I were ever apart.'

'She didn't go with you?'

'No, son. That's what we argued about. I wanted to get married and take her with me. She thought it was all too soon; we'd only been walking out about six months by then. Didn't want to uproot herself or leave her parents. All I could see was a brand-new country, a new exciting start. A good promotion for me an' all.'

'So you went?' Rick prompted gently.

'So I went. And left the love of my life back here. Of course, we could only manage the odd phone call and write letters.' Keith put a finger to his eye and flicked a tear away. 'The letters got fewer and further between. I was convinced she'd found another beau so I cut the contract short and came home. Knew by then that, even though I loved Canada and the life I had there, I loved Susan more.'

'August's flowers,' Mia interrupted. 'Sunflowers! Loyalty and pride.'

Keith was obviously tiring but he smiled at her. 'Indeed. Took a while to persuade her to go out with me again, to get engaged but, as I kept saying, I've come halfway around the world just for you, what else can I do to convince you?' He gave a wan smile. 'So then she gave in and we got wed.'

'September's flowers,' Daisy whispered. 'We've just put them on Susan's grave. Carnations.'

'Love, devotion and blissful pleasure.' Mia gripped Keith's hand. 'It's a wonderful way to tell your story.'

'And my mother's too,' Rick added.

Keith gazed at him, his pale-blue eyes opaque with age. 'Run-of-the-mill story. Same as happened to lots of folk, but special to us.'

'Very special, Dad.'

Father and son smiled their love at one another.

Jan blew her nose, Mia wiped tears away and even Marion dabbed at her immaculately attached false lashes with a tissue. Keith and Susan's story had affected them all.

Daisy watched, through eyes blurred with tears, as a gull cried mournfully overhead against a dazzlingly blue sky. It caught a thermal and turned away to the west, the sun lighting its white underbelly into a blazing white. Keith was a wonderful man, full of humour and love. She thought of the blue glass heart Jago had given her and which was hanging in pride of place in her flat. Once her heart was like it, hard and brittle. If Rick had half of his father's warmth and compassion, devotion and caring, then her own heart was safe.

# Chapter Thirty-Five

October's bouquet
*Michaelmas Daisy – Aster amellus*
*Farewell, loyalty.*
*Pansy – Viola spp.*
*I think of you, think of me.*
*Myrtle – Myrtus communis*
*Love in all seasons, marriage.*
*Forget-me-nots – Myosotis sylvatica*
*Enduring, true love.*

An early October wind rustled leaves off the sycamore trees in the cemetery and whipped up the sea into a frenzy which they could hear in the distance. Keith, with a walking stick in one hand and Rick helping him on the other, made his unsteady way towards his wife's grave.

Daisy followed clutching the last bouquet. She thought back to the very first one and the mystery it had sparked. Now, though, she knew who it was for and why it had been ordered. She studied the flowers in her hand. A bunch of Michaelmas daisies, interspersed with winter pansies and a good sprinkling of myrtle. Small, unshowy, humble even.

Mia, though, had thoroughly approved. 'Daisies are for farewell and loyalty,' she'd explained, tears glistening. 'Pansies for the message, "I will think of you".' She sighed a little with the poignancy of it all. Now they all knew the story behind the flowers it seemed even more touching. 'And myrtle is for marriage and love in all seasons. Keith and Susan must have been very happy together.'

The symbolism had struck Daisy hard. 'It's a plant I've sneaked into so many bridal bouquets, not knowing its true significance,' she'd replied, giving Mia a hug. 'It's just perfect, isn't it?'

Keith had also stipulated forget-me-nots, but they were out of season. Daisy had suggested, instead, she pot up some seedlings and plant them in a decorative tub to be placed permanently on the grave. Everyone thought it such a good idea that Daisy and Jan planned to do the same for her father. As Mia had pointed out, the little flowers' symbolism was both obvious and apt.

Unfortunately, Keith hadn't recovered quite as quickly as expected so he'd moved into a flat in a warden-controlled block. With a communal lounge should he wish to be social he was in his element, especially when Doreen moved in too. Together they snaffled the best cake and biscuits, held court dominating the best seats in the lounge and ran the poor staff ragged.

Daisy's relationship with Rick had gone from strength to strength and she couldn't be happier. Every instinct about how her heart would be safe with him was correct. They had scraped snatched moments, when not devoted to setting up Rick's business or developing *Va Va Bloom!* to spend together. In a way, it felt all the sweeter and more exciting. To Daisy's amazement, Rick had even asked her to move into Beech Tree House but she'd held off, thinking it too soon. At least Minty was off their conscience. Word was she'd found herself a millionaire, was living in Dubai and very happy. Marion, wild with envy, thoroughly approved.

Daisy considered it an honour to accompany Rick and Keith to place the last bouquet on Susan's grave. She waited while Rick tidied it and then handed over the flowers. Now she knew its purpose she'd made it more robust with thicker wrapping and more securely tied. Keith's face when he'd seen it told her all she needed to know. She stood back to give them some space and then wandered off to her father's grave.

Standing in front of it, nestling her face into her collar, her nose as rosy red as her coat due to the chilly breeze, it felt right that she talk to him. Inevitably, the blackbird landed a few feet from her, its glossy feathers sheeny in the autumn sunshine. She reached into her coat pocket for the biscuit she'd brought especially, crushed it and threw the crumbs. 'See,' she said softly. 'Told you I wouldn't forget.'

She watched for a few moments as the blackbird was joined by a robin, the birds hopping about pecking and then she turned to her father's grave. 'Well, Dad. A lot's happened since me and Mum popped by in August. I think Mum told you about Colin? She seems to have bagged herself a good 'un, and a pet dog too. A spaniel called Fleur who is adorable. Mum dotes on her. I think you'd like Colin. He seems a decent bloke and obviously adores Mum but then who wouldn't? We did a joint FaceTime with the twins and told them. They were surprised I think, and a little shocked, but I backed Mum up when she said how good Colin is for her. And he really is, Dad. She's blossomed.

'We went to Colin's barbeque and met his daughters. It was okay, a bit awkward at first but his grandchildren were fun and once we'd rescued Fleur, they were trying to put her in the paddling pool can you imagine, the ice was broken. I suppose none of us knew quite how to navigate the situation but after a couple of glasses of wine, we all relaxed. I think everyone could see how much Mum and Colin are besotted with one another.

'He's very different to you, of course, but I've seen Mum laugh more in the last month than I have in a long time. She's finally embracing her early retirement, about time, eh? She's putting in fewer hours in the shop and has even joined the Knit and Natter Group. Not sure that's totally a good thing, to be honest; she's knitted me this lime-green-and-orange scarf. It really doesn't go with my red coat but I wear it to make her happy. You know they've found the culprit who was vandalising the yarn bombing? Whoever would have thought it would be Colonel Smythe of all people with a grudge against all the lovely knitted stuff that goes up in town? Always such a stern upright pillar of the community. He often popped in to buy his wife some roses. Apparently, he's got early-onset dementia so it's all really sad. Just goes to prove you never know what's going on under the surface with people.

'Think the Ninjas Knitters are planning on even bigger and better things than last Christmas and who could forget the wise man they created last year with that phallic purple present at his feet? I've heard rumours they're planning on a life-sized knitted nativity scene to put in the castle grounds. Mary and Joseph, the shepherds, a donkey and even a camel. Hope they've got enough brown wool!

'Mia and Ben are going strong. Love's young dream. She's begun her second year of A-levels and Ben is tutoring her. She's an absolute star in the shop. I hope she stays on when she starts university. She wants to go to Exeter which will keep her local, although I've a feeling it's not proximity to a florists that's keeping her in west Dorset but more a hunky primary school teacher who bears an uncanny resemblance to Jamie Dornan. Who could blame her?

'Ben is wonderful and the age gap doesn't seem to matter as much as Mia thought it might. I always said Mia had an old head on young shoulders. Actually I didn't, did I? I prejudged her terribly. How wrong could I be? I really learned something about myself there, Dad. I'm finally learning never to prejudge people.

After all, look at Colonel Smythe. On the surface all respectability and underneath a raging anti-knitter and a really poorly man. I promised myself I will not make any judgements about people ever again until I've got to know them, and maybe not even then. It's amazing what being happy can do to you.

'On the subject of making judgements about people, Marion continues to be a pain in the backside. She'll never change and, to be honest, we all love her the way she is, despite her many faults. Brittany has finally found her mojo and joined Emirates. She's training to be cabin crew. Says the uniform is dead sexy and she likes all the travel. Rather her than me. I love staying put in Lullbury Bay. Don't want to live anywhere else, although Rick and me are planning a holiday in Thailand next year when things have settled down with the businesses. Can you believe I'll finally get there? I've always wanted to go.

'Poor old Maz, though, is suffering empty nest syndrome now Brit has finally left home and Cassius has gone back to university. She keeps coming up with wild things to try out which is fine but she ropes me into them! Last week she got me to try a hot stone massage. But do you know what? I quite enjoyed it. This week's is "Creative Writing Channelling Your Inner Diva". Think she might win that one!

'The business is doing well. The WebFlorist status has meant trade rocketing. I'm even looking into taking on another assistant. Well, I may need to train someone up if I lose Mia to academia. I've got plans for the shop but I'm still working on most of them. Work on the conservatory begins next week and I'm drawing up landscaping plans for the garden. Think I'm going to expand into plant sales and pots. You know, have a mini garden centre out there eventually. Makes sense as the nearest one is Bridport and people don't always want to trek all the way there if all they need are a few daffodil bulbs.

'I'm looking into selling more cards and gifts too. Oh, and indoor plants in the conservatory. I've decided to keep Primrose though. I'm so fond of her, I couldn't trade her in. She's going to have an engine refit instead. Colin knows a good bloke and I might even get a swanky new radio, one that isn't stuck on Bay Radio. It's all go. If I move in with Rick, which I think I might, you know, at some point, I'll be able to rent the flat out which will give me a bit more income to invest in the shop. Imagine me living somewhere like Beech Tree House! Maybe I'll finally find out what's in the turret? Let's hope it's not a mad wife, as Mia thinks. All this change is really exciting, Dad. A bit scary but exciting. And now I don't feel I'm doing it on my own.'

Daisy glanced up. Rick was walking towards her. 'I've got to go now, Dad. We've got to go and put the finishing touches to The Old School Kitchen. It's opening night tomorrow and I want it to be perfect. Oh, Dad,' she whispered, tears thickening, 'I love him so much. I wish you could have met him. I think, no I *know*, you would have loved him too.'

As Rick neared, the blackbird and robin flew off. Smiling through her tears, she knew they'd done their job. Had listened well. She greeted Rick with a kiss. 'All okay with Keith?'

'He's fine. Emotional but fine. He's sitting in the van out of this cold wind. Speaking of emotional, are *you* all right?' He fixed her with a penetrating look.

Daisy nodded. 'Just having a moment. You know.'

He folded her into his arms. 'I know.' They stood for a while, arms around one another seeking and giving comfort. 'Your dad will be with us tomorrow.'

She reached up and kissed him lightly on the nose. It was pink and delightfully cold. 'As will your mum. Now, come on.' She took him by the arm and steered him back to the car park. 'We've got work to do!'

# Chapter Thirty-Six

Rick had worked ferociously hard to get The Old School Kitchen ready. There had been last-minute hitches. Despite his optimism about the kitchen, one of the industrial ovens didn't work and had to be replaced, and the plumbing firm employed to install the new loos had only just finished. Daisy had helped out whenever she could and she and Rick had spent hours of their weekends sanding and scrubbing floors, trawling auctions for tables and chairs, tasting food and drink from suppliers and interviewing staff.

Hot on the dying embers of the holiday season, two chefs had been taken on, but it had been trickier finding waiting staff now the students had returned to college. An unexpected ally had been Caroline, the owner of The Station House, who had been generous with her advice and contacts. Her daughter Eleanor had even mucked in to help with cleaning and painting. As had Mia, Ben, Jan and Colin. Marion, notable in her absence, had chimed in on décor and recommended an interior designer. He'd quoted a startlingly large amount of money to suggest a steel and grey industrial look which they'd dismissed out of hand.

Daisy paused in her task of giving the dining room parquet

floor one last sweep and looked around. Although they'd had to work into the early hours, the restaurant was finally in launch party readiness.

Rick came up to her, took the broom out of her hand and gave her a hug. 'Time to stop working and get your glad rags on.'

Daisy looked down at her jeans and filthy white T-shirt. 'What d'you mean? Can't I attend dressed like this?'

He kissed her cheek. 'I prefer you in far less,' he joked, making her insides curl, 'but think we might have to make an effort if the press is coming.'

She giggled. 'I suppose. Although we might get a bit more coverage if I turn up naked. Is Bay Radio still coming along?'

Rick nodded. 'Along with all those lucky enough to receive a personal invite, local dignitaries and anyone who's pitched in to help these last two months.'

'So the launch party will be later this afternoon and you're still going ahead with opening tonight too?'

'Yup. I'm gambling on a few folk staying on and eating with us. We'll keep the kitchens open. Steve and Kostas have agreed to work throughout the day.'

'They've been stars.'

'They have. I'm lucky to have them on board. We've got a good team around us.'

Daisy liked his use of the word 'us'. She cuddled into his side, high on a wave of exhaustion. 'It's been manic.'

'Certainly has.'

Together they studied the results of their labour. Long scrubbed oak tables, designed for sociable eating and drinking were positioned about the room, along with smaller tables to sit the romantic duos. Rick had scored a bulk buy of chairs from a recently redundant chapel. Solid hardwood, they bore the original hymn-book holders on their backs, giving them a quirky look. To make the renovation as straightforward as possible, due to lack of time, they'd painted the walls a warm cream and the ceiling white, and kept the lighting simple.

Daisy had sourced a stash of antique green glass bottles of varying sizes and had filled them with silver-dollar eucalyptus, cream roses, white carnations and frothy gypsophila. She'd added fragrant lemon verbena to scent the air. A tempting grazing board stretched across two tables and groaned with locally grown apple slices, grapes, figs, locally sourced charcuterie and cheeses, Kostas's special feta and spinach pies, quiches made with rich Devon cream and cheddar, vibrant salads, walnuts, silver onions, and poppy seed savoury crackers from an artisan bakery Rick knew of.

On another bench, nearer the door, stood sparkling glasses on a snowy white cloth, ice buckets, bottles of red wine 'breathing', and a selection of soft drinks flavoured with elderflower and lavender from a small company in Cornwall, and water. The champagne, and the chilled Hampshire white wine would come out at the last minute.

Daisy's tummy rumbled; she'd had no time to eat.

Rick pulled her closer. 'I couldn't have done it without you, you know.' Turning her to him, he kissed her properly. The broom fell unnoticed to the floor.

She broke away reluctantly. 'I have to go and grab a shower.'

'Now there's a delightful thought,' he murmured against her lips. He chuckled through his exhaustion. 'I don't know what it is about this space but it makes me incredibly–'

She gave in and kissed him some more, interrupting him. She felt exactly the same. Giggling a little, making their kisses vibrate, she thought back to when he'd rubbed aftersun in and they'd been interrupted by–

Someone clearing their throat had them springing apart.

Daisy wheeled around. Surely it couldn't be Minty *again*? Relieved, she saw it was Eleanor reporting for waitressing duty. She'd kindly offered as extra staff just for today.

'I see you guys are going strong.' She winked at Daisy. 'I have to say, out of all the blokes I've seen you with, I think this one's a keeper.'

'*All* the blokes?' Rick queried, looking taken aback.

'I'll tell you later.' Daisy laughed, enjoying his jealousy. She glanced at the enormous antique wall clock. 'Haven't time now though. Gotta go.'

By the time she'd run up the high street to the flat above her shop, showered and pulled on the only vaguely decent party outfit she owned – a pair of black wool trousers and a sparkly top – and run back down to the party, it was in full swing.

She made a beeline for the food and ate a tiny spinach and feta pie jewelled with pine nuts. It was delicious so she ate another and then heaped up a poppy seed cracker with some Sharpham Ticklemore. The Devon cheese was so delicious she moaned.

'Loading up with carbs, Daisy? You naughty girl.' Marion reached past her and picked up a couple of olives. Tossing them into her mouth, she surveyed the party. 'Good turnout, sweetie. Quite right too, for all our hard work.'

Daisy nearly choked on her mouthful. 'I know. I don't know how you managed to put all those hours in.'

Marion rose above the sarcasm. 'What do you think of my outfit? Weeks of planning.' She preened and held out one leg to show off the vividly patterned silk of her jumpsuit. 'Moschino, darling,' she explained smugly. 'Cost a fortune.' She looked Daisy up and down over the rim of her champagne flute and raised one perfectly micro-bladed eyebrow. 'One has to make an effort, doesn't one?' Her meaning was clear. 'But you'll have your day to shine, no doubt. And it might be sooner than you expect.'

Daisy had no idea what she meant but was too happy, and too tired, to be irritated or ask the woman to explain. Marion was Marion. Always would be. 'You look lovely, Maz. Is Barry here?'

Marion's face shut down. 'No. He had to go to Dusseldorf on business.'

'Oh, I'm sorry.' A sudden pang of sadness for her shot through Daisy. Now she thought about it, the woman was always on her own, with her husband permanently working away. It was even more apparent now the children had flown the nest. No wonder she filled her days with hot yoga and cruising discount designer websites. She put an arm through the older woman's and hugged her nearer. 'How's Brittany getting on?'

Marion brightened slightly. 'Just about to finish her training. So exciting. I'm hoping to grab a cheap flight, staff discounts, don't you know, and get over to Dubai to see her. Such a glamorous place.'

'I've heard it is.'

'Oh, and are you free next week? I've heard of this simply marvellous new yoga class. Yoga with Goats. It's on at a centre just out of Beaminster.'

Daisy was about to scoff. Yoga with goats? She couldn't imagine anything worse. *What about those cloven feet? What about if they pooed?* She recalled the flash of lonely vulnerability Marion had exposed briefly and relented. It could be fun. 'Oh, go on then, after all I quite enjoyed the poetry writing while channelling your spirit animal. It sounds a blast. But what do the goats actually *do*?'

'I've no idea, honeybun, but the woman who runs it makes face creams and soaps which are goats' milk based. Thought she'd be a useful contact. Might be great for the shop.'

'Might well be. Good idea.' Daisy watched as Marion drifted away to talk to the mayor's wife who looked faintly alarmed at being accosted by a statuesque forty-something dressed in flowing pink, green and yellow silk. Daisy smiled fondly; Marion was an irritating snob, but she had a genuine heart and always made things lively.

'Daisy, there you are.' Jan approached, glass of fizz in hand. 'I was worried you'd miss the speeches.'

'Sorry, Mum. Worked here until the eleventh hour then had to wash off the grime.'

'You look lovely, chickadee. Happiness suits you.' She gave her a kiss on the cheek. 'You must be so proud of all you and Rick have achieved. Well done. I approve of that young man completely. He's perfect for you.'

Daisy was taken aback; her mother was complimenting her more and more lately. There was definitely something up with her, what with Marion's odd comment and now her mother's. Maybe she was overthinking things? She put it down to exhaustion. 'Thanks, Mum. He is. Just perfect. And we are proud of all we've done. There were times I didn't think it would happen and I don't just mean the restaurant.'

'You've been through a lot, my lovely. Your dad dying and losing your way, getting stuck in a career you hated, branching out on your own with the business and all the worry that's brought. Not to mention having Marion as the most challenging employee.'

Daisy glanced over to where Marion was now looming over the mayor, pointing out the flower displays and handing over a *Va Va Bloom!* business card. 'Oh, I don't know, she's got her plus points.'

Jan laughed as she followed Daisy's look. 'Perhaps she has. You handle her ever so well, lovie. If I was her employer I think she would have been out of the door by now.'

'Don't forget she introduced us to Mia and Mia is an absolute superstar.'

'True.' Jan put an arm around her daughter's waist. 'But I can see how everything knocked you sideways. I could see all that lovely bubbly confidence you had as a little girl get knocked out of you by everything you've had to deal with. And, on top of all that, came Neville.'

'And then came Neville,' Daisy agreed. 'He nearly finished me off.'

Jan hugged her closer. 'But you got through it all. Dealt with all that rubbish stuff and I can see my little girl again. I know you've got your lovely Rick now but I suspect even without him you would have come up trumps anyway. It's good to know I've got a strong independent daughter.'

'Oh, Mum.' Daisy hugged her mum hard. 'Thank you, that means so much.'

They released one another, not quite knowing what to do with all the emotion that had suddenly been stirred up.

'I'm ecstatic to be thought of as a strong independent woman. I'm even happier to be a team with Rick. I think it's amazing what we've achieved in such a short time. But we haven't done it alone, you know. We're immensely grateful for everyone's help. Rick was very impressed with Colin. He's been a superstar getting that electrician in at the very last moment.'

Jan flicked a glance to where Colin was standing talking to Caroline from The Station House. 'He's a legend.'

'Can I say back,' Daisy said gently, 'that happiness suits you too? I admit you having a relationship threw me off kilter a bit at first but now I can see how right Colin is for you.'

'Thanks, Daisy.' Sudden tears sparkled in Jan's eyes. Then she resorted to form. 'Now come on, enough of this sentimentality,' she said gruffly, 'let's get you a drink.'

'And something to eat. I'm starving.'

'Tell me something new.' Jan laughed and led her back to the grazing table.

The restaurant was filling up now; it was crowded. The champagne was flowing, people were eating the food with obvious relish and Eleanor and her team of waiters in white shirts, black trousers and long sandy-coloured aprons were squeezing through the crowds making sure guests' glasses were topped up. It was looking like a success. Rick sat at a table surrounded by journalists from *The Lullbury Bay Echo*, the *Dorset Country Life* magazine, a blogger from the *Southwest News and Views* site and the reporter from the local radio station. Even from here Daisy could see he was charming them. The change of career suited him but more than that, she knew he had the skills and talent to make a success of it. She couldn't be prouder.

Sipping her fizz she quietly surveyed the scene. Jan and Colin were talking to newlyweds Jago and Honor. All four looked loved-up. Again, Daisy reflected on how good it was to see her mum happy. Mia and Ben were having an animated conversation with Tom Catesby, perhaps booking a school trip to his animal sanctuary. Bee from the bookshop and Bella from the bakery were giggling over something Brenda Pearce was showing them on her phone; quite possibly Aggie's latest blog piece on Sex for Boomers. Daisy suppressed a shudder hoping her mother hadn't read it. Tracy from the Sea Spray Café, along with Verity and Jamie and her cousin Lucie stood next to a gaggle of noisy Wiscombes and Keith and Doreen sat in a couple of specially designed upright chairs borrowed for the occasion. Doreen looked splendid in an enormous fuchsia-pink feathered hat. Daisy giggled. She hoped Marion hadn't spotted it; it would be the perfect accessory for her Moschino jumpsuit.

Most people here were the ones dearest to her. Her town. She couldn't be prouder of being part of it and its community. She picked up a cracker and loaded it with some creamy Somerset Brie. It was so good.

Rick appeared to have finished with the press junket and was making his way over to her, hampered by everyone wishing him well and stopping him to chat. Daisy ate two slices of locally cured ham while she waited. These grazing tables were a nightmare. You couldn't stop eating.

Eventually he reached her. 'Hello, you.' He kissed her on the nose and lovingly flicked away a smudge of cheese.

'Hello, you.' She smiled at him idiotically. She loved looking at him, would never tire of it. He was formally dressed today in an ice-white shirt and dark-grey trousers. Although there were lines of fatigue showing, his face was alight with excitement. He'd had his hair cut especially for the party so it was shorter than usual but the rebellious cowlick still flopped over his forehead. She loved him so much.

'You look beautiful.' Edging nearer, he pulled her to him by looping an arm around her waist. He whispered into her ear. 'I love you.'

'And I love you.' She kissed him. 'How did the press interviews go?'

A wide grin split Rick's face, radiating through the stress and exhaustion. He nodded. 'Great. Think we're going to get some good publicity in the *Dorset Country Life* mag and *Southwest News and Views* has even offered us a spot on their website showcasing west country restaurants.' He gazed at her intently. 'Can we escape for a moment, do you think?'

They glanced around the restaurant. The atmosphere and noise levels had increased to a happy buzzy level. Everyone looked to be contentedly eating and drinking.

'I think they'll manage without us for a while,' Daisy answered, puzzled at what he had planned.

# Chapter Thirty-Seven

Daisy's bouquet
*Jersey Lily – Amaryllidaceae*
*Good fortune.*
*Dahlia – Asteraceae*
*Staying graceful under pressure, following your own unique path.*
*Michaelmas Daisy – Aster amellus*
*Loyalty.*
*Pansy – Viola spp.*
*I think of you.*
*Orange roses – Rosa spp.*
*Fascination, passion, deep emotions.*
*Passionflower – Passiflora caerulea spp.*
*Devotion.*
*Myrtle – Myrtus communis*
*Love in all seasons, marriage.*

Rick led her into the kitchens and nodded at Steve and Kostas. 'Can you give us a few minutes, guys?' They grinned and disappeared outside for a break.

He turned to Daisy. 'It's not the most romantic of venues for this but I didn't want to do it in public, in front of all the hordes out there, and put you under unfair pressure.'

Daisy sort of guessed what was coming. And she sort of guessed what she'd say.

'Wait for just one second.' Rick steered her to a high stool and she clambered onto it. He disappeared into the passageway which ran alongside the kitchen, where the chest freezers were stored, along with any supplies which needed to be kept cool.

Daisy waited, wondering why an engagement ring had to be stored along with the fruit and veg. She gazed around her. Prepped food as far as she could see. Enormous bowls of chopped vegetables and onions covered in cling film, neatly stacked containers of salad ready for the restaurant's first proper night's service, cooking stations marked out, colour-coded chopping boards at the ready on the immaculately clean steel work surfaces, all along with platters of food to replenish this afternoon's grazing tables. It all looked professional and efficient, and Daisy prayed Rick and his team would have a good opening night. Bay Radio played quietly in the background. The Bee Gees, 'How Can You Mend a Broken Heart?' She had a feeling hers might be about to be finally healed.

Rick returned and flourished the most enormous bouquet Daisy had ever seen. But he didn't hand it over. Instead, he stood in front of her and cleared his throat nervously. Daisy peered more closely at the flowers; most of them looked suspiciously familiar.

'This was tricky to pull off,' Rick began to say. 'Mia and Jan both helped and Marion did an expert job at keeping you busy for a couple of afternoons so we could plan it and put it together.'

'The paddleboard Pilates and the gong bath sessions?' Daisy exclaimed.

Rick nodded.

'And there's me feeling sorry for her and trying to help her with the empty nesting!'

'Sorry. It was all a conspiracy to keep you out of *Va Va Bloom!* Timing was a nightmare. Too soon and they would wilt and last night there was no time to do anything but work here.' He examined the flowers anxiously. 'I hope they've lasted.'

'Welcome to my world.' Daisy giggled. 'They look in perfect condition. But why the conspiracy?'

He cleared his throat again. 'If you'll let me, I'd like to explain. You once said, rather mournfully, that no one ever buys a florist flowers so I thought I'd put that right.'

'And they're gorgeous. And I should know. By the look of them, they come from my stock!'

Rick grinned ruefully. 'They do. But there's a reason for this riot of mismatched colours and lack of style.'

'Well, I didn't like to say but I'd never put anything like that together. I mean, they're lovely, Rick, and I'm incredibly touched but the florist in me is cringing at the colour mix.'

'I agree. They clash horribly. Maybe they can start a new trend?' He looked at Daisy and pulled a face.

'Maybe,' she giggled again, 'but probably not.'

'Then let me explain.' He plucked out a pale-pink flower. 'Nerines. Meaning good fortune.'

Daisy took the flower from him and sniffed it. 'Jersey Lily, one of my favourites.'

He smiled tenderly. 'And I've had the best fortune in meeting you. Fate brought me into your shop that day back in May.' He wrinkled his nose. 'Was it only May? I seem to have known you forever.' He handed over a bright-orange bloom. 'Dahlias. Grace under pressure. Over the last few weeks, I've seen you display that countless times. When the paint failed to turn up–'

'And when it did it was the wrong colour.'

'When the bottled water supplier let us down at the last minute and you trekked into KashKost in rattly old Primrose to buy replacements. When we found the damp in the roof. When I had to give up the idea of knocking through to find the old chimney. When I had a hissy fit at the water company for mixing up our account.'

'Well, you were stressed,' Daisy acknowledged. 'It was understandable.'

'I couldn't have done any of this without your steadying influence. I owe you so much, Daisy. You are a wonder.'

'I am,' she replied. 'I'm pretty remarkable, aren't I?'

'You are.' He laughed and handed over a vividly purple Michaelmas Daisy. 'A daisy for my very own Daisy.'

'Cheesy. But I love Asters so I'll accept it.'

'Yes, it is cheesy,' Rick admitted. 'But the word Aster means star and that's what you are to me.'

'Oh.' Daisy, lost for words, clutched it to her and blushed.

Rick tugged out a rose from the many in the bouquet. 'An orange rose. It means fascination, passion and deep love.' He put it into her hands. 'Because you fascinate me and will never stop fascinating me. And you must know by now how passionate and deep my love is for you.'

Daisy blushed even harder. She nodded and buried her hot face in the flowers.

A passionflower was next. 'It stands for devotion,' Rick explained. 'Have to admit this one's a stretch as I'm told it's really about religious devotion, but I want you to know I'm devoted to you, Daisy, and promise to be always devoted to you. Through the good times and the less good. Through riches and poverty. Whatever comes our way, I want to see it through with you.'

They gazed at one another for a second, breathless.

'And besides, they're really pretty,' he added, breaking the emotional tension.

Daisy smiled, holding back tears, and studied the spiky purple-and-white flower which to her always seemed exotic and slightly alien-looking but which was actually a fairly common garden rambler.

When she looked up Rick was holding a spray of something with glossy dark-green leaves and fuzzy white flowers. He'd put the rest of the bouquet on the steel food prep counter and was holding in his other hand a tiny open box. Inside was a perfect solitaire.

'Myrtle,' he began.

'Marriage,' Daisy breathed, her eyes misting.

'And love in all seasons. I love you, Daisy. I'm in love with you and always will be. Through all the seasons. Through all the years to come. I know we haven't known one another for very long but in a way I feel I've always known you–'

'And we've spent so much time together working on the restaurant–'

'That we fast-forwarded to seeing one another at our worst–'

'And best–'

'And we've made a brilliant team–'

Their words tumbled over one another's in their eagerness to agree.

Daisy slid, on wobbly legs, from the stool, put her flowers on the side to join the others and slipped her arms around Rick's waist. 'Of course I'll marry you,' she whispered, emotion making her voice hoarse and tears closing her throat. She kissed him passionately. 'Yes please, I'll marry you.'

'I haven't asked you yet!'

'You don't have to. Will *you* marry *me*, Rick?'

He slipped the diamond onto the third finger of her left hand. 'Yes, Daisy Wiscombe. It would be my delight and honour to marry you.'

They kissed, oblivious to the noise of revelry filtering in from the restaurant, not noticing Steve and Kosta's return and then exit again hurriedly, ignoring Eleanor collecting a tray of refills for the grazing tables.

Eventually, they broke apart.

'We ought to go back to the party.' Daisy nuzzled Rick's neck and then kissed him again. 'You've got a speech to make. Maybe you can tell everyone our news at the end of it.'

He laughed against her lips. 'They already know.'

'Oh, of course. The meanings of the flowers in the bouquet.'

'All Mia's work.'

'It's lovely by the way. The best I've ever been given.' She licked the collar of his shirt away and kissed just under his ear where she knew he was most sensitive.

He gasped, tightening his hold. 'Daisy, what are you doing to me?' Then he focused, pushing her away but holding her face between his hands. 'How can it be the best you've ever had? You've never been given a bouquet before.' He smiled his love.

'That's true. I forgot. Kissing you makes me very distracted.'

'Good.' His lips twitched.

'I suppose, seeing as everyone already knows we're engaged,' Daisy reached up and kissed his nose, 'we could stay here for a bit and kiss and you could distract me a while longer.'

Giving in to temptation, he answered, 'I think I could. Just for a little while longer.'

So they did.

THE END

# Also by Georgia Hill

New Beginnings at Christmas Tree Cottage

## Acknowledgements

Like Mia, I researched the fascinating Victorian language of flowers with books and the internet. For how a florist's shop worked, though, I had help in the human and kind forms of retired florist Una Tromans, and Julie from Flowers of Hagley. My grateful thanks go to them both as they gave of their time very generously. I must add all mistakes are my own. For Spurs knowledge I thank footie fans Steve Nichols and Cait Kidd. Ditto!

I loved spending time in Lullbury Bay again and hope you do too. Just remember, next time you receive a bouquet of flowers, examine them carefully for the hidden message!

# A note from the publisher

**Thank you for reading this book**. If you enjoyed it please do consider leaving a review on Amazon to help others find it too.

**We hate typos.** All of our books have been rigorously edited and proofread, but sometimes mistakes do slip through. If you have spotted a typo, please do let us know and we can get it amended within hours.

**info@bloodhoundbooks.com**

Printed in Great Britain
by Amazon

37748708R00158